KILLER Candy

HOLLY BLOOM

KILLER
Candy

LAPLAND UNDERGROUND
BOOK ONE

HOLLY BLOOM

To the voice inside your head that says you can't do it…
fuck you.

PROLOGUE
KITTEN

"You like this?" Raphael grunted. His hand pumped up and down his dry shaft like he was trying to yank his damn cock off. He took the phrase choking the chicken to a whole new level. "You want a piece of this, huh?"

Once upon a time, he may have been considered attractive. Now, he was old enough to be my father. His belly hung over the dirty waistband of his jeans, trying to escape. That, and the Jacobson signet ring on his finger, made me want to vomit.

Instead of throwing up, I ran my tongue over my red lips and stared at him in wide-eyed wonderment. The type of smoldering look to con him into believing a drop of his cum would be the best present he could give me. I had the whole 'innocent but a freak in the sheets' look nailed to perfection.

"I love it!" I moaned, kneeling before him to give an eyeful of my cleavage. It was no accident I'd chosen to wear a killer black dress to show off my best assets. "You are *so* big!"

Well, as big as my pinkie finger chopped in two.

Men gobbled up compliments over the size of their dicks every single time. Why did they all think their spunk was spun from fucking gold? Give me a chocolate milkshake any day of the week.

"You're a bad girl, aren't you?"

A high-pitched, sickly sweet giggle erupted from the back of my throat. Eurgh, it made me cringe to think about what the job had reduced me to. In another life, I'd have made a damn good actress.

Well done, Kitty. I could almost hear Hiram purring in my ear. *You've got him right where you want him.*

Sweat dripped down Raphael's forehead from the exertion. Getting hard at his age must take some effort. The poor chump looked like he'd run ten marathons. If he wasn't about to die, I'd have warned him about friction burn and given a lecture on the benefits of lube.

"Suck it," Raphael ordered. He pointed his man meat in my face like a small angry marshmallow. Hell, I'm sure he'd whip it out for anyone who looked in his direction because he was so fucking proud of it.

I tried not to gag as I took the disgusting slug into my mouth. I'd need to get a tetanus shot and gargle disinfectant for weeks to feel clean again afterward. Raphael didn't notice. Men like him were used to getting anything they wanted. A blow job was just another transaction. I'd bet he went through more whores than underwear judging from the look of the stains.

Raphael groaned and pushed my head down deeper. His sticky pubes smelt like fried chicken left in the sun for weeks during the height of summer. His eyes rolled back in his head. "I'm close."

Fuck, no!

Enough was enough.

I may be a professional, but I still had limits.

I bit down as hard as I could. Sinking teeth into flesh is more difficult than it sounds. A penis isn't quite as easy to chew as your standard hotdog. The situation played out the same every time. First, a brief pause when the guy doesn't know what's happening. After that, the pain and panic set in like someone lit their balls on fire.

"Fuuuuuuuuuuuuuuuuuuck!"

Raphael screamed like a wounded animal. He grabbed a fistful of my hair. His shit wouldn't fly with me. He may be bigger, but I had all the power. I once watched a documentary about how crocodiles kill their prey. That's exactly what I liked to do.

I locked my jaw down in a motherfucking death grip and ripped straight through. Thrashing around didn't do him any favors. The more he struggled, the more he tore.

Oomph. A kick to my stomach loosened my hold enough for the bastard to pull away.

"You crazy bitch!" he yowled, clutching onto his split dicklet. *How disappointing.* I'd been hoping for a clean break. He staggered to his feet to make a desperate hobble for the door. "Somebody help!"

In his eagerness, he tripped over the corner of the rug and landed with a thud. What better way to be found? His pants around his ankles and spouting blood from his dick like a fountain. It had a poetic ring to it. After building his wealth on the exploitation of others, this was exactly what he deserved.

"No one is coming," I said, wiping his blood from my chin with the back of my hand. I'd been waiting to do this for a long time. I wanted to savor every second. He'd spent the last thirty years trafficking and selling underage girls. The fucker was gonna pay for what he did. "It's just the two of us."

"Why are you doing this?" He trembled. Seeing him like this made me realize how weak and pathetic he really was. How could I have ever been afraid of him? There was nothing impressive about picking on those who couldn't defend themselves. "What do you want?"

He reached for my ankle, but my reactions were quicker. Didn't he know stilettos could be as sharp as knives?

"This isn't my first rodeo," I hissed, driving my heel straight through the palm of his hand and pinning him to the floor.

He didn't bother calling out this time. Raphael may be a monster, but he wasn't stupid. There was no point in pleading when we both knew he wouldn't be leaving the room alive. His body would soon be decomposing in an acid-filled oil drum or chopped up and forced through a meat mincer... I hadn't decided yet.

"W-w-who are you?" he stammered.

I seductively ran a hand up my thigh, pulling the fabric away to reveal a blade tucked into my stocking. His gaze traveled to the distinct red scar. The letter **R**. A letter he had burned into my skin with a hot poker years before.

"What's the matter, honey?" I cocked my head to the side. "Do you remember me now?"

His eyes blackened with fury. The twisted sicko had never expected this day to come. I wanted him to die knowing exactly who had brought him down. Before he could say another word, I took my knife to his throat and slit it wide open.

I grinned down at my work. "Karma's a bitch, right?"

ONE

THREE YEARS LATER...

I pulled up outside the strip club. Unlike every other building on the block, the pink neon sign hadn't succumbed to graffiti. That could be for two reasons, either: the owners took care of the joint, or the vandals were scared to get close. If it was the latter, the people inside were bad fucking news, which was the last thing I needed. But what other choice did I have? Taking off my clothes would beat living on a dumpster-diving diet, or worse…

Selling my jewelry had gotten me this far but, now, I was on my own and out of diamonds. I needed to make rent on my new place. It was a total dive and the cheapest apartment in town, but it was *mine*. If I could keep up with the payments. Apart from that, the only thing I owned was a beat-up old car stolen from a gas station a few months back. It'd been a miracle the cops didn't pick me up before I switched the plates.

It's not like I hadn't *tried* to look for an ordinary job. I'd wasted weeks canvassing neighborhoods for work in rundown diners and stores. Snotty hiring managers took one look down their noses at me and said they had no positions available, despite the clear-as-fuck vacancy sign still hanging in the window. People tend to make certain assumptions when you have tattoos, pink hair, and fake tits. *Judgmental jerks.*

Let's be real though, I'm hardly an employer's wet dream. A twenty-one-year-old with no qualifications or experience — well, none that'd be traditionally accepted anyway. Unlucky for me, being 'trained to kill assholes who deserved it' was not a pre-requisite on a barista job application. That's why I decided to move to Port Valentine. There were other ways to make money in a town like this… if I wanted to.

Over the decades, its rundown streets have been an epicenter for illicit activities. But, before resorting to my unconventional ways, I wanted to try something that didn't involve slashing throats.

Lapland was my best bet.

It wasn't exactly what I had in mind when I left Hiram to live a normal life. Then again, what did someone as damaged and broken as me know about normal? The only thing I knew for sure was that I needed cash. Fast. Stripping was a realistic option and playing a role would be nothing new. Besides, I'd done a hell of a lot worse than batting my eyelashes, shaking my ass, and twirling around a pole for money before.

I'd parked far enough away from the door to be concealed from view. As I turned the handle to get out, a crashing noise stopped me. Had I imagined it? Old habits were hard to shake when you'd spent years watching your back. I took a deep breath to pull myself together — hell, I'd been less jittery when I'd seduced a congressman!

Moments later, the side entrance to Lapland burst open. Three shaven-headed beefcakes dragged a sniveling man into the alley. From a glance, I could tell his nose was broken, and, judging from his whimpering, he'd probably bust a few ribs too. The gang of baldies threw the guy to the floor and gave a signal to someone inside.

This is where the fun would begin.

A giant mountain of a man filled the entire door frame; almost as broad as he was tall. Imagine a literal embodiment of The Hulk, but not green and covered in tats. A distinct diagonal scar ran from his cheek to the corner of his mouth, which curled into a snarl. His biceps were so big he'd be able to fold the guy on the floor up into a suitcase as easily as making an origami bird.

I knew a killer when I saw one.

The Hulk didn't make his move straight away. He was biding his time and making it clear who was in control. I couldn't risk lowering the squeaky window to hear what they were saying, but I'd be damned if I could look away.

I'd bet the guy on the ground had shat himself and offered up his only child on a plate by now. You'd be shocked to find out how low people sunk once they realized their life was balancing on a knife edge. None of them seemed to understand bribery, almost always, made things worse. When someone decides you're going to die, there's nothing you can do about it.

The Hulk pulled out a gun. He could rip someone's head straight off their shoulders with his bare hands in his sleep. Wasn't using a weapon a bit of a cop-out? A little too easy? Or, perhaps he did it so often that he didn't feel in the mood to pound bones to a pulp tonight? The thought sent a shiver up my thighs.

I liked how he had no idea that I was hiding in the shadows, watching him. It's rare to get the chance to see another artist at work and, there I was, getting my own private show. A unique insight into the mind of a beast. I should want to get away. After all, it'd been me who had wanted to leave my old life behind and start afresh. Maybe I'd been naïve in thinking I could ever get on the straight and narrow.

The muscled monster squeezed his finger on the trigger. I didn't even blink as the gun fired and splattered chunks of brain all over the bricks.

The Hulk looked down at the remains with a grim smile of satisfaction, making the hairs on the back of my neck stand on end. It was an expression I knew all too well. He'd done what he had to do. I'd found someone like me. Someone who had danger running through their veins. If you cut him open, he'd bleed havoc and destruction. He was the last person you'd want to run into in the dark and every father's worst nightmare rolled into one.

The beast kicked the corpse for good measure and disappeared inside. I slunk back in my seat, as his merry band of security appeared to tidy the mess he left behind. It'd be a nasty clean-up job, but nothing a jet wash couldn't fix.

What did it say about the club if people weren't afraid to shoot someone in a spot where anyone could walk on by? Shady underground shit had to be going on within those walls.

The best thing to do would be to drive away and pretend I'd not seen anything, but I wasn't about to do that. Danger had a strange way of drawing me in and, perhaps, it was time I accepted an ordinary life wasn't for everyone...

Inside, Lapland was definitely not an icy kingdom home to Santa's workshop. Picture crushed red velvet, black leather, low lights, and drapes hiding one too many dark corners. It was seedy enough to attract the drunks and give the appearance of being *just* another strip club, but something more sinister lurked in the shadows. This was a place where dirty deals were struck; where players exchanged cash under poker tables and lives were traded like gambling chips.

The air had a distinctive smell too: whiskey, cigars, cheap perfume, and a whiff of desperation... or that could have been the group of suburban dads hoping to get their dicks wet when their wives were away for the weekend. *Fucking idiots.* They didn't know how lucky they had it.

Hawk-eyed girls clad with sequined pasties worked the crowd, looking out for the guys with the biggest wallet and lowest self-esteem. You could spot the more experienced hosts a mile away, already grinding on laps in high-backed booths. Under UV light, those seats would glow like they were freaking radioactive.

Across the floor, dancers writhed on poles and in cages on several podiums, but it was easy to see where the main action happened. Spotlights pointed at the stage right in the heart of the club. It was higher than the other platforms, like a prized spot in a trophy cabinet. In the middle of it, a ten-foot pole painted with red and white stripes resembled a giant candy cane. Whoever danced there would be the star of the show for the evening. That's where the big money was and where I needed to be.

The barmaid glared at me from underneath blunt bangs that looked like they'd give you a paper cut if you accidentally brushed by. Her black bob streaked with fiery red made her porcelain skin look almost iridescent, and an inverse labret stud drew my attention to a cupid's bow so sharp it looked like she'd penciled it on with a fucking ruler. Aside from that, the main thing I noticed? Her fake as fuck expression told me she thought her shit didn't stink.

"What do you want?" she eventually snapped, after serving everyone else in sight.

"Vodka," I said, unperturbed by her complete lack of customer service. "Double."

"Ice?" She looked like she'd rather be glassing me with a bottle instead of pouring a drink out of one.

I smiled, which only seemed to piss her off more. "Of course."

The bitch slammed my drink down on the counter and shoved it toward me. One sip was enough for me to realize she'd cut it with water. I downed it one.

"Another," I demanded.

She narrowed her eyes. Clearly, she wasn't used to being challenged.

"Have it your way," she said, as I handed over my last five-dollar bill for an even more diluted excuse of a vodka. I wasn't dumb enough to give her a reaction — not yet, anyway. There would be plenty of time for games later but, right now, I'd come on a mission.

"Who do I speak to about getting a job around here?" I asked.

"You want to work here?" She raised one perfectly plucked eyebrow and crossed her arms over her chest. "Not going to fucking happen."

I was seconds away from tearing her septum piercing straight out of her face and attaching it to the back of my car when a voice behind me froze my feet to the spot.

"Oh really, Vixen?" A voice so fucking cold it'd make the flames of hell turn to ice. "Since when do you have that authority?"

"We don't need someone like her, Zander," Vixen spat, looking at me in disgust. "Just *look* at her."

"As one of the Sevens, you should remember I'm the boss and this is my club," Zander said, holding up a hand to silence her. I hadn't heard of the Sevens before, but I assumed it was the name of the gang in charge. A gang he was the leader of. A gang I should avoid if I knew what was good for me. "And I choose my girls."

My girls.

His words should make me want to run, but I didn't. Instead, I turned to find myself staring into the stormy gray eyes of a devil in a perfectly fitted black suit. A chokehold of tattoos enveloped his throat and crept over the top of his crisp white collar. An inked silhouette of a single rose adorned the side of his face; the thorns cut across the razor edge of his cheekbones like a warning to stay away. If we were in a fairytale, he would be the type of prince who'd fuck the princess senseless, destroy her happily ever after, and… she'd still be begging for more.

"You." His dead stare locked on me with such an

intensity it made the rest of the room fall away. "What's your name?"

"Candy."

"Candy, what?"

"Uh…" I stalled, looking around for inspiration and landing on the first thing in sight. "Cane."

Okay, it sounded a *little* ridiculous. But I'd have to own it. It shouldn't be hard, considering I'd already spent most of my life explaining to people that Candy was my actual name and not something I'd made up to sound cute. Cute is the last word I'd use to describe myself.

My full name is Candy Green, but it'd been years since I'd gone by that identity. The story behind my name is a funny one. When my two-week-old baby self got dumped on the doorstep of Evergreen kid's home, my fate had been sealed. Every abandoned baby was automatically given the last name 'Green' and whoever discovered them was given the honor of choosing the first name. Unfortunately, the brat who found me was a toddler with a sweet tooth.

"Candy Cane?" Zander repeated. The corner of his mouth twitched up in what could be the beginning of a smile or a snarl, but it was too hard to tell.

"Yep," I said, popping the p. "That's me."

He paused, as his eyes trailed up and down my body with the precision of an X-ray machine. They lingered a little too long on the stretch of skin where my crop top ended and shorts began. That one look told me all I needed to know. He had the power to tear people down, rip them apart, and shatter their souls into little pieces. Lucky for me, I wasn't made of glass. Finally, a twisted panty-dropping grin spread over his face. "You have one dance."

"You've got to be kidding, Zander," Vixen objected. I got the feeling she would give anything to claw my eyeballs with her pointed talons. "You're out of your fucking mind!"

"Show Candy backstage," Zander ordered. His decision was final. "What difference will one more slut make?"

Vixen stayed silent as I followed her into the dressing room, where twenty other girls were practically pulling at each other's extensions to get closer to the mirrors. You'd think they were preparing to go on a catwalk, not the stage of a seedy titty bar.

"Who is *she*?" a girl hissed.

"The boss picked her out," Vixen declared.

Everyone spun around to stare me down. What a great start. I'd only just walked in, but they had already made me public enemy number one. There was nothing like slicing someone open before throwing them into a shark tank.

"Her?!"

"Have fun competing for the top spot." Vixen blew me a sarcastic kiss, making me hope she'd get a yeast infection in her skin-tight leather pants. "You're up last if you're still here by the end of the night."

"Lapland is only for the best." A leggy brunette cornered me. I resisted the urge to roll my eyes. Since when did strippers have a fucking A-Lister status? I must have missed the memo. "We don't have room here for trash."

"You're right, Bella," a blonde with a dodgy nose job agreed. "Cupid's always has openings, though."

"Even they are not *that* desperate," Bella added, looking pleased with herself as the rest of the group snickered in response. "They want high-class escorts."

I stood my ground. This wasn't a fucking playground, and her attempts to intimidate me wouldn't work. Bella may be the Queen Bee around here, but I didn't have a problem getting stung.

"Why don't you take it up with Zander if you have a problem?" I asked, cocking my hip and planting my hand there.

Bella flinched at the mention of his name, then regained her resting bitch face.

"You're only in the trials for the freak factor," Bella said. "You didn't think he was serious about you dancing here, did you?"

"What's wrong?" I questioned. "Are you feeling threatened, Bells?"

Everyone drew a sharp intake of breath. Bella may rule over her minions, but someone would have to put bullets through my kneecaps to get me to bow down to her throne.

"Listen up, you little whore!" Bella loomed over me. Puh-lease. Did she really think the sight of her under-boob would make me beg for mercy? I'd survived being tortured and locked in a prison basement for months. After that ordeal, it'd take more than unnaturally perky breasts for me to break out in a sweat. "Lapland has a certain reputation. They're not going to let in trailer trash. Everyone knows the top spot is mine."

Bella didn't *want* the top spot, she needed it. She'd be lucky to get another three years out of dancing before the partying and botched plastic surgery forced her off the main stage. Youth didn't last forever, and she fucking knew it. It would make taking her crown even sweeter.

"We'll see," I said, with a shrug.

"You'll regret—"

A megaphone requesting Annabella's presence on stage stopped her from finishing whatever threat she was about to throw my way.

I yawned. "And here I thought this would be a slumber party."

"This isn't over," she hissed in my ear, before flouncing away in a fog of cheap perfume.

Yep, I guess that meant we wouldn't be having a pillow fight and sipping hot cocoa arm-in-arm any time soon. Whoever said girls should stick together talked utter bullshit. We lived in a dog-eat-dog world and these girls were thirsty bitches.

My cell phone vibrating in my pocket jolted me back to reality like a taser shot in the ass. Stripper wars were the least of my problems. This could only be one person.

Missing me yet, Kitten? The message read.

Yeah, like a hole in the fucking head.

The mouthy brown-nosing blonde felt like now would be a great time to face off against me. "Where are you going?"

"I'm getting a drink." I clenched my fists, readying for a fight. "Do you have a fucking problem?"

"I don't know who you think you are; swanning in and—"

I was on top of her before she even saw me coming.

I grabbed her ponytail and twisted it around my knuckles like I was preparing to go into a boxing ring.

"Unless you want to have your nose rearranged again," I said, yanking her head back with full force. "I'd shut the fuck up and tell me you don't have a problem."

The rest of the sheep shifted nervously in their seats, but none of them made an effort to move. Since when did applying bronzer to your cleavage become more important than helping a friend? Spineless assholes. If they had each other's backs, they'd be all over me and I wouldn't stand a chance.

"N-n-no problem," Blondie yelped. "I don't have a problem!"

"That's what I thought," I sneered, releasing her and hoping none of them noticed the slight tremor in my voice.

Way to fucking go, Candy!

I'd lived in a world of violence for so long that it came as naturally to me as breathing. It'd been six months since I'd left Hiram, and he knew exactly how to get under my skin.

Missing me yet, Kitten?

I'd been a fool to think he'd let me go so easily. I may have worked hard to win my freedom, but it didn't change how Hiram saw me. He'd always believe I belonged to him. That I was his. I'd thought our contract would be enough to hold him at bay. Hiram might be the most twisted motherfucker around, but he was a man of his word. Even if he didn't plan to break our agreement, it didn't guarantee he wouldn't try to find a way around it and destroy me... again.

If he came for me, I'd have to be ready this time.

Over the last five years, Hiram had molded me into an unstoppable killing force. He'd made sure the sweet and innocent girl I used to be was gone. She'd been replaced by a fucking lion who could play him at his own game. I knew all his old tricks. Hiram was a dirty player, but he'd trained me to be a worthy opponent. The text was his way of toying with me. It'd only be a matter of time before he played his next move. All I could do was wait until he showed his hand.

Right now, I had to address more immediate concerns. I needed to get my head together before I attacked another stripper and blew any chance I had at getting a job. Up on the main stage, Bella humped the pole to the beat of the music. One look at her smug, money-grabbing face made me want to punch something. I needed to…

"Hey, watch where you're going!"

I wiped my watery eyes from the force of the blow. Goddammit, I'd been too busy fantasizing about breaking Bella's legs I'd walked face-first into a human built like a literal fucking house. What the hell were his pecks made from? Bricks?

Oh, shit.

One glance confirmed my suspicions.

It was him.

The killer in the alleyway.

"Why aren't you backstage?" Vixen appeared out of nowhere. "This isn't a whorehouse. You need to do more than just spread your legs to get paid here."

For once, being called a whore was a welcome

distraction. I could deal with a snarky bitch like Vixen any day of the week, but the hulk-like man? I didn't trust what I'd say if I opened my mouth around him.

"I'm getting a drink," I replied, not daring to look up at the beast at her side.

"No alcohol on the job." Vixen scowled, then addressed the man. "West, our guest has arrived."

I followed their gaze to a booth where Zander was clinking glasses with a man with cropped dark hair and a sharp nose. He was traditionally handsome but made me uneasy. I'd been in enough tricky situations to trust my gut feeling and something about him made my skin crawl. When his guest looked the other way, Zander expertly emptied his glass into the ice bucket with one seamless motion. Judging from Vixen's eyes darting back and forth, a deal was going down and it was important nothing fucked it up.

Vixen zeroed in on me again like a hungry Rottweiler. "What are you still doing here?"

"Struggling to control your girls, Vix?" West mocked. The deep husky growl of his tone simultane-ously made my blood run cold and ignited a fire between my legs. "We don't need airheads running around here. Girls like her are only good for one thing."

"Here I was thinking you were enjoying my compa-ny," I quipped back, then instantly regretted it.

God help me. Why couldn't my damn smart mouth control itself? I knew exactly how trigger-happy this man could be.

"I wouldn't even pay for your company," West said, causing Vixen to cackle.

"You said you wanted a job," she snarled. "So fucking prove it."

The other dancers mustn't have been as stupid as I first thought. On my return to the dressing room, none of them were brave enough to look in my direction without their Queen Bee around. My little performance with Blondie had sent them all a clear message. Play with gasoline and you're gonna get burned.

As a late addition to this evening's line-up, there were no spare costumes for me to wear. Whilst the rest of the girls strutted around in tiny scraps of fabric, I had to get creative. Bella may think this was a classy club, but I knew from experience how powerful men had an appetite for things that were a little less refined.

I took scissors to my crop top to shorten it even further and leave it sitting just under my boobs. My denim shorts were basically hot pants anyway — thankfully, they were so well-worn I could move in them fine. I hit the jackpot by finding black tape at the back of the lipstick drawer and used it to cover my nipples. It'd sting like a bitch to pull off, but I needed to rock the 'down and dirty' look. If it meant having X's over my tits then that's what I had to do.

"Now, for the final dance of the evening!" The host's introduction rang through the club. Did they *have* to make my entrance sound so dramatic? "I present to you, Candy Cane!"

I piled my pink waist-length hair into a high ponytail and slipped off my boots. They were great for kicking men in the balls but not so good for hanging upside down on a pole. The audience would have to deal with the fact I wasn't eight feet tall, in skyscraper heels, like everyone else.

The beat from Marilyn Manson's 'Tainted Love' cover played as I stepped into the spotlight to take the stage like it was my fucking territory. I may not have a diamond G-string up my ass, but that didn't mean I couldn't work my way around a pole. Lapland may only be reserved for the best, but I would show them what it meant to be real.

As I climbed the striped pole, I tried not to think about how Zander and West were sitting somewhere in the audience. I hadn't always been a natural performer, but Hiram's training forced me to shred every one of my inhibitions. Now, stripping for a crowd came as easily to me as brushing my teeth in the morning. At the top of the pole, I locked my ankle in place and dropped into a perfect leg hang which made the clapping go wild.

The chanting started getting louder.

I whipped back upright, straddling the metal between my legs, and gave the audience a cheeky wink before corkscrewing down into an angel pose. You didn't honeytrap as many men as I had without having a few moves in your repertoire. I needed to hold on long enough to get them panting.

I shook my hair out of the ponytail and dropped to the floor, giving the crowd a good eyeful of my booty. Five crisp fifty-dollar bills fluttered down at my feet, which felt like a middle finger to the more distinguished dancers who were hellbent on throwing me onto the sidewalk.

I looked up to catch the eye of my admirer who I recognized as the guest Zander had been entertaining. Behind him, Zander whispered furiously in West's ear.

"I have more where that came from," their guest

bragged, pulling a thick roll of cash from his pocket and confirming my earlier instincts.

The only people brave enough to carry around that much dirty money knew no one would be stupid enough to try to steal it. I dubbed them the 'Untouchables'. They could be gang leaders, drug lords, corrupt politicians, or media moguls who had so much filth on corporations they could bring them down with a single click. It didn't matter which category he fell into. Money was power, and he had a shit tonne of it.

I bit my lip and leaned forward to tease him with a glimpse of my cleavage. He tossed another bill my way. This was too easy.

Bella better be watching from the wings and taking notes because I wasn't going to make it rain... I'd make it fucking pour.

TWO

"You've got to be fucking joking!" As usual, my zero-filtered mouth acted before my brain had time to catch up. "Did you even see me dance?"

No one could question whether I'd outperformed the other dancers during the trials. The crowd got so crazy there were calls for an encore at the end of my routine. I'd made five hundred dollars from Zander's creepy guest too — shouldn't she be showing me a little gratitude? My motor-boating skills would have helped to sweeten whatever deal they were making.

"Bella has the top spot," Vixen repeated to the group, then turned to me. "The sooner you learn your place here, the better. If you want to stay, you're starting right at the fucking bottom. If you don't like it, I'd suggest you walk out the door and never come back."

"You'd be doing us all a favor to crawl back to the gutter you came from," Bella chimed in.

Oh, I'm sure she'd love that. The bitch may wear my crown, but we both knew she didn't deserve the top title. The fact I'd earned it didn't matter. In Lapland, it would never be a fair fight when nobody played by the rules. Bella had another thing coming if she thought I'd roll over and give up so easily. Her days were fucking numbered.

"If I'm not dancing," I said, "then, why did you even call me back here?"

Vixen smirked as the evil cogs turned in her mind, reminding me of a nutty professor planning the apocalypse. She must have had serious shit happen in her own life to be this determined to make mine miserable.

"You're going to be our new cleaner."

I flashed her my most dazzling smile which I usually reserved for right before I rip off somebody's toenails. "When do I start?"

She'd underestimated me if she thought scrubbing spunk off seats would scare me away. Unlike the other bimbos, I was no stranger to getting my hands dirty. Breaking a few nails had to be better than breaking bones for a living, right?

"Tomorrow." Vixen eyed me with suspicion. "You'll be first here and last out at night, is that clear?"

"Crystal," I said. "Whatever you say, *boss.*"

I may start by mopping the floor, but I had no intention of staying at the bottom for long. The only way to bring down a hierarchy was from the inside, and there was serious money to be made here. If I couldn't dance for tips, I'd have to figure out what operation Zander was running… and how I could use it to my advantage.

Zander may be the boss of Lapland's underground business and the elusive gang known as the Sevens, but

Vixen ruled over the daily running of the club. Her Majesty ruled with an iron fist and nothing was good enough for her exacting standards. She'd screamed for twenty minutes at the delivery guy because a bottle had accidentally smashed in transit; I counted myself lucky she'd only asked me to clean the urinals three times over.

"Well?" Vixen appeared in the dressing room, where I was busy buffing the mirrors. She had a nasty habit of materializing like the Grim Reaper when you least expected it. "When're you going to change? We're opening soon."

"Nobody mentioned a uniform."

Since when did you have to dress up to clean toilets? My comfy as fuck jeans and baggy T-shirt were all I needed.

"We're a strip club, if you haven't noticed," Vixen spoke in a slow, patronizing drawl. "You'll be clearing empty glasses on the floor. You can't wear *that*."

"Fine." I crossed my arms to stop myself from shoving the cloth down her throat. "Where's my uniform?"

"Here," she said, placing a bag down and leaning back against the wall to watch my reaction. "It'll be perfect for you."

"Wow." I glowered at the contents. A French maid outfit complete with matching stockings. Couldn't she have tried to be more original? "I can see you put a lot of thought into it."

The costume had been bought from a budget fancy dress store meaning I'd look even less like the other dancers in their boutique lingerie. It could have a silver lining, though. Rich men had a thing for maids, so maybe I could find a way to work it for extra tips.

"Don't even think about speaking to customers," Vixen snapped as if she'd read my mind. "We have hosts for that. All you need to do is collect empty glasses and clean up the mess. Think you can handle it?"

"Just about," I muttered.

Oh, honey... you have no idea what I can handle.

"My cousin may have picked you out, but that doesn't mean you're fucking special." Her eyes flashed in warning, showing a whole new level of crazy lurking under the surface. Vixen and Zander being related explained why he hadn't fired the charmless psychopath yet. "You don't want to make an enemy of me, Candy."

"I'm the one you should be worried about," I murmured under my breath, as the bitch stomped away in her New Rock boots.

Vixen may think she's an ice queen, but it wouldn't be enough to extinguish the inferno that burned inside me. Being around Zander made her untouchable at work, but it didn't make her invincible. She wouldn't know what hit her if I went Guy Fawkes on her ass. If I didn't need the money, her house would already be burnt to the fucking ground and I'd be dancing in the ashes.

My first shift didn't improve after changing into my compulsory uniform. I flashed my panties every time I bent over in my short dress. Sleaze balls took it as an invitation to pat — yes, fucking PAT — my ass. The slimy bastards didn't even leave a tip because they thought it was the correct way to show their gratitude for collecting empties. With their manners, it's no fucking surprise they had to pay women for company.

The club was quieter on a Sunday night, as no big performances were scheduled. Bella and her followers had descended upon the floor to reel in horny desperados for private dances. Judging from her overzealous hair swishing, Bella would give the old guy with false teeth a lot more than a lap dance by the end of the night. He'd already ordered the best champagne and Bella hung on his every word, lighting up every time he swiped his platinum card.

Out of the corner of my eye, I clocked Vixen slipping out from behind the bar to the side entrance. Shortly after, she resurfaced with two men by her side, donning a rare smile. Only one thing would make her grin like that: cold, hard cash. I pressed myself against the wall and edged my way around a group of drunken revelers to get a closer look.

Vixen showed the guests into a private booth and, a few seconds later, she emerged alone. The dancers were too busy grinding on stranger's boners and the customers were too distracted by trying not to cum in their pants, to even notice people slipping in undetected under their noses. Nothing got past me, though. I'd lived in a world where survival depended on noticing what other people missed. Everyone knows if you're oblivious, you're as good as dead.

Over the next hour, more men arrived. The same thing happened each time. Vixen had the whole slick routine nailed. You didn't have to be a rocket scientist to work out there must be a hidden door somewhere. There was barely enough room to house two people in the space — let alone seven!

Whatever was happening, I wanted in.

I planned my move carefully. As soon as Vixen went to greet the next arrival, I positioned myself close to the booth and waited for the perfect moment. Then, like clockwork...

"Oopsie!" I stumbled from the shadows and, miraculously, found myself in the arms of a stranger. I mean, what had Vixen expected from a ditzy, clumsy maid who lacked the coordination to be a dancer?

The man looked down at me. "Well, aren't you a sight for sore eyes?"

"You're my hero!" I beamed at my savior as he helped me to my feet. The fabric of his suit was expensive to the touch, and the thick gold chain around his neck almost blinded me. "Thank you."

It was a cliché move, but it's a classic for a reason. What man doesn't want to save a poor damsel in distress? The helpless princess always lands the handsome prince or, in this case, a ticket to a private gathering taking place in a strip club.

He spoke in a strong New Jersey accent, "You need to be careful where you're stepping in those heels."

"I'm so clumsy." I shook my head and squeezed his arm in thanks. "If you hadn't been there to catch me, then I don't know what I'd have done..."

Vixen bared her teeth in a lackluster attempt at a smile. "Don't you have work to be getting on with, Candy?"

If looks could kill, the daggers she was shooting would have impaled me. Luckily, even she wasn't stupid enough to make a scene in front of a client. Who knew she had it in her to be so professional?

"You can't be all work and no play, Vix." The man playfully nudged her in the ribs — a move that would have had many others castrated. "Why don't you give the girl a break?"

"Vixen's right." I bit my lip and pulled down the hem of my dress to flash an extra pop of cleavage his way. Yet another classic maneuver that never failed. "I should get back to work. I'm sorry again for being such a klutz."

It would only take... 3... 2...

"Candy, is it?" The man held out an outstretched hand. "I'm Vinny."

"It's so rare to meet a proper gentleman."

Vinny was in his fifties and, from his puffed chest, I could tell I'd hit his sweet spot. Underneath the tough guy act and firm grip, he was still a stickler for old-fashioned values. No one got to the top of their game without doing some damage, but he'd be the type who'd feel bad after killing a man who had a wife and kids at home.

"I've had an idea!" Vinny's eyes lit up in excitement, still completely oblivious to the subconscious mind games I'd been playing. "I think this little minx may just be the good luck charm I need tonight."

"Me?" I gasped and put my hand to my mouth in mock surprise. "A good luck charm?"

"You know the Sevens' rules, Vinny," Vixen warned. "No girls."

"I'll tell you what, how does an extra ten G's to seal the deal sound? I'll also forget about the little favor Zander owes me?" he suggested. "Tonight is a game amongst friends after all."

Vixen paused to consider his proposal, then nodded sharply in agreement. "Done."

"Now, tell me…" Vinny pulled open the curtain and led me into the booth. "Are you as sweet as your name suggests?"

"Oh, Vinny." I giggled. "You have no idea…"

What can I say? The fairytale formula gets proven results. No one expects Sleeping Beauty to have a knife under her pillow.

Vinny loved the sound of his own voice. From the moment we passed through the not-so-secret door and down the hidden staircase; all I had to do was laugh whenever he took a break for air. Whilst he was blathering, I made a mental note of the door's keypad combination when he typed it in. 6-9-6-9. Real fucking mature, but remembering it could come in handy someday.

"I'm feeling really lucky tonight, Candy," Vinny exclaimed, rubbing his hands together. "What d'you think? Am I gonna win big?"

Once upon a time, Vinny may have been a big shot. Now, he had more money than sense and only enjoyed having a pretty young piece on his arm to stroke his ego. The most pathetic part of all? He didn't realize it only made him look more desperate and irrelevant. It wouldn't be long until he faded into insignificance entirely and the wolves closed in to take his place.

"Definitely," I chirped, playing the part of the personal cheerleader he wanted me to be. All I needed was pompoms to shake along. "I'm your good luck charm, remember?"

We made our way through the underground corridor, where closed doors beckoned me like shiny invitations. Most women fantasized about their dream weddings, but me? I got my kicks from unearthing secrets people wanted to stay buried. I was damn good at it, too. One of the first lessons Hiram taught me was how money could buy you anything, but knowledge had the power to rip it all away. Empires, careers, and lives can be destroyed in an instant when information gets into the wrong hands.

"This is our stop." Vinny opened a door for me to pass. "Ladies first."

Black leather chairs surrounded a poker table. The smell of cigars, whiskey, and testosterone hit me like a cum shot to the face. I'd been in rooms like this many times before. A scent combination like that meant the big boys were here to play. I was about to discover who sat on these thrones and ruled the kingdom.

As soon as my heel hit the tiles, heads snapped around to gawp in my direction. I bit my tongue to stop myself from making a joke about whiplash. You'd think this was the first time they'd ever seen a woman.

"No girls allowed." A gigantic figure rose from his seat. Trust the fucking Hulk to have a problem. He was on a constant man period. "Rules are rules."

Vinny waved his hand nonchalantly. "Vixen agreed Candy will accompany me."

"She didn't run it past me," West hissed. "Or the rest of the Sevens."

How many people made up the Sevens? So far, I knew West, Vixen, and Zander… was that all of them?

Or were more monsters skulking around in the shadows who I hadn't met yet? I made a mental note to find out.

"Come on, West!" another player, the same bag of shit who'd made my stomach turn and tipped me generously last night, said. "I've always had a soft spot for maids."

"Candy is with me this evening," Vinny said stiffly. From the change in Vinny's tone, he wasn't a fan of the guy. Either that, or he didn't want to have wasted ten grand for someone else to pull me from under his feet. Men acted like dogs; they loved to piss on women to claim their territory. "She is *my* guest."

West shot a venomous glare in my direction. Being in the company of others gave me immunity, and we both knew it. I didn't allow myself to think about what would happen when he next got me alone.

"You sit next to him and don't say a word," West ordered.

I nodded dutifully, enjoying the way a vein protruded from his forehead in anger. He seriously needed to work on keeping his emotions in check. If he kept going like this, his blood pressure would put him in an early grave before someone from a rival gang did.

"She won't be any trouble," Vinny promised, pulling out a chair for me to sit down. That was easy for him to say when he had no idea who he'd really invited along. "Will you, Candy?"

"No, sir." Well, not tonight anyway. "You won't even know I'm here."

"Atta girl!" Vinny patted my thigh. "See, West? Everyone's happy!"

Well, almost everyone. I wasn't exactly overjoyed at

the prospect of having to act like Vinny's fucking golden retriever for the evening.

"Let's fucking play," West growled. He returned to his chair, which was larger than the others to accommodate his muscular frame, and nodded for the dealer to shuffle. I'm surprised he hadn't ground his teeth to the bone with how hard his jaw was clenched. Someone needed to teach him how to cut loose.

The dealer started to lay down the cards. It was time for the real games to begin. I may have entered the lion's den, but none of them suspected a new predator was now in their midst.

As the night wore on, it became obvious Vinny didn't know a rat's ass about poker. Being clueless didn't stop him from laying down twenty big ones on a shit hand. It was easy to see why everyone treated him like royalty here. He burned through cash and expensive liquor faster than a car lit up by a petrol bomb.

"What do you say, Candy?" Vinny asked, already pulling out a fat roll of cash. He had more money on him than Mr. fucking Monopoly. "Winner takes all in the last game?"

Between fluttering my eyelashes and flicking hair over my shoulder, I'd been watching the players closely. Three of them, including Vinny, knew fuck all about playing the game. They'd only been invited to make up the numbers and crank up the pot. The remaining four all had some skill, but West was the one I had my eye on. He knew his way around the deck but the big guy wasn't playing to win. No, he'd carefully orchestrated the game like a conductor by pre-empting every move to strike up a perfect balance of wins and losses. Just enough to give the players a flavor of victory to keep them reaching into their pockets and coming back for more.

"Why don't we make things a little more interesting?" The suggestion came from the heavy tipper perve who had spent most of the evening ogling my tits from across the table. "Candy should play."

The muscles in West's neck tensed. "You know the rules, Cheeks."

From listening to their conversations, I learned Cheeks was a bent cop drunk on power. He seemed to know everything that was going on in Port Valentine, or at least that's what he wanted everyone to think. If something dirty was going down, you'd bet he'd be around to smooth things over and collect a cheque for his troubles. Cheeks could be schmoozing the Mayor one evening and making sure an arms delivery arrives without a hitch the next. He had to be a twisted bastard to make an oath to protect people, then help murderers and rapists stay on the streets.

"I'll buy her in." Vinny counted out a stack of crisp hundred-dollar bills. "What do you say?"

"Be a sport!" One of the older gents clapped West on the back in encouragement. "What harm could it do?"

West could treat me like the devil incarnate all he liked, but hello? It's not like I'd asked to play. Letting me join a game was a small commiseration for having to sit around listening to this group of animals measuring the size of their dicks for hours.

"I'll let her play, but it's your money you're wasting."

West shrugged. "You don't pay a girl like *that* to use her head."

As if I hadn't heard the same line before. A good ole misogynistic spreading the legs quip grew old fast. For someone smart enough to mastermind an illegal casino, West was surprisingly unobservant.

"Tell you what." Vinny refilled his scotch. "We'll go 50/50 if you win."

"But I've only played a few times before..."

It pained me to act all dumb and innocent, but it got the response I wanted.

"Don't they play poker at the trailer park?" West rebutted, taking my bait.

The prick. Didn't anyone ever teach him never to underestimate an opponent? I'd been planning to go easy on him, but it was about time someone taught him a lesson. By the time I'd wiped the floor with him, he'd be slurping his words through a straw.

"You ignore them, darlin'," Vinny said. "You're my good luck charm tonight, remember?"

Vinny may be a schmuck, but he'd lost thousands tonight. The least I could do was get him back the money he'd paid for my invitation. Besides, the winning pot now stood at fifty grand and the extra money would come in handy. Rent was due in a few days, and I craved food with more nutritional value than a packet of mac and cheese.

"What did I tell you, Candy?" Vinny grabbed my face and kissed me on both cheeks. "You're my lucky charm."

"Oh my gosh, I can't believe it," I said, dragging out my words to do my best bimbo impersonation. "I guess it must be beginner's luck."

West's stare cut through my core like molten lava as his eyes flicked from me to the straight flush laid on the table. He knew this had nothing to do with luck. If only he'd seen through my bluff sooner. Who would have suspected the pink-haired stripper was a poker pro?

West threw down strong moves throughout the game, but he had diverted his attention to the other players long enough to give me the upper hand. It wasn't until the river he noticed something was wrong. By then, it was too late... he was already drowning.

Over the years, I'd accompanied Hiram to casinos and watched from the shadows. Learning the rules of poker was one thing, but it wasn't enough to make you a winner. The game is as much about analyzing the other players as the cards. It's a good thing people are easier to read than books because I've cataloged the full fucking library. I'd never lost a game.

"It's the first time I've won in ten years," Vinny said. He scooped up the prize pot with all the glee of an addict getting their next shot of snow. Technically, I'd won... but I wouldn't ruin this moment for him. Logically, he'd have to 'win' at some point, right? "I had a good feeling about you, Candy."

"I just can't believeeee it!" I crooned.

"I'm a man of my word," Vinny said, slipping me my cut of the cash. *Thank you very much.* It'd sort my bills for the next year. "You buy yourself something nice, won't you?"

"Oh, I will."

I stashed it inside my bra and flashed West a

sparkling smile, which he met with a scowl. The puppet master wasn't happy to learn he hadn't been the only one pulling the strings.

"You're a lot more than a pretty face, Miss Cane," Cheeks leered. Yep, this 'pretty face' actually had a brain and the ability to ram a corkscrew down his urethra without hesitation. "Why don't I take you up to the bar and buy you a drink, huh?"

Before I could respond, West cut in.

"She has work to do," West said, saving me the effort of coming up with an excuse. Although, I had a funny feeling he wasn't trying to do me a favor. "If she still wants to keep her job."

"He's right." I threw my hands up in the air to signal it was a completely hopeless case. "I need to clean up in here."

Thankfully, Vinny was too caught up in his winning high and the potential of making a dent in the bar's liquor stash to object. Thank fuck. My sweet and stupid act was souring fast. How did people smile all day without their face aching like they'd sucked a dragon chode? It was a full-on workout routine.

Cheeks winked at me over his shoulder as the party filed out. "I'll be seeing you soon, Candy."

The only place I'll be seeing you is in hell, motherfucker!

The man tipped well, but my intuition didn't lie. Learning he was a bent cop only proved it. I'd need to give Cheeks a wide birth, even if it meant having to face the wrath of West with no crowd immunity.

West slammed the door shut behind the last player. Hopefully, the building had firm foundations because the floor shook from the force. I braced myself for the worst, but West didn't say a word and whipped out his phone. On the screen, he pulled the club's CCTV footage and watched them move along the basement corridor. He waited until the final figure slipped back into the club, then turned to face me.

It was just the two of us.

Alone.

Just breathe, Candy. It's not fucking hard. You do it all the time.

"Where did you learn to play like that?"

West took a step closer and backed me into a corner. The walls suddenly felt like they were closing in. If it wasn't for his delicious smell — a mixture of rum, sandalwood, and a fancy cologne I couldn't remember the name of — I'd have thought he'd put a bag over my head and this was an astral experience.

"What's wrong?" My voice came out breathier than usual. "Upset about being beaten by a girl?"

"Don't fucking push me."

He punched the wall to the right of my head. The plasterboard breaking snapped me back into the moment, but I didn't flinch.

"Is that supposed to scare me?" I asked.

He could do better than that…

"It should do."

One wrong move would be like waving a red flag under the nose of a raging bull, but I never ran from confrontation.

"What're you going to do?" I cocked my head to the

side and arched an eyebrow in mild bemusement. "Take me to the parking lot and shoot me, too?"

He spluttered. "How did you—"

"Chill out, okay?" As much as I enjoyed making him squirm, I didn't want to have to answer Zander's questions if West ended up tearing apart the entire room. "Your secret is safe with me. But, a little tip for next time, maybe you should be more careful next time you take out your garbage?"

West looked at me. Like, *really* looked at me. As if he was only seeing me for the first time. "Who the fuck are you?"

"I'm just another airhead," I said. "Remember?"

Why did it feel so fucking good to be noticed by him? I'd been the one who'd insisted I wanted to skip into the sunset to live a normal life and look at me now! I stood face-to-face with a cold-blooded killer who had the tattooed muscles of an alternative Greek god. The worst thing of all? I didn't even care. Hiram may have been right all along when he said some people were destined to become monsters.

"We split the money down the middle," West growled, returning to his usual grisly self. "It's club policy."

"Club policy, or Seven policy?"

He narrowed his eyes. "Both."

"How about we make a deal?" I suggested, twirling a strand of hair around my finger. "I'll split the cash *if* I'm promoted to dancer and you give me permission to burn this outfit as soon as I take it off."

"Done." His mouth quirked upwards at the corners. Then, just as quickly, the ghost of a smile vanished. "What the fuck did you say your name was again?"

"Candy," I said. Remember that. I may sound sweet, but I'm the type of girl who'd break your teeth if you cross me. "Candy Cane."

West averted his eyes as I pulled the cash from the front of my dress. Well, who knew he could be such a gentleman? It pained me to part with the money, but I needed to play the long game. If I could make this amount in one night, think how much more I could earn over a few months… if Zander and his gang trusted me enough.

"Be careful, Candy." His stare scorched me with a soulless intensity only serial killers possessed. "You don't want to make an enemy of me."

"Don't worry," I said, sashaying out of the room on my heels. "I'll go easy on you next time."

My face broke out into a grin at the crash of a table being upturned behind me. I guess that's one way to deal with your masculinity being threatened by a stripper dressed as a maid. He didn't scare me. Not when I'd already been to hell and back.

I didn't run from the darkness… I fucking welcomed it.

THREE

I strutted into the dressing room like I owned it. "Did you miss me?"

If only I had a camera to film their reactions. Jaws hit the floor quicker than Bella dropped her panties for a wrinkly millionaire with saggy balls. From my observations, that was almost faster than the speed of light.

"What is *she* doing here?" Bella turned to Vixen in accusation. "I thought *she* was the help, not a dancer."

"*She* has a name," I reminded her.

"We've had a staff restructure," Vixen explained, refusing to admit her authority had been overruled. "It seems some of our clientele have lower standards and Candy will be filling the gap."

The bitch never failed to miss an opportunity to twist the knife in, but it didn't matter. We both knew the real reason why I was still around. All West had to do was click his fingers to get what he wanted. She wasn't as all-powerful as she thought. That would be killing the control freak inside her.

"None of our clients are that desperate." Bella tried to wrinkle her nose but the botox made her look constipated instead. "She was more suited to cleaning the bathroom."

"If you want me to be Cinderella, what does that make you?" I asked. "One of the ugly sisters?"

"You think you're so clever, don't you?" Bella snarled. "You won't last here. You're not the right fit."

"That's what everyone said to Cinders before she tried on the slipper. Haven't you read until the end of the story?" I asked. "The future doesn't look good for you"

She'd die old, ugly, and alone with only her bitter heart and poisonous tongue for company. Not that I believed in happily ever afters for people like me. They didn't exist. Life was no fucking fairy tale. Love was an excuse adults used to justify sleeping next to the same fat snoring bastard for fifty years.

"You bring any more trouble here and you're out, Candy." Vixen pointed one of her black-painted claws my way. "And I don't give a shit what West says."

Boss from hell, much? I resisted the urge to give her a one-finger salute as she stomped out of the room, cursing under her breath.

"West?" Blondie wailed, almost falling off her chair. I'd heard rumors she and West were seeing each other. Her reaction only confirmed it. I didn't understand how West could be interested in someone with zero backbone… or why the thought of him fucking a Barbie-wannabe made me want to rearrange her face.

"He wants to see me dance." I shrugged like it was nothing and made myself comfy at a vacant dressing table. "That's not a problem, is it?"

Blondie kept her mouth clamped shut. Almost scalping her must have made a lasting impact.

"She's lying, Scarlett," Bella said, patting her arm. "Ignore her. West is interested in you."

"What do you think? Will West like it?" I held up a lipstick. If winding them up was a sport, I was going for a gold medal. "Mm, it tastes like sour cherries."

"West wouldn't be interested in a slut like you." Bella looked down at her nose like I was a piece of shit caught in her stiletto and smiled knowingly to herself. "West likes classy women, just like Zander."

I snorted. Surely they weren't naïve enough to think they were living in a stripper version of the Stepford Wives? These men were using them like taps to get their dicks wet on demand. If Bella wasn't such a bitch, I'd feel bad her only source of genuine pride was wearing the fact the boss boned her like a badge of honor.

"At least I don't need to bang the boss to hold down a job," I pointed out.

I may have been an expert seductress in the past, but I'd never had full-on sex with any of my marks. It was another one of Hiram's rules. Not that I'd have wanted to. My vagina was a complete no-peen zone. The closest I'd got to sex was biting cocks off, although I wouldn't really count it. There's a blurred line between pleasure and pain but severed penises cross the line.

"They wouldn't want you, anyway. Who knows what diseases you have?" Bella scoffed. "I bet you don't even know how many men you've slept with."

She couldn't be any further from the truth. It wasn't hard to keep count when only one guy had ever been inside me…

One guy who I'd never been able to forget.

One guy who had single-handedly been the catalyst for ripping my entire life apart.

Falling for him was the biggest mistake I'd ever made, and the most soul-shattering part of the whole thing? I'd been stupid enough to believe he loved me when the only real desire he had was to screw me, then screw me over. The bastard handed me over to Hiram like a gift-wrapped present. If our paths ever crossed again, I'd make sure he lost more than his cock for what he did.

"At least every one I've fucked still had their own teeth," I said, dabbing the corner of my mouth to perfect my lipstick. It was exactly the same shade as a two-day-old bloodstain. "Can you say the same, Bells?"

"You're going to wish you never said that." Bella's cheeks flushed red in anger. She had no reason to be annoyed when I was only telling the truth. If she was happy to trade gummy kisses for cash, then she should fucking own it. "There is a hierarchy here, and you? You're right at the bottom. No one crosses me and gets away with it."

She threw her long dark hair over her shoulder and flounced away with Scarlett. *Good fucking riddance.* I needed to concentrate on my winged eyeliner without worrying someone would stab me in the back with a curling iron.

"You don't want to get on the wrong side of her," someone whispered in my ear.

I turned to face a petite beauty. She wore glossy purple hair in two cute buns on the top of her head and looked like a legit anime character from outer space. I'd seen her around a few times. She kept quiet and tried to blend into the background. Apart from the quirky hair color, she was essentially my total opposite.

"Bella will make your life hell." She spoke so softly that I struggled to hear, but something about her vibe made me warm to her instantly. She didn't have an ego like the others. "Bad things happen when she targets you."

"Thanks for the warning, but I don't need it," I replied. "She doesn't scare me."

"She should," she whispered, glancing around to make sure none of the minions were listening. They were all too absorbed in their reflections to pay us any attention. "I don't agree with what she does, okay? It's just easier this way."

Something being easy didn't make it right. Everyone else may be okay with getting squashed under the Queen Bee's massive fucking superiority complex, but I wouldn't stand for her bullshit. If she wanted a war, I was going to put on my big girl pasties and bring it.

"What's your name?" I asked.

Her eyes widened in shock. I may as well have asked whether she liked to take it up the ass. In Lapland, bitches were hiding around every drape waiting to tear you down. A simple question, with no ulterior motive, came around as often as a customer wanting you to put more clothes on. *Fucking never.*

"It's Mieko."

"Well, Mieko," I said, "I think it's about time someone taught those bullies a lesson, don't you?"

Mieko didn't answer, but a tiny smile flickered over her lips as she turned away to fix her false eyelashes.

It looked like I'd found an ally in the hive.

West may have gotten me promoted, but Vixen wanted to make damn sure I started at the bottom. I'd spend the evening trying to flog diluted shots and avoid being molested by the creeps who had crawled in from the gutter.

"Come and sit with me," a chubby man leered, beckoning me over with a fat finger. I'd rather lie under a bus and ask the driver to run me over, but I smiled politely on the off-chance it'd earn me a few dollars.

The man had a round pink face that looked like sliced ham. Immediately, my thoughts moved to how easy it would be to strip his layers of fat away with a blade. As I approached, the clammy sweat of his paws seeping through my shorts made me want to throw up in my mouth. He gave my cheek an extra greedy squeeze like he was trying to force the last of the ketchup out of the bottle.

Hell fucking no, did he just do that!

I placed the tray down on the table carefully. Spilling the merchandise would only give Vixen another excuse to get rid of me.

"If you touch me again," I bent down to whisper in his ear and sunk my nails into his arm, "I'll fucking break you."

"But I thought you were selling," he whimpered. "One of the girls told me you were."

I tightened my grip. "Selling, what?"

He squealed like a piglet. If I didn't need this job, I'd take great pleasure in roasting him over an open fire. Bella waved over at us from the other side of the club. If rumors were being spread about me, it was no fucking mystery where they were coming from. A big bullseye had been planted on my booty from the moment I'd stepped through the sparkly silver doors.

"Bargain blowjohhh—Yowchh!"

His wrist would snap with another swish of my hand. From his quivering bottom lip, he fucking knew it too. For him, losing the ability to move his right hand would be worse than losing a best friend. How else would he fill his time?

"Candy." Vixen's glacial tone made me drop his trotter. Goddammit, he'd live to jerk another day. "You're up in the cage."

"I'll see you soon, handsome," I said, flashing the lump of lard my pearly whites. He didn't know how lucky he really was. No one ever laid a finger on me without paying for it. Not anymore.

I followed Vixen to one of the three cages and spotted Mieko kicking ass in another. Holy shit, the girl was flexible. She flew around like a crazy trapeze artist. I couldn't help wondering what had led her to this place. She could do better than this seedy joint with such raw talent.

"At least your hands won't be able to stray behind bars," Vixen hissed.

"Maybe they wouldn't need to if people kept theirs to themselves."

"What's wrong? Did he undercut your little operation?" She locked the cage behind me. It's a good thing we had a barrier between us because I'd have loved nothing more than to wipe the smirk off her smug face. "I heard you were offering ten dollars to swallow."

I may be under Vixen's lock and key for now, but she

had to remember wild animals could do damage when they were unleashed.

I knew now why Mieko wound herself around the cage like a circus performer. The less time you spent on the ground, the less opportunity the foot fetish guys had to stroke your toes. I'm all for people having their kinks, but I was not in the mood for anyone to play a game of little piggies on me.

A sticky-fingered bastard yowled as my heel trapped his forefinger underfoot. "Ouch!"

Oops. A girl can't help it if she's ticklish, right?

Thankfully, a toe-ring wearing dancer distracted the group of footsies away from my podium. The cheap piece of sterling trash was a twenty-carat diamond in their eyes. With them gone, the minutes passed quickly. It was easy to forget the club was filled with people. When I went into my own world, everything else became background noise.

My teachers used to call me a daydreamer for staring into space. It didn't win me any popularity contests in class. The other kids called me a freak — not that they dared say it to my face. *Spineless assholes.* There was an unspoken rule at school not to mess with the Evergreen group home kids. If you did, there was always the risk of your daddy's BMW being burnt to a metal crisp or your garage turning into a meth lab when you were on vacation. The Evergreen kids were trouble, and I was guilty by association.

"Oh, look!" The distinct whine of Bella cut above the bass like the scraping of frost in a freezer. "Vixen said she wanted to keep the chlamydia outbreak under control. Up there, she can't infect anyone."

Sticks and fucking stones. I'd been up against bullies like her my entire life. To survive growing up in Evergreen, you didn't just need thick skin... you needed a bulletproof vest. If Bella thought she could break me by spreading a few rumors, she was even stupider than she looked.

Whoever said drama got left behind when you graduated was a liar. The truth is, high school never ends. If you don't believe me, look at any politician. Corruption goes all the way to the top. There's nothing you can do. When I was younger, being invisible was my way of coping. Now, I'd take down the system with a sledgehammer if I had to.

"Are you even listening, Candy? Hey!" Vixen rattled the bars to get my attention. "I said, Zander wants to see you. Now."

What had I done wrong?

Vixen escorted me through the building. Correctional officers had more trust in convicts than she had in me. What did she think I was going to do? Make a bomb out of lube in the ladies? Raid the clubs' lifetime supply of tissues and rubbers? Pfft, they had nothing worth stealing — at least on the upper levels, anyway.

A bronze plaque reading 'The Boss' emblazoned on Zander's office door could either be a stroke of irony or a hint at his inflated ego. I'd put money on the latter.

I scowled as Vixen raised her hand. "I am capable of knocking myself."

"Have it your way." She grinned, pushing it open and shoving me inside. Who doesn't want to make an entrance with the grace of Bambi on roller skates after a nasty LSD trip?

"You should have knocked." Zander's chair faced away, but I detected the underlying contempt in his tone. "Did no one ever teach you manners?"

"I must have missed that lesson."

The rest of the dancers seemed happy to throw each other under a moving train, but I was no snitch.

Zander slowly turned and gestured towards a chair that looked as comfortable as a medieval torture device. "Sit."

"If you're going to fire me, just get it over with." I put my hands on my hips and didn't move an inch. "I didn't even hurt the bastard's wrist. It's not my fault he was a fucking crybaby—"

"What are you talking about?"

Way to go, Candy. I may as well have put an apple in my mouth and hogtied myself. *Just don't say anything else.*

"I'll only ask one more time." Zander drummed his fingers on the desk impatiently. My heart jolted at the sight of the 'no mercy' tattoo over his knuckles. For most people, they'd see that as a bad omen. But I had to drag my mind out of the gutter to stop thinking about what other ink might be hiding underneath his flashy suit. What the fuck was wrong with me? "Sit."

I plonked my ass down. At this point, did I really have anything to lose?

"What do you want?" I asked.

"Are you always this direct?"

"It depends." I lifted my chin to meet his unblinking stare. "Are you always this mysterious?"

"Tell me about the poker game." He reclined and propped his feet on the desk. "Where did you learn to play poker?"

I shrugged.

He raised one eyebrow, making his rose tat dance. "Now, who is being mysterious?"

"I got lucky one time," I said. I wasn't about to spill my life story to a stranger because West was a sour loser over being beaten by someone with tits. "So what?"

"Your act may have fooled Vinny, but this isn't a game." Zander's face turned to stone, giving me a glimpse of the predator prowling under the surface. "When I ask you a question, I expect you to fucking answer it."

He looked at me like I was a freshly baked cookie he wanted to sink his teeth into. Zander was no amateur. If he took a bite, he'd leave no crumbs behind. He'd devour you whole and wipe any trace of you from existence.

"You got your cut," I replied. "What more do you want?"

"Your cooperation."

Unfortunately for him, cooperation wasn't usually one of my strong points.

"West is taking you on a date next Friday," Zander continued. "There's a high-stakes poker game at Briarly Manor I'd like you to attend."

I'd heard enough whispered conversations in the dressing room to know Briarly Manor was the multimillion-dollar estate of a family, who'd made their fortunes through generations of drug smuggling. Nobody stayed at the top for that long unless there was something to fear. And the Briarly's? They were a fucking institution in Port Valentine. But it wasn't playing poker or visiting the manor that bothered me about Zander's proposal…

"You want me to help you win," I said, reading between the lines and putting aside my reservations. What's the worst that could happen if I went on a fake date with a man who hated my guts? "What do I get out of it?"

"Keeping your job and a new dress." My skin prickled as he looked me up and down with distaste. "West can't be seen with someone who looks like *that*."

"The arrangement doesn't work for me." The last time I checked a pretty dress didn't pay the bills and, given the Briarly's reputation, there would be a lot more at risk than losing money. "I want twenty percent *and* a pair of Louboutins."

If Zander wanted to dress me up like a doll, then he'd need to give me the full fucking package. When I left Hiram, I had the clothes on my back and as much jewelry as I could wear without arising suspicion. Beautiful shoes had always been a guilty pleasure of mine… or maybe I just really enjoyed how they could do serious damage? Either way, watching Bella choking on her veneers when she found out about my new gift would be priceless.

Zander threw back his head and laughed; a sound that would give Lucifer himself the chills.

"Brains and a pretty face." He let out a low whistle. "You'll get five percent *if* you win."

Before I could argue, Vixen charged into the office unannounced. She had the crazed manner of a meth addict hunting down their next fix. The chick's default mode was angry, but this was on a whole new level.

"You sent Red after the Razors?" she blazed. "Are

you insane? There will only be three of the Sevens left by dawn. If he fucks this up, they'll kill him!"

Red, whoever he was, must have got himself wrapped up in seriously messed up shit to have whipped the ice queen into this much of a frenzy. She had also inadvertently answered another one of my questions. I now knew who the members of the Sevens were: *West, Zander, Vixen, and… Red.* Despite the name, there were only four of them. Although, they may be down to three if Vixen was right. If the elusive fourth member was anything like the others, maybe his imminent death wouldn't be a bad thing.

"Red knows what he's doing," Zander replied coolly. "Ask him yourself tomorrow."

Vixen's nostrils flared like a bull preparing to charge. It was not the answer she'd wanted.

"What the fuck are you still doing here?" She turned on me, the nearest thing to a punching bag in sight. "Get back to work!"

As much as a Vixen-Zander showdown would have been entertaining to watch, you'd have to be missing brain cells to risk being sucked into the middle of that hurricane. When I reached the doorway, Zander called after me.

"Oh, and Candy?" As if he'd let me walk away so easily. "Don't ever think about lying to me again. It could be the last thing you ever do."

How could someone have the bone structure of an angel, but be a fucking demon on the inside?

"Where have you been?" Bella descended upon me like a vulture as soon as I stepped back onto the club floor. "You're late."

"Late for what?" I rolled my eyes. "Don't tell me you've been missing me already?"

She pointed up at the empty stage. The club lights were dimmed, and the spotlight pointed at a big fat nothing. *Fuck.* After my whirlwind conversation with Zander, it completely slipped my mind I was part of the line-up.

"How much longer?" An impatient drunk threw a beer can. "We want boobs! We want boobs!"

The crowd grew more restless with every passing second like a bunch of sugar-starved toddlers at a birthday party. If they were gagging to see a half-naked woman, they'd be better off going home to their long-suffering girlfriends or watching porn. Hadn't they heard of the internet?

"Get up there," Bella ordered. "Now!"

I bit my tongue to stop myself from telling her to go fuck herself and that I'd perform in my own sweet time. However, it wouldn't be long before Vixen returned. She was already on the warpath tonight, and I'd be damned if I was gonna be a casualty of her bad mood.

"Better late than never!" The announcer introduced me as I strutted onto the stage. "But will she be worth your wait? Candy Cane, everybody!"

The song 'Wicked Ones' by Dorothy blasted from the speakers. All I had to do was throw down a few simple moves to keep the pond scum happy. I let the rhythm wash over me and allowed my body to respond to the music. I gyrated my hips, moving slowly, trying to hypnotize them with my swaying. The leeches couldn't get enough of it. Dollar bills were already being tossed my way.

It wasn't until I began to climb the pole that an uneasy feeling swept over me. Bella and her army of tramps were standing shoulder-to-shoulder at the bar with shit-eating smirks on their faces. If those bitches were happy, something was wrong.

By then, it was already too late...

The moment I dropped into a rainbow pose, I saw the large bucket precariously balanced on the drapes above my head. All it took was the quick tug of a rope for it to overturn completely, showering me in a red and sticky substance.

"What the hell is this?" a customer gasped, wiping his spattered glasses. The liquid had sprayed every man in the front row. It'd be interesting to hear how they'd describe away the stains to their dry cleaners. Now, that would be a story worth writing about.

Mieko was easy to spot in the crowd. Her eyes were like saucers and a shaking hand covered her mouth. Hey, at least I had something to be thankful for. No one could fake a reaction like that, so she mustn't have known about Bella's plans to go Carrie on me.

Now, it made sense why Bella was so eager to get me on stage. It would have been difficult to source this much pig's blood at short notice — maybe she'd sampled the butcher's special sausage? In any case, it was hard not to be impressed by how little time it had taken for her to orchestrate this master humiliation plan.

It was a shame her efforts would be wasted, though. Hadn't anyone ever told her the show must go on? I flipped upright to let the metallic-tasting liquid run down my face and twirled down the pole to end in the splits.

Choke on a big fat pig's dick, Bella.

The audience went wild as I shook my hair and flipped onto my front to crawl through the puddle. It soaked my white clothes through as I writhed around and caressed my curves. It wasn't every day you went to see a strip show that ended like a scene from a slasher movie.

Lucky for me, I was no stranger to bathing in blood.

Thunderous applause filled the club as the song ended. Against all odds, Bella's plans to sabotage me had spectacularly backfired and I'd pulled it off. She'd not considered how good I looked in a wet T-shirt. This may have been my baptism of fire, but she was the one who'd got burned like a rasher of crispy bacon.

At the back of the crowd, Zander watched on with a stare as dark as the secrets he kept. A wicked grin crept over his lips as I caught his eye. He raised a glass. A part of me felt a twisted satisfaction at drawing his attention, whilst my instinct sensed it was anything but good fucking news.

I ran my tongue over my lips and savored the metallic taste on my tongue. Zander may be the big bad wolf around here, but Little Red wasn't a helpless young girl anymore. She'd got lost in the woods and turned into a woman with a hunger for blood... and an appetite for monsters with face tattoos.

FOUR

"Can you smell something rotten?"

As usual, Bella's nasal voice grated on my soul like freshly manicured nails down a chalkboard.

Scarlett sniffed the air. "I can't smell anything."

"Look!" Bella elbowed her in the ribs and nudged her head pointedly in my direction. "Over there."

As much as I was over the drama in the club, I'd actually been looking forward to my shift. Anything was better than spending another hour in my mold-ridden apartment. My teeth had only just stopped chattering from the three hours I'd spent scrubbing blood off my scalp with cold water.

"How funny, the only thing I can smell is a dried-up old cum rag. Oh, wait…" I said, smiling sweetly as my eyes landed on her. "That must be you."

Bella pursed her lips. It was rare for her to be in this position. No one else had dared to stand up to her and keep coming back for more. She'd better get used to it because I always came back swinging.

"I really should thank you for last night, Bells," I continued. "I made a sweet stack of Franklin's."

I planned to save every dime. Unlike Bella, who spent her earnings on coke and designer clothes, I needed a fallback plan. You didn't get as high as I did in Hiram's ranks by making friendship bracelets and singing Kumbay-fucking-ah. Bad people wanted me dead and, if any of them came sniffing around, I needed to get the hell outta town in a flash.

"Make the most of it while it lasts," Bella said. "Because I'm only getting started."

Bella may have been smart enough to not pull the rope herself at yesterday's show, but she was unknowingly wrapping another tighter around her neck. Getting into a war with me was not one she would win.

The club felt emptier than usual. Zander and West sat in their usual booth, where Bella and Scarlett hung off their arms like flies buzzing around shit. Their simpering giggles made me want to slice out their voice boxes and rip off my ears. Bella had clambered onto Zander's knee, and Scarlett looked like she was trying to light a fire in West's lap. I was busy wishing their cocks would shrivel up when a voice crept up behind me.

"Hello there, beautiful," it said. I painted on my fake-ass smile and turned to face Cheeks. His gaze was automatically drawn to my chest. The guy was incapable of looking any girl in the eye for longer than two seconds. "I've been looking for you everywhere."

"Well, you've found me…"

I'd already started weighing up the best escape options in my head. The last time I'd seen the bent cop was at the poker game when I'd hoped it would be the last.

"I'm going to a Maven party tomorrow night. It's an exclusive crowd, if you know what I mean?" Well, duh. You'd need to have lived under a rock for years to have not heard about the insanity that goes down at the Maven. "It's going to be a crazy night."

"Mhmm." I did my best to feign interest as Cheeks bragged about his connections. The guy spouted more shit than an explosive bout of diarrhea after popping a pack of laxatives. "Yeah, it sounds crazy…"

"Vixen told me it was your night off." Oh, I bet she had. I'd been trying to forget about it. Working kept my mind busy, and having an entire day with no plans was not something I was used to. "So, how do you fancy being my plus one?"

My mouth hung open.

No.

Fucking.

Way.

An invitation to a Maven night was one of the rarest tickets in town. Scratch that, it was like finding a fucking red diamond in the dirt. People traveled from all over the country to visit the underground club. It only opened a handful of times a year. Hiram's cronies, who'd done business in this area, had told me about it before. Sometimes, Hiram even went himself. Rumor had it they completely redecorated after each party because things got... messy.

As much as I didn't want to breathe the same air as Cheeks for any longer than necessary, it was hard to deny the prospect of going to the Maven had piqued my curiosity. Before I had time to reply, Zander appeared out of nowhere like a black cloud of doom ready to rain down hell.

"She's not going," Zander said flatly.

"This is a Maven party we're talking about," Cheeks insisted. "Why don't you let the girl speak for herself, Zander? Candy would like to go, wouldn't you?"

It was probably the first time in his life that Cheeks had requested a woman speak up for herself.

"My decision is final," Zander said. I opened my mouth to speak, but Zander shot me a look in warning. "You're not going."

Who was he to tell me what to do? He'd spent the evening wrapped around his in-house floozy. He was my boss — not my fucking keeper.

"It's my night off." I crossed my arms. "I don't see a collar around *my* neck."

As if to illustrate my point perfectly, Bella sidled up to Zander like a mangy cat. Her inflated lips were pouting so hard they resembled a severe case of hemorrhoids.

"Babe," she whined, pawing at Zander's arm. Her tone was ten times past desperate. If you dipped your dick into that level of crazy, you deserved to have it cut off. "You said we'd have some special time tonight."

"What good is a loose pussy to me?" Zander growled. She dropped her hand and yelped as if he'd slapped her. "You'd have to pay me to fuck you."

If Bella wasn't such an egotistical psycho hellbent on screwing me over, I *might* have felt sorry for her. But I didn't.

"You can't keep all your girls on a leash," Cheeks said, ruining his moment of redemption by slapping

Bella's ass as she slunk away. "Why don't we let Candy decide?"

"I'll think about it," I replied.

Zander's stare scorched into my skin like he was trying to brand me as his own. He needed to get it through his skull that I wasn't his property, especially if he wanted me to be a part of screwing over the Briarly's on their home turf next week. Not every girl in Lapland would do what he wanted on command.

"I'll pick you up here at ten." Cheeks took anything other than a straight 'no' to be a yes. Then he winked at Zander, adding, "She won't regret it."

Zander's eyes were dead inside as he watched Cheeks leave the club and disappear into the night. This spelled out a disaster waiting to happen.

"You won't go to the party if you know what's good for you," Zander warned. His breath sent goosebumps racing down my spine as he leaned in closer. "Every action has consequences."

A sane person would see his words as a threat, but I never ran away from a challenge. Zander thought he could break me, but I'd put myself back together more times than I could count, and maybe... *just maybe*... a small part of me wanted to see exactly what conse- quences Zander had in mind.

"He's really into me," Bella told Scarlett as they reapplied their lip gloss for the millionth time. How many layers of gloss would it take for them not to be able to speak again? "Have you noticed? He can't keep his hands off me tonight."

I disguised my snort of laughter as a bad fart from within the bathroom stall. I couldn't believe what I was hearing. What part of him saying 'you'd have to pay me to fuck you' didn't she understand? You had to admire her ability to bounce back.

"Can we double-date?" Scarlett asked. "West is, like, so... tall."

West was a lot of things, but *tall* wasn't the first thing that sprang to my mind when I thought of him.

"Zander just wants us to be alone, sweetie," Bella replied. "He's been begging to take me to a new French restaurant opening. Can you believe it?"

Puh-lease. The only place Zander would take her for dinner was the fucking kennels where the specials were a bowl of dog food and a side serving of cold shoulder.

Scarlett sighed. "You are *so* lucky."

"I am," she agreed. "Just think how much a man like him is worth. I can't wait for him to take me shopping."

Zander blowing her off like a used sex doll wasn't a deterrent when she was only interested in his bank balance. How was it possible for your vision to be so clouded by dollar signs that you'd throw yourself at someone who treated you like a hole in the wall? Maybe I was old-fashioned, but I believed sex should mean something and be with someone you cared about.

After they left, I gave it a few minutes to make sure the Queen had returned to her throne. Bella may be happy to pretend things were fantastic, but Zander's dismissal will have made her more resolved to mark her territory. It wouldn't be long before the hive was abuzz with the news of my Maven request which would only give them more reason to make my life unbearable.

As I made my way back to the bar, a clumsy idiot

stepped right into my path. The drink in his hand went flying over the pair of us and...

Fuck.

This couldn't be real.

"Candy?" The glass slipped through his fingers, shattering with a smash. "Is that you?"

It couldn't be, could it?

"What are you doing here?" I demanded, praying he didn't notice how much my hands were shaking. I'd been dreaming about this moment for years, but being caught off guard and drenched in tequila was never part of the plan.

"I could ask you the same question," he said, taking in my hot pants and crop top. His deep brown eyes looked troubled, and his caramel skin bore more scars than before. Good, I looked at them with satisfaction; I hoped they'd fucking hurt. "Last time I heard you were working with—"

"Why pretend you give a shit, Rocky?" My adrenaline kicked into overdrive, and I pulled my pocket knife out of my bra. I went nowhere without it. "I could gut you right here if I wanted."

I wasn't the same helpless girl he'd left behind five years ago. Back then, we were teenagers from the wrong side of the tracks who dreamed of getting out of a shitty situation. I'd been too young to see him for what he really was. Now, I knew the truth.

Rocky Marshall had no heart.

He was pure, unadulterated evil.

"If you touch me," Rocky said, "you'll have Zander to answer to."

His voice was just as I remembered, but malice had replaced any hint of playfulness. Did he seriously think him knowing Zander would stop me? I held the blade to his stomach. It would take seconds to make an incision and run with his entrails down the corridor like a party streamer.

"Let him come," I spat through gritted teeth. I pushed the knife in deeper, enough for a round pool of red to seep through the white fabric of his shirt. "Maybe he'll even finish the job if he finds out what you did to me?"

His rough hands closed around my throat in a flash.

"You don't know what you're talking about," Rocky hissed, using his full body weight to slam me backward into the wall and fingers to crush my windpipe. "I saved you."

"Saved me?" My mouth twisted into a snarl. He may think he has the upper hand, but I gripped the handle tighter. "You *sold* me!"

Rocky faltered, loosening his hold. "You think you know the full story, but you know nothing."

"I know everything I need to." None of his bullshit would change what happened. A few hours after I'd lost my virginity to him, Rocky delivered me to Hiram like I was nothing more than a pepperoni pizza. He knew the life he was signing me up for when he'd handed me over. The bastard doused me in gasoline, struck the match, and left me to burn. I walked through fire and came back stronger every time. Now, I'd become an inferno that'd tear down his entire world. "I'm going to hurt you just like you hurt me."

"Go on. Do it." He pressed his muscled frame closer toward me, forcing the blade in further. "I dare you."

I hated Rocky with every fiber of my being for what he'd done, but the heat of his body against mine stirred something else inside me… which made me detest him even more than I thought possible.

"Everything has always been a game to you, hasn't it?" I said. He'd played with my life. Trusting him had been the biggest mistake I'd ever made. "You won't get away with it."

"I know you don't want to hurt me, C," Rocky murmured.

He was right about one thing. I didn't *just* want to hurt him. I wanted to make him suffer. He needed to feel the pain of having his heart cut out and ripped to pieces as he'd done with mine.

Vixen's sharp voice hit me like another drink in the face. "What the hell is going on here?"

Neither of us spoke. Rocky's hands wrapped around my neck and me holding a knife to his crotch must have been an interesting sight to stumble upon.

"Do I have to make a new rule about no S&M in public places?" she sneered. "It didn't take you long to meet the new resident whore, Red."

Red?

No…

Rocky couldn't be…

"What can I say, Vix?" Rocky took advantage of my surprise by swiping the knife from my hand in a slick motion. "I've always had a sweet tooth."

"Don't let Zander catch you with a blade," she scowled.

Rocky winked and pocketed my weapon. "What he doesn't know won't hurt him."

Vixen shook her head in mock disapproval, but her shield had significantly thawed. I'd never seen her attitude rise above freezing before. The boy I'd grown up with would never have been friends with a slave driver like Vixen. It was only more proof he'd never been who said he was. That person had never really existed. All the time we'd spent together was built on lies.

How had the boy who broke my heart transitioned into the man now known as 'Red'?

"And, Candy?" Vixen's frosty glare returned with vengeance. "Don't think screwing one of your new bosses will change your place here. Go and sort the costume closet, before I change my mind about firing your ass."

I caught Rocky's eye. "I'll watch out for the skeletons hiding in there."

He may be one of the Sevens, but I would never follow his orders. His quick thinking and smooth move may have saved his balls this time, but the clock was already ticking down. History had a way of coming back to life and biting you in the fucking ass.

———

"Are you okay?" Mieko ambushed me amidst the growing piles of funky-smelling latex littering the floor. "I swear I didn't know what they were planning yesterday."

"I'm just peachy," I said. Well, if you didn't count learning one of my new bosses was responsible for destroying my entire future.

"I never thought she would do something like that." Mieko grimaced. "All the blood everywhere…"

"Are *you* okay?" I pressed gently.

"Fine," she replied, a little too fast.

Unsaid words hung in the air. We didn't know each

other well, but I recognized a haunted look when I saw it. She shot me a small smile that said *thank you, but I'm not ready to talk*. Hell, I understood better than anyone how some wounds could take a lifetime to heal.

"I wanted to talk to you about something else." Mieko chewed her bottom lip. "I overheard the girls talking tonight. Apparently, they found a video of you."

"A video?"

"A..." she said, then mimed, "sex tape."

Laughter bubbled out of me like a popped cork. I mean, come on, have you ever known a stripper who was too afraid to say the word 'sex' aloud?

"What's so funny?" She frowned in confusion, which only made her even more endearing. "Aren't you worried?"

Mieko's concern was sweet, but Bella's childish pranks were the least of my problems. The bitch would get what she deserved eventually but, right now, the only revenge I could think about involved spilling the blood of a man who I'd fantasized about killing for years.

I shrugged. "It'll be a fake."

Anyone could trawl through the internet to find someone with a similar body type or pay a shady hacker to do a deepfake job. The only semi-compromising footage of me ever taken had been used for blackmail. It didn't look great when married politicians were filmed in a hotel room with a hooker, did it? Hiram would never have allowed it to leak into the public domain. Covering your tracks was one of his rules. He was too thorough to let anything lead back to him… or me.

"How many hours do you think it took her to find my porn star doppelgänger?" I asked. With any luck, the actress would have a killer bod and I'd be able to use it to my advantage. "No wonder she was begging Zander for the D tonight."

A giggle escaped Mieko's lips and, within seconds, the pair of us were wiping rolling tears from our cheeks. I'd lived in the darkness for so long I'd forgotten how freeing it was to laugh again. When I lived in Blackthorne Towers with Hiram, my only real happiness came from my friendship with Crystal… but it was too painful to remember.

"I'm so glad you're here, Candy," Mieko said, blotting her mascara. "I'd never be brave enough to stand up to her like you do."

Not yet, anyway. Mieko may not realize it, but I sensed she was stronger than she gave herself credit for. All she needed was more confidence and belief in herself. If she hung out with me for long enough, she'd be kicking ass in no time.

"There's nothing wrong with lying low," I pointed out. "Sometimes it's the only thing you can do."

In this cut-throat world, we all did what we had to do to survive. Everyone had their own pasts and demons to battle. It just so happened mine sat in the next room with my knife in his pocket.

Mieko glanced up at the clock. "Vixen will be wondering where I am."

"Go," I said, throwing a pair of cum-stained stockings at her face. She shrieked in horror. "I'll see you in there."

A lone soldier couldn't do the same damage as an army when it came to taking down a hive, but having Mieko on my side would help to take the bitches in Lapland down.

If I found one more pair of unwashed crotchless panties, I'd...

Shit.

Bile rose in my throat at the buzz of my cell phone. Only one person could make this evening any worse. I looked down at his latest text.

Want to come home yet, Kitty? Just say the word.

This was the bastard's way of testing me.

I knew exactly how Hiram's mind games worked. He wanted to assert his dominance and remind me of where he felt I belonged. He didn't understand that Blackthorne Towers had never felt like a proper home. Ever. I may have had my own room, but it changed nothing. Deep down, I'd always known what the place was. A five-star fucking prison. If he wanted me back, he'd have to drag me across the country in a body bag.

"What are you doing on your phone?" Vixen roared, blowing up like a volcano and almost shattering my eardrums. She didn't even look at the rows of outfits that I'd spent the last hour organizing by color. Freaking color! I'd be lucky not to have caught a sexually transmitted disease from the pieces needing dry-cleaning. "You're supposed to be working."

"Why don't you buy a whip and be done with it?" I muttered under my breath, pressing delete and stashing my cell away. If only erasing Hiram from my life would be as easy.

"Scarlett's disappeared, and it's her shift at the bar," Vixen continued. No doubt she'd disappeared down a backstreet to give someone a cheeky hand job. "I need you to cover her. You have worked behind a bar before, haven't you?"

"Sure have," I lied. I mean, how hard could it be?

Everyone had gathered around the main stage to watch Mieko dance, leaving very few customers waiting to be served, which suited me just fine. We were in the hazy stage of the evening, where people were already too wasted to care what they were drinking anyway.

A storm rolled in over the bar as I ducked underneath to collect a clean stack of glasses.

"I told you." I recognized Rocky's voice instantly. My body tensed, knowing he was only inches away. "It's all good, man. It's under control."

"That's what you said last time," West replied in a low rumble. "Remember what happened then?"

"Enough." Zander silenced them both. "We can't afford any more mistakes."

"There won't be any," Vixen hissed. Whatever they were up to left no room for error. That meant one thing. Danger. "We'll talk later."

I rose to my feet slowly, hoping to draw as little attention to myself as possible. It failed. Zander detected the smallest sign of movement like a bloodhound.

He clicked his fingers. "Bourbon."

At least it was something I knew how to pour.

I decanted a shot and slammed it down with a bang. He may look like a gentleman in his suit, but wearing a fancy tie didn't excuse having no fucking manners. Then again, who needed to say 'please' when girls dropped their panties for you at a single glance?

"When he says bourbon," Vixen snarled. "He means Old Rip Van Winkle that we store *under* the bar. Not the cheap gasoline we serve to customers."

"Here's an idea," I said, unable to stop the words from firing off my tongue. "Maybe you should treat your colleagues with a little respect?"

"Don't even pretend we're on the same level." Vixen's jaw clenched. "I'm nothing like you."

"Oh, honey. I think we're a lot more alike than you think." I met her seething stare. "I know a cold, hard bitch when I see one."

Vixen looked like she'd fallen straight on her ass, as West threw his head back and laughed. I'd pay for that another time but not being thrown out on the street instantly felt like a win.

"She has you there, Vix," Rocky agreed, looking at me with a mixture of shock and admiration. The teenage girl he used to know wouldn't have dared to call someone out. She would have preferred to blend into the background and pray no one noticed her. Because of him, that girl no longer existed. "Maybe you should take her advice?"

"Of course, you'd say that," Vixen said. "You've only been home five minutes and already—"

Zander twisted his head sharply. "Already, what?"

I used to be able to tell what Rocky was thinking. Under Zander's scrutiny, I could have sworn a flicker of fear crossed over his moody features. Then, just as fast, it vanished.

"Is it a crime to check out a new piece of ass?" Rocky shrugged, returning to his zero-shits-given attitude and lightening the weird tension between them.

Rocky wanting to keep our history a secret from his

fellow Sevens didn't surprise me. Whatever motivations he had for keeping quiet suited my agenda. If no one knew about us, there would be no reason for anyone to suspect me when he ended up dead.

"That piece of ass is going to the next Briarly game," Zander said.

"If the shoes fit," I added.

"I can handle it on my own," West grumbled, crossing his arms. The giant killing machine was pouting and it was freaking adorable. Did he even realize he was doing it? Making him sulk might become one of my new favorite hobbies. "I don't need any help."

"We'll see," I said, making him pout harder.

"In that case," Rocky raised his glass, "let the games begin."

Bring it on, motherfucker.

He had beaten me once but, now? I played to win.

FIVE

I teased my pink hair into loose waves. To play it safe, I'd opted for a slick of red lipstick and a smoky eye. You couldn't go wrong with a classic combo, right? Besides, a Maven night was no high-society event. It was a place where shit went down and things got dirty.

Every action has consequences.

Zander's words sprung into my mind as I pulled on ripped black high-waisted shorts over fishnet tights. It paired well with my loose white crop top, which was thin enough to show off my leopard print bra and the snake tattoo which coiled from my hip to rib. I didn't know what the dress code was, but this should fit the bill.

Against the paleness of my skin, my beautiful pair of traditional inked roses stood out on my collarbones. Permanently altering your body wasn't for everyone, but it had offered me a lifeline. I traced a finger over the dagger tattoo on my thigh to feel the scar hidden underneath. The dagger plunging into a colorful heart had been my second big 'fuck you' tattoo.

Getting inked had been a healing process, allowing

me to take control and reclaim my skin as my own. Who gave a shit about what other people thought? My opinion was the only one that mattered. Decorating my skin with stunning artwork reminded me of who I wanted to become every day: a bad-ass bitch who didn't answer to anyone. Including Zander.

I didn't care about defying his orders. A Maven invitation was just that. *A Maven fucking invitation.* This was a once in a lifetime chance to go to one of the most exclusive clubs in the country. I wasn't about to throw it away because my boss demanded all his girls lick his shoes clean.

From the cab driver's reaction, my whole look must have worked together because the perve nearly crashed the car checking me out in the rear-view mirror.

"Pull up here," I demanded. I'd rather walk two blocks to Lapland than have him know where I worked. Having one creep like Cheeks hanging around was bad enough. I didn't need a fan club. "Anywhere's fine."

"The pleasure is all mine," he said, attempting to rub my hand as I handed him the bills. The creeper wouldn't be washing his palm for a week.

I waited until his headlights disappeared before walking in the right direction. Thankfully, I'd chosen not to wear heels and it wasn't far away. My trusty pair of black knee-high boots were perfect for dancing and their steel toe caps doubled as a great ball cruncher. As I turned down the next street, an uneasy feeling came over me.

Someone was watching.

I was not alone.

In my pocket, I closed my fingers around my pepper spray cleverly disguised as a lipstick case. Sure, I could go straight for the throat, but that wasn't what normal girls would do. Killing someone would draw too much unwanted attention.

Footsteps grew closer behind me. I reacted fast. I spun around, wielding my lipstick and ready to blast the fucker.

"Woah!" Rocky jumped back. He stood six feet away with his hands up. "Can we talk?"

I turned and kept walking in the opposite direction. He wasn't worth wasting my spray on. That'd be too kind. When I made my move, I'd make it count. Rocky sped up in pursuit. The bastard used to be on the football team, so I stood no chance of out-running him.

"Hey!" He caught my wrist and pulled me into an alleyway. "All I want to do is talk."

"Most people would take the fucking hint," I hissed, yanking myself out of his reach like his fingers were on fucking fire. "What do you want?"

"Zander told me about Cheeks." He put his hands against the bricks on either side of my head to box me in. "You're going, aren't you?"

I jerked my chin upward to meet his furious glare. "What I do is none of your business."

"Cheeks is a bad guy." Rocky was the last person in the world who had any right to lecture me. "You should stay outta his way."

"Don't tell me you're concerned about me now," I mocked. "It's not like you cared when you handed me over to the fucking devil."

Compared to Hiram, Cheeks was as threatening as the tooth fairy.

"What happened to you…" Rocky sighed, chewing his lip to think of the right words. It didn't matter what he said. Nothing would be good enough. "I had no choice."

"No choice?" I laughed bitterly. "Of course, you had a fucking choice."

His shoulders slumped like his entire body had caved in, then stood to run a hand through his dark floppy hair.

"I never wanted to hurt you," he whispered.

"Too fucking bad," I snapped. "What did you think would happen to me? I'd skip off into the sunset at Blackthorne Towers?"

Growing up in Evergreen wasn't easy for anyone. We first met when I was fourteen and Rocky was two years older. The other kids never tried to talk to me, but he hadn't been like the rest of them… or so I'd thought. The two of us used to hang out, share a joint, and talk about how we wanted a better life. Over time, we grew closer and our friendship turned into something more. Something I thought was special. We had a dream of starting afresh together, somewhere new, away from all the bullshit. Then it all fell apart…

"I did what I had to." Rocky looked down at his sneakers. I noticed the outline of something in his pocket. Something that belonged to me. "There was no other way, C…"

Rocky had been so much more than someone I used to date. He'd been my best friend. My rock. The person I trusted more than anyone else in this screwed up world. If something got stolen from my room in Evergreen, he made sure I got it back. Whenever I felt upset, he brought me candy to cheer me up. We didn't have much between us: no family, no money, no home, but we had each other... and hope.

"There's always another way," I snarled. "You didn't even fucking try."

When Rocky kissed me for the first time, it shocked me. I didn't understand how he could have been interested in someone like me. Back then, I was the weird freak who everyone avoided. Rocky was the opposite. He'd been popular. The cool, funny guy everyone picked first in gym. Even though we were different, I still believed him when he said he loved me… and was stupid enough to have loved him back.

"I get that you don't trust me. I don't blame you," he said, shuffling from one foot to another, then meeting my gaze with a newfound determination. "But I'm trying to look out for you. Fucked up shit happens at the Maven. It's not safe."

"I'm not the same girl you used to know." I narrowed my eyes. "I don't need anyone to look out for me. I can handle myself."

Betrayal and pain had twisted my soul in ways that made it impossible to put back together. I could kill a man in less than thirty seconds and castrate him in less than ten.

Rocky sighed. "Zander won't be happy when he finds out."

"Zander isn't my fucking keeper."

"You don't want to get on the wrong side of him, C. Zander and West are like my fucking brothers, but that doesn't make them good people," Rocky warned, stepping forwards to close the gap between us. "Disobeying an order will have consequences. You know that, right?"

"I'm not afraid of consequences," I said. "Not anymore."

He gently stroked one finger down my cheek, leaving a burning trail behind. "Maybe you should be," he whispered.

Wham! I slammed my knee into his groin like I was doing a kick-up with a soccer ball. He groaned, steadying himself against the wall to stop himself from falling. It'd be a while before he'd be able to move again.

"Don't ever touch me again," I hissed, pushing aside the tingling left behind by his touch and reaching into his pocket to retrieve the knife he'd stolen. "I'm taking back what's mine."

I stormed towards the neon lights. My skin may scream out for more, but my heart would never forget the feeling of being ripped out and blasted to smithereens.

After ensuring Rocky would piss red for days, I needed a drink. Fast.

"Double vodka," I barked at Scarlett, who, for a change, had shown up to her shift on time. It was most likely a rare stroke of luck over her ability to read the time, as there was nothing but air in her blonde weave. "Don't even think about watering it the fuck down either."

It was still early, and Cheeks hadn't arrived to pick me up yet. Typical. Where was the louse when you needed him?

Bella surrounded my barstool and formed a circle around me with her cronies. "Look who it is."

"It's always a pleasure, Bells." I downed my drink in one. It hadn't even touched the sides. I could drink men twice my size under the table. "Another."

"You know," Bella smirked, pulling out her phone and dramatically scrolling over the screen. "A certain video is going around."

"Really?" I played dumb. "What video?"

"You never mentioned you'd been in porn before," Bella drawled. "I'm not surprised. Everyone knows you love the attention, but who would want to watch that?"

The others giggled behind her like a pack of hyenas staring down at a dead carcass. I'd already lost my shit with Rocky once tonight, and Bella was treading a very thin fucking line.

"Your technique isn't even that great..." she continued.

As she was about to spin the screen around, a quiet voice piped up behind her.

"Zander is looking for you," Mieko squeaked.

Bella turned like a starving shark, and her nostrils flared like she'd got a whiff of a fresh kill. "Where?"

"In the back," Mieko said.

"Get out of my way!" Bella shoved her followers to the side. If she was driving, she'd have mown down every person who stood between her and Zander without batting an eyelash. Had no one ever told her desperation was unattractive? Zander wanting his cock sucked was not a life and death situation. "Move!"

Mieko caught my eye and nudged her head to the left, gesturing for me to follow.

"Is everything okay?" I asked.

"We don't have long before Bella finds out I lied…"

Mieko's voice trailed off as I followed her into one of the private booths. Something had to be seriously wrong for her to risk bringing down the full wrath of the Lapland monarchy on her head. Bella would not be happy when she realized the boss's boner wasn't waiting for her.

I pulled the drape closed behind us. "What is it?"

"I know you weren't worried." Mieko wrung her hands. "But you need to see this."

She passed me her phone, which displayed the still-image of a hotel room. Room 29. Adrenaline sent my heart racing like I'd robbed a fucking bank.

Fuck.

It can't be… but, it is… fuckety-fuck-fuck-FUCK!

I hit play.

"I'm so sorry, Candy," she whispered, having the decency to avert her eyes as the scene played.

In the video, a man with hairy legs and a fat belly perched on the edge of a bed. Only the lower half of his body was visible, but I could almost smell his reeking body odor through the screen. A few seconds later, a blonde-haired woman stepped out of the bathroom wearing a silky black robe. It was like watching a stick of dynamite explode in slow motion and knowing exactly what would happen next.

I clenched my teeth to stop myself from retching. "How long does it go on for?"

"I didn't watch it," Mieko said. "As soon as I realized what it was."

My retinas were burning, but I couldn't bring myself to look away. The woman peeled off her robe and stroked her curves over expensive lingerie. Her hair color may be different, but there was no mistaking it was me.

I fast-forwarded, being assaulted by a frame of Raphael Jacobson's dirty hands holding my head down. The slimy feeling of his *thing* in my mouth was hard to forget. Worse, if anyone found out his identity and what happened to him… I was dead.

I skipped to the end of the clip, where it abruptly cut off. If it continued for a second more, Raphael's dick would be flapping around his thighs and he'd be bleeding out on the floor.

My mouth was dry and words came out in hoarse breathy rasps. "Did Bella say where she got her claws on this?"

"She said someone sent it to her," Mieko said. "Who would do something like that?"

I knew someone who would.

There was a bitter irony in the fact I used to make videos to blackmail others. Now, the roles had been reversed. I'd offended Hiram by ignoring his attempts to contact me. This was my punishment. He wanted to show he had the power to destroy me. Raphael may have been an evil son of a bitch, but there were still people interested in finding out why he'd disappeared. And who was responsible.

If Hiram had held onto this, what other evidence did he have?

During the years I'd spent with him, he must have been storing incriminating evidence in case I ever dared to leave. He may have agreed to my release, but he never promised to stop following me or leave the past behind. Hiram must have sent Bella the video because he knew I'd see it. He knew exactly where I was.

"Who else has seen it?" I pressed, even though I already knew the answer.

Mieko gulped. "Everyone."

My tongue turned to sandpaper. I didn't care that the stripper bitches had seen it. Hell, I knew most of them had featured in a porno at some point. No, what bothered me was how nothing happened in this club without the Sevens knowing. If Zander and West didn't make enough jokes about me being a whore already, they sure would now.

"Candy," Mieko called after me, but my feet were already moving. "Wait!"

I didn't know where the fuck I was going, but all I knew was I needed to get out.

Far away from here.

I raced through the back of the bar towards an exit. As I threw the door to the kitchen open, I stopped dead in my tracks. Ahead, a girl sat astride the counter with her legs spread as someone chowed down on her pussy like an all-you-can-eat buffet.

The life-size barbie threw her head back. "Ohhhh-hhh, Vixen."

Her moans were overly theatrical, which meant that Vixen didn't give good head or the girl had an even better reason for faking it. It also explained the mystery of how Vixen hung out with hot guys all day and didn't break out in a fucking sweat.

"What the fuck!" Barbie's thighs slapped together around Vixen's head so tightly that it's a wonder her brains didn't leak out her ears. A part of me hoped it would. Anything would help distract me from the memories of my time with Raphael flooding my senses.

"What're you looking at, huh?" Vixen snarled, standing and wiping her mouth as if she'd been snacking on a bag of chips.

"Isn't she the whore from the sex tape?" the girl asked. The longer I looked at her, the more she resembled a plastic toy that had been left in the sun for too long. "Babe, she was filming us."

I hadn't even realized Mieko's phone was still in my shaking hands.

"You may want other people to watch you fuck," Vixen's girl sneered, "but not everyone's into that."

"I wouldn't—"

Before I could finish telling her how no one would be interested in watching her groan like a dying horse, she ripped the cell straight out of my clutches. My reactions were too slow. I had to use all of my self-control to squeeze my eyes shut and block the images trying to take over my mind.

She pressed play, and the sound of Raphael's voice filled the room.

"You like this, huh?"

It felt like a weight had been strapped to my chest.

I was sinking.

Every breath more shallow than the last.

I needed air.

I may have made sure Raphael would never hurt anyone again, but his voice still haunted my nightmares. Often, it was the last thing I heard before waking up screaming in clammy sheets. Hearing it again transported me straight back.

When I'd first moved to Blackthorn Towers, Hiram

believed every girl should go through, what he liked to call, a 'breaking in' period. Raphael took his job as 'the breaker' seriously. He was a sick bastard who got his kicks from causing inexplicable pain. He got hard off your tears and laughed through every bloodcurdling scream. Three days in a dungeon with Raphael would be enough to make the strongest person beg for death — let alone a sixteen-year-old girl. That's what Hiram wanted; he needed you to be willing to do anything to stop the pain. After Raphael broke your bones, Hiram stepped in to break your fucking spirit.

"What's wrong with her?" Vixen's girl giggled. "What a fucking freak."

They were still talking, but I couldn't hear a word. My vision blurred like a television set losing signal. I vaguely made out Mieko's phone, bouncing off the wall and hitting the floor with a smash, but it seemed so far away. I gripped the counter to stop myself from falling. The only thing worse than having a breakdown was having one in front of people who were already waiting for any excuse to tear you apart.

"Just leave her," Vixen said. She sounded like she was underwater. "Let's go, Charlene."

The two of them linked their sticky fingers together and pushed past me like I was invisible. With them gone, I slumped down the wall and started to count back from five hundred in intervals of seven.

500…

493…

It was the only thing that worked.

486…

I'd do it for however long it took to force the memories back into their coffin.

63…

Footsteps hitting the tiled floor made my head snap up. Fresh bleeding moons cut into my palms and stung from my clenched fists, but the discomfort grounded me enough to get my shit together. *Raphael can't hurt you anymore,* I reminded myself, *he's dead.*

"Cheeks is looking for you." West scowled down at me with his arms crossed over his muscled chest. "He doesn't like being kept waiting."

"Fuck you." I sniffed, wiping my eyes with the back of my hand and standing before he could see. "Go to fucking hell."

"Calm down, Pinkie." West's silver-plated canine winked at me under the fluorescent light. He didn't smile often, and it made the hairs on the back of my neck stand on end. "I don't bite."

"But I do."

My teeth had torn straight through Raphael's flesh like razor blades. I'd slain a monster that night, and I'd fucking enjoyed every minute of it. Killing him had been the best birthday present Hiram had given me, and I didn't regret it. Just like I didn't regret leaving behind my life under his rule.

The video may only be the start of his plans to get me back, but I couldn't let him win. I'd weighed up my options. I could pack a bag and flee, but what good would it do? He'd hunt me wherever I went. No, the best thing I could do was wait for him to come to me. I stood a better chance of survival if I knew the area. Besides, I had other reasons to stick around…

Stripping in Lapland may not be the future I

dreamed about, but I was only beginning to scratch the surface of the Seven's operations. Powerful people were close by and there were opportunities to make money. The Briarly Manor poker game would help. Port Valentine also offered me something I couldn't get anywhere else. Revenge on the one person to blame for the fucked up mess my life had become. I wasn't going anywhere until I'd mounted Rocky Marshall's bleeding heart on the candy pole.

West paused. "Maybe you will survive a night at the Maven after all."

"Aren't you going to tell me not to go?" I asked, cocking my head to the side. Rocky and Zander had already made their opinions pretty clear. "Everyone else around here seems to enjoy telling me what to do."

"It's your funeral." West shrugged. "But I do have one piece of advice."

I snorted. "And what's that?"

A wicked grin spread over his face as his electric blue eyes met mine. "Don't do anything you wouldn't want to be caught on film."

"I'll try to remember." I'd rather scrape my skin off with a cheese grater than let West get under it. "Do you get off on watching trailer trash now?"

"If I want to see someone suck cock." West's voice became a dangerously low growl. It had an animalistic quality that made my legs feel shaky again. "They'd be choking on mine."

"Get outta my way." I shoved him and bruised my shoulder in the process. I really needed to remember his muscles were hard enough to cause serious damage.

West's laughter followed me. If the sword in his pants was as big as his head, I'd bet he'd break my jaw.

Getting down on my knees for West would be like bowing down at the devil's altar, and… a twisted part of me couldn't help but like the thought.

The sight of Cheeks was enough to extinguish any faint flutters West had ignited in my core. I wrote it off as being down to the shock. Adrenaline could do weird shit to our brains.

"Hi, gorgeous." Cheeks dropped a wet kiss on my cheek, which made me cough because of the strength of his cologne. He needed to come with a hazard warning label. "I've been looking for you everywhere. Not having second thoughts, are we?"

Tonight had seriously messed with my head. I didn't want Zander to think I was following his orders, but partying was the last thing on my mind. Plus, I didn't have a gas mask. A few more minutes around Cheeks would bring on a fucking migraine.

"Actually, about that—"

"Before you say anything else," Cheeks interrupted. His shoulders tensed like I'd poked him with a cattle prod. He pulled a USB stick from his pocket. "There is something on here that I'm sure you don't want anyone to see. One of your dancer friends sent me a video she thought I'd be interested in."

"You're too late," I said. Being a cop and having a badge didn't give him the authority to blackmail me. The Maven may be a once in a lifetime opportunity, but it wasn't worth throwing my principles out the window for. Rule number one: don't take shit from a dirty slimeball who thinks he has the upper hand. "Everyone's already seen it."

"As much as I loved watching you, that's not what I'm talking about." Cheeks ran his tongue over his lips. Eurgh, he made my skin crawl. Those pixels would be the closest the fucker ever got to touching me. "There was something else in the video that interested me more. Did you know that only one family wears that particular ring?"

An icy shiver trailed down my spine.

How the hell hadn't I noticed the ring before?

As much as I hated to admit it, Cheeks was onto something. With the right technology, someone could easily sharpen the video enough to see the crest on Raphael's golden ring.

Raphael Jacobson hadn't only worked for Hiram. Sure, he regularly worked in Blackthorne Towers to break in the new girls, but he was part of a family whose fortune was built on sex trafficking. Raphael had been the youngest of six brothers and the black sheep of the family. He'd been too disorganized to get involved with the operational side and too unpredictable to procure girls, so he did his own thing. When he went missing, his family thought he'd crossed the wrong people and got himself killed. He was too much of a liability to be missed, and they were grateful his disappearance didn't bite them in the ass. Still, the other Jacobsons wouldn't be happy if they found out what happened to their baby brother. It didn't matter how much of a pain in the nuts he was; they were still blood.

I needed to tread carefully. Leaving Hiram's rule and starting over hadn't erased my past. All the big underground criminal organizations and networks were interconnected. Cheeks might have even heard rumors about the Kitten, Hiram's mysterious female protégé. If he had, or if he shared the video with any of his associates, Hiram coming after me wasn't the only danger I faced. The list of people who held grudges against me filled a motherfucking bible.

"I think the Jacobson family would be interested to know who their brother was screwing," Cheeks continued. He may know who the guy in the video was, but he didn't seem to suspect my involvement in Raphael's death. "Don't you?"

"He paid for sex all the time," I said, playing along with his assumption. If Cheeks believed I worked as a prostitute, then I wouldn't need to kill him... yet. "What's the big deal?"

"I'll bet a piece of ass like you doesn't even know what happened," Cheeks gloated. He didn't know he was talking to Raphael's murderer. "Didn't you hear?"

"Hear about what?"

"Your client disappeared around the same time the video was filmed." If Cheeks spent the same amount of time doing his actual job as he did jerking off to a grainy porno, then the town's crime rates wouldn't be so damn high. "I checked the time stamp."

"Really?" I gasped. "No way."

"I'm sure his buddies would like to have a chat with one of the last whores to fuck him." Cheeks leaned in closer, almost knocking me out with his toxic smell, to whisper in my ear, "I know you're nothing but a sweet ripe pussy, but they may not see it that way. Not all men are as gentle as me."

I had to grind my teeth together to stop myself from snapping his fingers. "I don't do that anymore."

"Sure you don't." Cheeks tucked one of my loose tendrils behind my ear, but the underlying threat lingered. He wanted me to go to the Maven and would not take no for an answer. "I've already ordered a cab."

I fluttered my eyelashes. "Sounds perfect."

Well, as perfect as using pliers to peel my toenails off one by one in a vat of battery acid…

"I thought that's what you'd say." Cheeks smirked, stashing the USB safely into his pocket and pulling out a jewelry box. "I almost forgot, I got you something special to wear."

He opened the lid to reveal a diamond choker. It looked like a tacky, sparkly dog collar. Not the type of accessory anyone would choose to wear to a rave known for its brawls. Diamond knuckle dusters would have been more appropriate.

"It's beautiful," I lied. "Can you fasten it for me?"

From across the bar, Rocky's eyes burned into us. He watched our every move like a lion prowling in the undergrowth, ready to pounce on his prey at any second. I turned around and held my hair up. Rocky jumped to his feet, causing his stool to screech across the floor. It looked like I'd touched a nerve. He needed to get it through his skull that my life, and the decisions I made, were none of his fucking business.

"Everyone will know you're mine tonight," Cheek said. His slippery hands snapped the clasp in place. "See? All mine."

The cool stones felt heavy around my throat. I tipped my chin upwards to meet Rocky's thunderous glare in defiance. His fists were balled at his sides. His usually brown eyes turned black, penetrating me with a venomous fury that wanted to poison the deepest depths of my soul. He'd never been an angry person before but, now, I saw a whole new side to him. A monster lurked under his clenched jaw, begging for release.

"Let's go." I shot Cheeks my best attempt at a charming smile, but it turned into more of a grimace. Luckily, he was too busy staring down my shirt to notice. "I think I heard a car outside."

As much as I relished the chance to make Rocky suffer, I couldn't afford for him to compromise my plans. I needed to lull Cheeks into a false sense of security, so I could wipe evidence off his devices. It'd be easier to kill him, but murdering a cop was never a good idea, even one as icky as Cheeks.

Keep your friends close and your enemies closer, right?

SIX

The cab ground to a halt at the rusty gates of an old shipping yard. Some girls got taken to fancy restaurants, but girls like me? We were taken on dates to places that looked like fucking crime scenes. Metal containers in varying shades of rust loomed above us like skyscrapers, surrounded by a graveyard of broken machinery. I hadn't expected a red carpet, but this? It wasn't exactly impressive for somewhere so infamous.

"We're here," Cheeks declared proudly like we'd pulled up at the Four Seasons.

We waited until the cab disappeared before heading towards a hole in the barbed wire fence underneath a danger of electrocution sign. As if that would keep the type of people on the guestlist out.

"Ladies first." Cheeks eyed the warning warily and proved me wrong. It turned out even the Maven had a handful of cowards attending. "After you."

I rolled my eyes and ducked under. It was an eerily still evening, like the opening scene in a horror movie. When evil acts take place, they leave behind a residual energy you can feel in your bones. My intuition told me this yard had more ghosts than a fucking cemetery. This was where many people had drawn their last breaths. Half the containers were probably stuffed with rotting corpses who held grudges.

Cheeks led us deeper into the metal jungle.

"How much further?" I asked.

Where was everyone? I'd expected axe-wielding murderers to be jumping out from every unlit corner. This was supposed to be a wild, hedonist's wet dream.

"Not far," he said. "We're nearly there."

We turned a corner and approached the filthiest container of them all. From its appearance, it looked like it had been at the center of an atomic bomb drop with large dents on the top and sides.

"This is the VIP entrance," Cheeks bragged.

"No champagne?" I muttered sarcastically. It wasn't exactly a luxury retreat.

Cheeks pounded on the door, then jumped a few steps back like he was playing a game of ding-dong ditch. Suddenly, the metal groaned to life to reveal a small gap. Out of it, an arm shot out and pressed the barrel of a gun into my forehead.

I didn't flinch.

Please. If they were going to pull the trigger, I would be dead already. It wasn't the first time someone had pointed a weapon in my face; although I'd be mighty annoyed if the ring of gunpowder ruined my make-up.

"Don't worry, princess. Let me handle this," Cheeks said. He stepped in to play the role of savior and mumbled a few hushed code words to grant us access. Had he forgotten he'd been the one quivering behind me a few seconds ago? It's not like he was saving me from imminent death.

The gun lowered, and the hinges swung open to let us inside. If this was the VIP entrance, I didn't even want to think about what other shit you had to do if you came in the other way.

"In," the doorman grunted. It was hard to make out his features from the number of piercings on his face. How the hell did he towel dry without catching one of those things? I only had my belly button pierced, and it hurt like a bitch whenever it got caught. The pierced troll stepped off a steel trapdoor and nudged Cheeks with the gun to pass. "Go through."

"Ladies first," Cheeks insisted.

Chivalry had nothing to do with it. The guy was a fucking limp dick. The feel of his sweaty hand on the small of my back made me want to scrub my skin clean with a scouring pad.

The killer bass hit me as soon as the trapdoor opened. It revealed a rickety metal staircase that vibrated with the volume of the music and looked close to collapsing. The stairway to hell led down into an underground cave where a swarm of people was crammed inside. Strobe lights mounted in the rock face bounded off every uneven surface.

Now, this was the Maven.

The dance floor was a fast blur of tits, leather, and tattoos. Chains hung from the walls like a medieval torture chamber, and bloodstains smeared the stone like cave paintings. This is what happened when you stuck all the worst people in the same place. A total cesspool of fuckery.

Cheeks pulled a vial out of his pocket and sprinkled white powder on the back of his hand.

"Want some?" he offered, snorting a line. "It's the best in town."

"Maybe later."

The night was young, but a bubbling tension already lurked under the surface. I needed to stay alert. It would only take the smallest thing for the whole situation to explode. Although, helping Cheeks get off his face wouldn't hurt.

We edged through the writhing bodies to the bar.

"Absinthe," Cheeks barked. He pointed at the dusty green bottle with wide, dilated eyes.

Cheeks chugged his down in one. Thankfully, they'd mixed it with water for me. No one but Cheeks wanted to drink that shit straight. Every mouthful burnt the back of my throat, but the minty flavor was good. It's what you'd get if you mixed petrol and mouthwash.

Cheeks slapped his empty glass down. "Another!"

"I'm gonna go to the bathroom," I said.

His high had kicked in, which made it the perfect time for me to slip away. With any luck, he'd have passed out by the time I returned. All I'd need to do was grab his cell, the USB, and his house keys to destroy any copies of the video. Then, somehow, figure out a way to take it down for good.

"Hurry back," he slurred.

I wouldn't be seeing any green fairies in the underground lair tonight; the only creatures around were horned fucking demons.

I scanned the packed crowd, trying to discern whether I recognized any faces. Hiram and his cronies only traveled to Port Valentine occasionally, but it didn't hurt to be too careful. So far, no one looked familiar, meaning there was no reason to make a hasty escape... yet.

I passed a group of brawling men who were a storm of fists and metal. Judging by the tattoos on their necks, they were from rival gangs. Behind them, a harem of young half-naked women surrounded an old guy, and a dominatrix led three barking men around on collars. Rules were non-existent.

"Want some company?" A straggly-haired man wiggled his tongue through the gap where his two front teeth should be. "I promise I won't bite."

Well, duh. He probably had to blend all his meals and suck them through a straw.

"If you want to keep the teeth you have left," I said, grabbing him by the scruff of his neck. "I'd think carefully about what you say next."

"Frigid bitch," he grumbled. He couldn't grasp how looking like he'd crawled out of the sewer may explain why someone wouldn't want to screw him. It was easy to understand why men subjugated women when rejection shattered their fragile masculinity.

I stopped myself from following him as he scurried off to try his luck on the next nearest vagina in sight. Forcing the Teenage Mutant Ninja Turtle's wrinkled grandad to kiss the ground may help release my pent-up anger from Cheeks's blackmail attempt and Rocky wanting to control me, but it was too much of a risk. I couldn't justify the attention it'd draw with Hiram breathing down my neck.

"Hey, watch where you're going!" A man called after me as I barged into him.

Wait… his voice sounded familiar.

I spun around to look up at the face hidden underneath the baseball cap. The surprise in his eyes mirrored my own.

"Q?!" I gasped, blinking hard to make sure I wasn't hallucinating. Surely, no amount of absinthe could resurrect the dead? Hell, I was sure Q's bones were dust by now! I'd always known Q was a stealthy lone wolf, but it was almost impossible to believe that someone could stay under Hiram's radar for so long. He had vanished without a trace after... what happened. "Is that really you?"

We first met in my early months of living in Blackthorne Towers. During my breaking-in period, Q had been kinder to me than the others. He'd tried to look out for me as much as he could. With the way things turned out, he must regret it now.

Whilst Q had never been one of Hiram's crew officially, he had been one of his most trusted allies until he disappeared. It had taken Hiram months to find a replacement. No one else could clean money quite like Q. What he could do with the filthiest dollars overnight was nothing short of magic.

"You shouldn't be here." Q grabbed me by the arm and dragged me to the side of the pit. All the while, his eyes darted around the crowd like he was expecting gunmen to descend upon us any second. "It's dangerous."

"What are you doing here?" I stammered. "I thought you were dead. Everyone did."

The last time we saw each other was forever

scorched into my memory; Q was covered in blood, jumping into the back of an ambulance. The look of horror on his face was something I'd never be able to forget. Even though it'd only been a year ago, it could have been a decade. Time hadn't been kind to him. Q was in his late thirties but looked older. His shoulder-length sandy hair was flecked with gray, and deep lines were carved into his skin. That's what happened when you went on the run and hid from Hiram.

Q put a hand to his lips. "Are you here alone?"

"I don't work with *him* anymore." The last thing I wanted was for him to think this was a trap. "I got out."

"He let you go?" Q frowned.

"Well, not exactly…" I paused. "It's a long story, but we made a deal."

"She always knew you'd find a way." Q shot me a tight-lipped smile, but pain hid behind it. The pain left behind by the absence of someone he loved. Who *we* both had loved. He ruffled my hair, like he used to do, then added, "Look after yourself, kid."

He turned his back on me and melted into the crowd like the invisible man, leaving so many questions unanswered. *Where had he been all this time? How had he evaded Hiram? And would he ever forgive me?* Instead of running after him, I stayed rooted to the spot. Q was entitled to his privacy. I owed him that much, at least. Maybe our paths would cross again one day, and we could finally talk about what happened… until then, knowing he was still breathing would have to be enough.

A girl shoved past, jolting me back to the chaos. "Move, bitch!"

For once, I couldn't find it in me to snap back a snarky response. Seeing Q had felt like a dream. It'd made defying Zander and Rocky's recommendations worth it. Even my worries about the video leak faded in the glow of knowing Q was alive. If he had started over, then maybe there was still hope for me. With the buzz of alcohol and newfound optimism, I set out into a tunnel that led further underground to find out what other secrets the Maven may be holding.

On my way, I passed ten couples either fucking or in different stages of undress. Seemingly, you had to battle past several orgies to go for a pee. I turned a corner to find myself face-to-face with a man lounging against the wall with his hands behind his head. I recognized the rose face tattoo and the smug smirk in an instant.

What the fuck was he doing here?

It took me a few seconds to register the two girls down on their knees, taking it in turns to pleasure him. Neither one was Bella. Zander averted his gaze from one of the dick suckers to catch my eye, then winked. Yes, he fucking winked.

"Enjoying the show?" Zander asked.

What kind of psycho stops to have a conversation when someone is giving them head? If he was trying to make me uncomfortable, it wouldn't work.

My cheeks heated in fury. "You didn't say you were coming tonight."

He wouldn't allow me to go to the Maven, but it was fine for him to do whatever the hell he liked. How was that fair? One girl pulled away and mumbled a few words in a language I didn't understand. To my surprise, Zander responded fluently. Whatever he said gave them added encouragement as their heads returned to bobbing around like they were raving to a song only they could hear. All the while, his eyes didn't leave mine.

"I'm not," he said, then grinned wickedly, "yet."

"You're a fucking hypocrite," I spat, turning on my heel.

I'd rather see Cheeks again than stand around watching Zander drop his load.

The atmosphere in the club had taken a dangerous turn. The rising testosterone levels in the air could have impregnated a virgin, and a few more drops of spilled blood threatened to start a full-on cage brawl. Pieces of rock falling from above covered the crowd in a cloud of fine dust, as it crumbled under the thumping beat. If people didn't end up killing each other soon, everyone might get buried alive by the end of the night.

Cheeks staggered towards me. "Where've you been?"

It was impressive he was still standing with the amount of absinthe and coke in his system.

"I couldn't find you."

At that moment, the action in the middle of the dance floor erupted. A man pinned another to the ground and started pounding into his face like he was trying to shape it into a burger patty. This was what everyone had been waiting for. Seconds later, bodies flooded into the pit and turned on each other with swinging fists. Sweat, fury, and pure blood lust turned everyone into animals. The darkness had been unleashed, and there was no going back.

"Le'ssss go." Cheeks grabbed my wrist in a vice-like grip and pulled me to the exit, as his instincts kicked in.

The man was a coward right down to the bone.

Cheeks may be a police officer by vocation, but he let others do his dirty work. We both knew he stood no chance if anyone threw a punch his way. They'd roast him over a barbecue and eat him alive.

"Leaving so soon?" The dungeon troll guarding the VIP staircase scowled, looking down at the crowbar in his hand like he was considering smashing it over Cheeks's head. I wished he would. Seeing Q had made this evening extra special, but being splattered in the asshole's brains would be the perfect cherry on top.

The crack of a gunshot and a bullet ricocheting off a nearby wall sent Cheeks flying forwards.

"Move!" he yelled, barging past.

The guard spat at his feet. Too fucking right. The Maven was not a place where you came to run from a fight. It seemed a shame to leave when it was just getting exciting, but I couldn't paint the town red every time I went out — especially when my sexy, insane boss was jizzing somewhere in the shadows.

Cheeks half-ran up the steps, nearly yanking my arm out of its socket. "Hurry up!"

The extra height gave us a bird's-eye view of the riot breaking out below. I glimpsed Zander's thorny face diving into the middle of the pit. His energy hadn't been drained along with his balls. I hoped the fight had ruined his happy ending. With any luck, someone would give him a black eye or break his perfectly defined cheekbones. Although any injury would only make him look more rugged and… *don't even fucking go there*, I willed myself. Those types of thoughts would send me over the edge of a dangerous cliff I wouldn't be able to come back from.

"I'ss nice we're alone," Cheeks said, releasing his hold on me as we exited the container.

Spotlights flickered overhead and cast shadows through the drizzling rain. There was nothing to suggest that complete carnage was unraveling beneath our feet.

"I'll call a cab," I said, heading towards the sound of the highway.

"Why so quick?" Cheeks's hand closed around my cell, leaving grubby fingerprints on the screen. "What's the hurry?"

I quickened my pace. "It's been a long night."

"But I think we should get to know each other," he said, then paused for a few seconds to remember the right word, "better."

"You're wasted."

"And you're *mine* for the night." His expression turned quickly to rage as his temper boiled over. It's funny how he was too scared to face off against the big boys underground but had no problem trying to intimidate a woman who only tipped over five-feet tall. "You're not going anywhere."

"I'm going home," I said firmly. "Alone."

"No, you're not." He snatched my phone from my hands and threw it against the metal side of a container, like a child unwilling to share his favorite toy. There goes the second one that had been destroyed in my possession. Clearly, I was cursed. "Not until you give me what I'm owed."

I glared up at him through my thick lashes. "I owe you nothing."

"You knew what you were agreeing to." He pointed at my neck. "Remember?"

"Not anymore." I ripped the choker from my throat,

sending stones bouncing and rolling into the darkness. Diamonds were overrated, anyway.

"You ungrateful whore!" Cheeks lurched forward and struck me hard across the face. The metallic taste of my blood was bitter on my tongue, but it made me feel more alive than I had in weeks. "No one disrespects me!"

"Just fucking watch me," I said, spitting the blood from my mouth on his shiny shoes.

He had messed with the wrong girl.

The stumbling bastard lunged again, but I was ready. My fist smashed into the center of his face. The satisfying crack of his bone felt wonderful beneath my knuckles. It had been too long since I'd heard that sweet sound. There was nothing I hated more than a person who picked on someone who was half their size, who they believed would be an easy target. Cheeks was a sniveling piece of vermin who hid behind his badge and had only gotten to where he was by brown-nosing the most powerful.

"Fucking bitch," Cheeks gasped, falling to his knees and holding his gushing nose like it was a fatal wound. "Call an ambulance."

"What's wrong?" I asked. "Is your mommy not here to kiss it better?"

"Call an ambulance," he begged.

"On what cell?"

"Come on," he pleaded. "This is all just a m-m-misunderstanding."

The only misunderstanding was him thinking I'd do whatever he wanted. I may have done a lot of things in my life that I wasn't proud of, but I still had my own rules. One of them was to only kill people who deserved it. Rapists, murderers, and traffickers were my favorite men to hunt, and Cheeks? Well, he fucking deserved it.

"You have something that belongs to me," I snarled. I knelt by his side and frisked his pockets. The closest to any action he'd be getting. He was too weak to resist, as I pocketed his phone and swiped the USB stick. He didn't have any keys, so I'd have to think of another way to get any additional copies. "Enjoy the rest of your night, Cheeks."

His eyes widened in panic as the realization of sleeping rough in a shipping yard festering with criminals set in. This wasn't how he'd expected the evening to end. "You c-c-can't leave me here!"

"Yes, I fucking can," I said. A part of me wanted to finish him off. Instead, I compromised by kicking his left side hard enough to break a rib. "And don't ever lay a finger on a woman again, got that? Consider this a warning."

Cheeks's yowls faded into the distance as I reached the edge of the perimeter and slipped back through the hole in the fence. I'd already deleted the video from his phone and the cloud. Now, all I had to do was destroy it. On the other side, a car screeched to a halt and its headlights almost blinded me. The window lowered.

"Get in," West growled from the driver's seat. "Buckle up."

I didn't have any better offers. It was either: accepting a ride, or having to hitch back looking like a hooker from a zombie apocalypse. As soon as I slipped in next to him, we sped off into the night.

"This makes us even," he snarled.

"Giving someone a lift doesn't equate to covering up a fucking murder," I snapped. "But it's a start."

West scowled. "What happened to your face?"

"Nothing I couldn't handle," I said, wiping my bloody knuckles on the expensive leather seats. I didn't know a lot about cars but, if he could afford this set of wheels, he could pay to get the stains out.

His biceps tensed under the thin fabric of his T-shirt. The roar of the engine was deafening as we raced down the empty highway. Maybe getting into a car at night in the middle of nowhere with a killer hadn't been a great idea after all.

Suddenly, and without warning, West slammed his foot down on the brake. Hard.

The tires squealed in objection.

We lurched forwards so fast that my insides felt like they were about to burst out of my skull. If we weren't wearing seatbelts, we'd have flown straight through the windshield like rag dolls.

"What the fuck are you doing?" I shrieked as we came to a halt.

A cocky smile spread over his face. "Just seeing what you can handle."

West usually came across as the sullen and moody type. Go figure it took almost giving me a heart attack to make him grin.

"So, you're trying to test that theory by killing us?"

"You seem to be doing a pretty good job of trying to get yourself killed on your own," he said. "Tell me what happened tonight."

"It's none of your fucking business." I tried the door. Walking home in the cold would beat riding alongside a crazy man who thought he was Mad Max. "Let me out!"

"I want you to tell me what happened," he pressed. "As long as you work in the club, you're my business. If someone hurt you, I'll deal with them."

A laugh escaped my lips.

West's brows furrowed. "What's so funny?"

"You pretending to give a shit," I said. West had taken every opportunity to rip me to shreds since the poker game, so seeing this new protective side of him had caught me off guard. "I'm not a damsel in distress, and I don't need you to fight my battles. I do just fine on my own."

"Cheeks hit you, didn't he?" West's expression was blank and unreadable, which made it even more worrying. I couldn't tell what was going on behind the muscles in his twisted mind. "Leave his cell with me."

"How did you—"

"It doesn't matter." West shut me down instantly. "You're not the only person who has a grudge against Cheeks."

I waited for him to elaborate, but he stayed silent. That was all the asshole was willing to share.

"Fine." I shoved the phone into the cupholder. I was only giving it to him because I'd already cleared what I needed to. He'd be doing me a favor in getting rid of the damn thing. "Are you going to tell me what you'll do with it?"

"No," he said. Of course, he wouldn't trust someone like me with such information. Whatever he had planned, it better be good. "Now, are you going to let me drive you home or what?"

"Only if you promise not to drive like a maniac."

My heart rate still hadn't returned to normal after our emergency stop. "And only because I don't have a better offer."

He turned the key in the ignition and didn't say another word until the car pulled up right outside my apartment block. Lapland wasn't the kind of place that kept the personal details of its employees on file.

I raised an eyebrow. "Are you stalking me now?"

"I think what you're trying to say," he said, "is 'thank you'."

"You lost my gratitude when you almost killed me."

I jumped out and slammed the door shut with a bang.

"Oh, and Pinkie?" West called. I didn't give him the satisfaction of turning around. "No one else needs to know about this."

Another secret I'd have to add to our growing list.

SEVEN

After doubling up on aspirin and gorging on junk food, I sauntered into Lapland with all the self-confidence I could muster. The dull ache in my head from last night hadn't fully lifted, but physical pain was the least of my problems. Zander knew I'd defied his orders by going to the Maven, and there would be consequences to pay. As if a hangover and slight concussion weren't bad enough…

I'd barely cleared the entrance when Rocky descended on me like a vulture. I wasn't the only one who'd had a rough night. He wore a loose hoodie over a pair of ripped jeans, and his crazed eyes were bloodshot.

"What happened? Who did that to you?" Rocky grabbed my arm, his fingers digging into my skin like he was holding on for dear life. "I told you not to go. I tried to warn you."

I may have respected his opinion once, but he'd lost the privilege long ago. His interference in my life had destroyed it. He was fucking delusional if he thought pretending to look out for me now would make up for the ultimate betrayal he committed.

"And I told you I don't do as you fucking say, remember?" I looked down at his groin in warning. "Move out of my way before I do some more serious damage."

He sighed and raised his hands in surrender. A wise move. A knee in the gonads had taught him to know better than to argue with me.

I headed straight for the dressing room, ignoring the other dancers' curious stares. There used to be a time when I was too shy to look anyone in the eye. Now, I walked into any place like I was fucking royalty. Confidence was easy to fake and no one could tell the difference.

"Oh my gosh!" Mieko dropped her comb and rushed to my side. "What happened to you?"

"I'm fine." I waved away her concern with a sweep of my hand, then winked. "You should see the other guy."

She dropped her voice to a whisper. "Are you sure you should be working?"

Bella's bat-like ability to detect vulnerability must have gone into overdrive because her chair spun around so quickly that the motion was a blur.

"Look who it is, everyone," Bella declared. "Frankenstein has arrived. Doesn't she look like a monster?"

"Frankenstein was the creator," I pointed out. Back in High School, gothic horror had been one of my favorite genres to read. "If you're going to insult me, at least get your fucking facts straight."

"No one wants to see someone with a face like yours dance," she sneered.

"Do you want me to level out the playing field?" I cracked my knuckles. "Let's see who does better."

Her smile froze momentarily as she weighed up whether I was bullshitting. Was saving face worth more than getting her own smashed up? She better think carefully, because I wasn't in the mood to be tested.

"What's going on here?" Vixen stormed in, then did a double-take in my direction. "You're not performing looking like that."

I played dumb. "Like what?"

"Like you've just walked out of a fucking ring."

The bruises on my face had matured like a fine wine; no amount of concealer could hide the bluish hue underneath. Not to mention my puffy bottom lip, which looked like someone had slipped when injecting filler.

"Maybe she's right, Candy," Mieko agreed. "You should rest."

"I'm fine," I insisted. Laying on the sofa planning Rocky's demise and binging trash TV wouldn't pay me. "I'm here to work."

"Not here," Vixen said. "Come back in a week. We'll see if your job is still around then."

"A week?" I spluttered, following her out and ignoring the snickers from the hive. "Can't I wear a mask?"

After dancing in a shower of blood, getting down in a balaclava didn't seem too outrageous.

"I'm done with your avant-fucking-garde performances," Vixen hissed. "You may have been able to charm Zander, but it's not going to work on me. My word is final. Lapland has standards."

"Fine, I won't dance." Now didn't seem the right moment to comment on how low her standards were if she let Bella front the show. Instead, I tried to level with her to strike up some kind of compromise. "But there must be something else I can do?"

"I thought you were too good for cleaning," she said. It'd only been a matter of time before she threw that back in my face. Bargaining with her was harder than taking blood from a heroin addict. "Remember?"

"C'mon, Vix." Rocky came over to intervene. "Cut her some slack, huh?"

He could shove his 'help' right up his ass. His trying to help only made me more infuriated. I wasn't the defenseless kid he used to look out for. The only thing he needed to be watching was his own back because I was coming for him.

"What the fuck is wrong with you, Red?" Vixen turned on him like a hungry Rottweiler and jabbed a finger into his chest. "You've been acting weird since you got back. The girls are my fucking business, not yours. You need to get your shit together. You're a mess!"

Rocky scratched his left ear like he always used to when he was trying to hide something. Would Vixen still think so highly of her precious Red, if she knew what he'd done to me? Hell, who was I kidding? The bitch would give him a medal.

Before Rocky could reply, Zander and West joined us. Zander wore his usual perfectly pressed black suit. He must have held his own in the Maven pit because all he had to show for it were minor cuts over his knuckles. It only made me hate Cheeks even more. I'd missed out on seeing Zander in action because of his spinelessness.

"What're you two arguing about now?" West asked.

"Red thinks I should cut her a little slack," Vixen explained. "We run a strip club, not a fucking freak show!"

"Speaking of shows," Zander said, turning his attention to me, "did you enjoy yours last night, Candy?"

Rocky's eyes flitted between the pair of us in confusion. The truth was, I'd been trying not to think about what I saw in the tunnel. Everyone knew Zander used women like tissues, and they were happy to be disposable for him.

"I've seen better," I answered with a casual shrug. "It didn't last long."

"You defied a direct order," Zander said. His gray eyes burned into mine like we were the only two people in the room. "I told you there would be consequences if you went to the Maven."

Was that a threat, or a promise? A shiver ran down my spine. Apparently, my beat-up face wasn't enough to serve whatever punishment he had in mind.

"What consequences?" I challenged, squaring my shoulders.

"You'll see."

"You can't let her go to the Briarly game now," Vixen huffed. "Not unless West doesn't mind looking like a wife-beater."

"Hey!" West slammed his glass down hard enough for it to crack. "She's not fucking going if—"

"Enough." Zander's steely tone signaled the conversation was over. "No more business talk here."

Vixen whirled around to face me. "Why are you still standing here? I told you to come back in a week."

"You heard her," Zander said. "Go."

"What about—"

"We'll be in touch," Zander interrupted. "But remember what I said, Candy."

The club fell into a hushed silence. In a seedy place, that only meant one thing. Serious trouble had strolled in off the sidewalk.

"He said he had to come in." One of the bald security guards hurried over to report to West and jerked his head toward a swaying figure. "I didn't know what—"

West raised his hand to silence him. "We'll take it from here."

Holy shit.

"You!" Cheeks's shrill voice echoed through the building as he pointed a shaky finger at me in accusation. "You sneaky fucking whore! What did you do with them? What did you do?"

He stumbled down the steps, and the floor cleared to make a path for him to pass. He looked almost unrecognizable. He was filthy, still in last night's blood-soaked clothes, and covered in bruises from head to toe. Both of his eyes were so swollen he couldn't see where he was going and kept tripping over his own feet. Sure, I'd given him a good beating, but he'd still been coherent when I'd left — well, coherent enough to have tried to attack me. After I'd gone, someone else must have got to him... but who?

"How did you do it?" Cheeks slurred, then mumbled a series of nonsensical sentences no one could understand. "All the copies... the... gone."

"I don't know what you're talking about," I said.

I may not be performing tonight, but we were certainly giving everyone a show.

"You heard her," West growled. He planted a firm

hand on Cheeks's shoulder, making him cry out in pain. "It's time to go."

"Not until she gives me them back. They're mine. Mine!" Cheeks shouted, wrestling to free himself. With his free hand, Cheeks grabbed my shirt and yanked me closer. The smell of vomit and liquor on his breath made my stomach heave. "I'll hand you over... I'll tell... I swear..."

"Get your hands off her," Zander warned. He unbuttoned his shirt cuffs and rolled up his sleeves to reveal more beautiful ink. "I won't ask you again."

"But, she—"

Zander threw a right hook that sent Cheeks toppling backward like a stack of Jenga blocks.

"You don't know who... you don't know..." Cheeks wailed as West yanked him to his feet. "You… mistake… she… you don't know who…"

Rocky moved to create a human wall between me and Cheeks. Seeing him stand next to West made me realize just how much he had filled out over the years. Rocky had always been tall and toned, but his shoulders were now broader and his muscles more defined.

"What the fuck is he talking about, Candy?" Vixen asked.

"How am I meant to know?" I rebutted. "Just look at him. He's on something!"

Roaring sirens outside grew closer.

"If you've brought trouble to our door, I swear I'll—"

Ten armed officers charged through the doors and flooded inside, drowning out the rest of Vixen's threat. Complete mayhem broke out. A stampede of clicking heels and high-pitched squeals echoed around the club as dancers fled into the backroom. Several customers ducked under tables to hide or scampered to the nearest bathroom in a desperate plight to flush whatever substances they had.

My heart hammered in my chest.

Why were they here?

Had someone tipped them off?

Did Cheeks tell them about my links to Raphael?

"Over here," one cop roared, beckoning the others to follow and heading in our direction.

Running would only make me look more guilty. This was it. The moment I got locked away forever.

"Get him," another said, as Cheeks tried to make a run for it.

They swarmed down on him in a flash. He stood no chance against them all.

"No!" Cheeks screamed in objection. They forced his struggling body to the floor and pinned his limbs in place. "This is a mistake!"

"Look what we have here." An officer pulled a bag of white powder from his back pocket. "Roy Checkersford, you are under arrest. You have the right to remain silent."

Last night Cheeks had carried a small vial of coke, but this would have been enough to tranquilize the entire dance floor. Even Cheeks wouldn't be stupid enough to carry around so much gear. West's words came flooding back: 'I'll deal with him.'

"No!" Cheeks thrashed around like a fish out of water. "Please, Billy! No! That's not mine! It's a setup… I can ex-explain!"

West watched the scene unfold with little interest. *Was it possible he'd orchestrated the whole thing?* His expression was as blank and unreadable as ever. Goddammit, it was easy to see why the guy was good at poker.

"Save it, Cheeks." The officer took great pleasure in forcing his colleague roughly into cuffs. Cheeks may have powerful connections outside of work, but it didn't look like they had made him a popular guy on the force. It was nice to know there were still cops who took their oath seriously. "You'll be going away for a long time."

"But it wa-wasn't me," Cheeks wept.

Watching him cry like a baby almost made my decision not to kill him worthwhile… *almost.*

The club buzzed with speculation as soon as the cops cleared out. Watching a powerful figure, like Cheeks, being escorted in a police van sent a massive statement. A big fuck you to the status quo and to those who pulled the strings in Port Valentine. The fallout from his arrest would be worse than the Chernobyl exclusion zone.

"Get everything under control, Vixen," Zander ordered.

She nodded curtly. A police raid was akin to throwing a grenade at Lapland's reputation for discretion. No doubt she'd have an empty bar by the time she'd finished smoothing over this mess.

"All of you." Zander signaled to the rest of us. "My office. Now."

From his rigid posture, he was using every ounce of his self-control not to explode. This was not a situation I wanted to get caught up in.

"If I'm not allowed to work—"

"Don't fucking test me, Candy," he said through gritted teeth. "Fall in fucking line."

This wasn't a battle worth fighting. Tension rose with every step. I felt like a naughty child being called to the principal's office; although Zander's punishments would be worse than writing an apology letter or a page of lines.

"Do you know what this means?" Zander reeled as soon as the door closed behind us. "The Briarlys are going to be furious. You know who they'll blame."

It didn't surprise me to find out the Briarlys had Cheeks on their payroll. Dirty cops helped crime families from the inside all the time; whether that was by feeding them information, helping them cover their tracks, or smoothing over any misdemeanors. It also explained why Cheeks carried a lot of cash. A family as prolific and wealthy as the Briarlys would have to pay damn well to ensure law enforcement looked the other way.

"But we didn't do anything," Rocky said. "Cheeks has fucked a lot of people over. It's not our fault he got sloppy and got caught with coke."

"Sloppy doesn't exist in our world." Zander paced back and forth. "I'm only going to ask this once. What do you know?"

Zander studied each of us. West didn't flinch under his scrutiny. He stared back at Zander with bored indifference. If West had gone against his fellow Sevens to handle Cheeks in his own way, then that was his prerogative. It was not my story to tell.

"What was he talking about, Candy?" Zander pressed. His piercing eyes searched my face for any hint of hesitation. "Copies? What did he mean?"

"He was talking shit like a crazy person," I dismissed. West wasn't the only person in the room who had a good poker face. "Nothing he said made any sense."

"You shouldn't hide anything from me, Candy."

"Come on, Zander." I rolled my eyes. "Anyone with a brain cell could see he'd lost his mind. The guy was too jacked up to function."

Zander pulled a gun out of his suit jacket and placed it on the desk. He turned to West and Rocky. "Why don't you two leave us alone?"

Rocky tensed at my side but inclined his head. Both of them obeyed and filed out. No one would dare question Zander's authority. Being stuck in a soundproof room with a gun and my boss was not an ideal situation.

I jutted my hip. "Well?"

Zander didn't reply. He let the silence stretch out to try to make me squirm. His tactic wouldn't work. If he gave me a recliner and a margarita, then I could chill here all night without saying a word if I had to. I'd spent a lot of time in solitary confinement in Blackthorne Towers, and my company was often better than the alternative.

"You've defied me once before," Zander said eventually. He cocked his head to the side, trying to figure me out. "Why should I trust you?"

"I could ask you the same question."

Trust was something to be earned. Zander knew better than anyone. Above all, I had to look out for myself. No one else was going to. I'd come into this world having to fend for myself, and that's the only way I'd get through it.

Zander picked up the gun and took a step forward.

I didn't move, but my heart rate started to rise. It wasn't the gun that made me nervous, but the thought of being so close to someone who wanted to ruin me. My vision wavered as his smoky bergamot aftershave enveloped me. He smelled nearly as delicious and dangerous as he looked.

"Do you always have an answer for everything?" Zander leaned in closer, the heat of his breath tickling my neck. "Anyone would think you had a death wish."

The feel of the cold metal running up my bare leg made me shiver.

"Maybe I do," I said.

Zander's knuckles gently grazed my skin as the gun slipped in between my thighs.

"I don't know what you're hiding." His stare scorched into mine as the gun slid further underneath my tiny skirt. "But I'll find out."

I tried to ignore how Zander's inked fingers brushing against me were setting every nerve ending in my body on fire. *How could something so bad feel so fucking good?* I didn't fear him shooting, but I'd rather die than give Zander the satisfaction of knowing the effect he had on me if he were to slip a few inches higher.

"I had nothing to do with his arrest," I said. "That's all you need to know."

Zander studied my face, then pulled the gun away and tucked it back into his waistband. Whatever he saw in my expression must have satisfied him. I smoothed down my skirt and flicked my hair over my shoulder, like having the barrel of a gun pointed at my pussy was a normal occurrence. He'd get pleasure from knowing he'd rattled me, and I refused to give him it.

"Do you like playing games, Candy?"

I arched an eyebrow. "Games?"

"No one takes me for a fool," Zander said. "When I play, I win. Every time. Whatever you're hiding, make no mistake, I will find out. And if you cross me, there—"

"There will be consequences," I finished the end of his sentence for him. "I know."

"You have no fucking idea," he spat. As much as Zander tried to portray the image of someone with full self-control, an unpredictable demon lived inside him that liked to rear its head when people least expected it. "Listen carefully to what I'm about to say. On Saturday, you're going to help us win the poker game at Briarly Manor. You will not see a cent because of the trouble you brought in tonight."

"But we had a deal."

"A deal you broke the moment you stepped into the Maven," he snarled. "You should be fucking grateful for the opportunity."

"What's stopping me from walking out of here and not helping you at all?"

"Nothing," Zander said, then paused to give the illusion he was deep in thought. "Unless you want the police to find out your new little friend's secret. What's her name? Mieko? Don't you think they'd be interested to know how she killed her own father?"

"You're talking bullshit," I said. A Care Bear seemed more likely to be an axe-wielding psychopath than the sweet girl who was too embarrassed to say the word 'sex' aloud. Sure, she'd seen some messed up shit, but killing her dad? She didn't seem capable of squashing a fly, let alone another person.

"Am I?" He stroked his chin, drawing attention to his perfect jawline. "Why don't you ask her yourself?"

The real question wasn't whether Zander was telling the truth about Mieko. It was what he was capable of and the depth he'd be willing to sink to.

"You're not a snitch."

Not snitching was the only rule all criminals held as fucking gospel. Snitches get stitches didn't become a truth universally acknowledged for no reason.

"Maybe not, but how sure are you?" He wouldn't mind screwing decent people over if it meant getting what he wanted. "Is it a risk you're willing to take?"

He was a master manipulator who could burrow under your skin and dig up vulnerabilities. It didn't matter whether he was lying. Seeing Q yesterday had brought back memories, and I'd already vowed I'd never let another innocent life be ruined because of my choices.

"Okay, I'll go to your fucking game." I scowled. "But I have one condition."

"This wasn't up for negotiation."

"Neither is this," I said. "If I do this, I want Mieko's history to stay buried. Forever."

"That depends."

"On what?"

Zander grinned wickedly. "On whether you can play by my rules."

Every fiber of my being screamed in objection. After leaving Hiram, I'd sworn never to follow someone else's orders again. Especially when those orders came from a gang leader who had serious control issues.

"Fine." I pursed my lips. Backing down wasn't usually in my nature, but this was an exceptional circumstance. Letting Zander believe he had the upper hand was the lesser of two evils. Allowing him to think he'd won would get him off my back long enough for me to pursue my personal agenda. "I'll try."

"Good," he said. "Just don't forget what happens if you break them."

There would be consequences.

EIGHT

A loud banging on my apartment door rudely interrupted my dairy coma. If my nosey neighbor had come to tell me to turn the TV down again, I'd blast metal at full volume for the rest of the day. Since when was the sound of Queer Eye so offensive? I didn't thump on her door every time she argued with one of her boyfriends.

"I'm coming," I shouted.

Since the Sevens had banned me from working in Lapland until my face healed, I'd spent the week involuntarily getting to know a little too much about the people who lived around me. In fact, the most productive task I'd done was turning my sofa into a blanket cocoon and devouring two tubs of ice cream in sixty minutes flat.

The knocking persisted.

If the TV was loud enough for her to walk across the landing, then she should have damn well heard me.

I swung the door open. "I already told you—"

"Before you slam the door in my face." Rocky

stepped forward to wedge his foot in the gap. "I have something for you."

He held a large shiny shopping bag that looked like it was from a fancy boutique I'd never be able to afford.

"Leave it there," I directed, nodding at the ground like it was a suspicious package and I was part of the bomb disposal unit. "Then back away."

"Aren't you going to invite me in?" he pressed.

"What's going on? What's that racket?" My neighbor's shrill voice floated over from across the hall. She shuffled out of her apartment with her hair still in rollers. She wore a leopard print silky robe and balanced a cigarette precariously in her hand. She looked Rocky up and down with distaste, then tutted. "Isn't it a bit early for gentleman callers? It's a scandal!"

"Can it, lady," I snapped back. Hello, we weren't in the 1920s anymore. Besides, she was hardly one to talk. I knew all about what *she* got up to. Wasn't it pathetic that even my sixty-year-old neighbor had a more active sex life than me? "If you don't want your husband to know what you get up to during the day, then you'll keep your mouth shut."

Rocky snorted in laughter.

From the look of shock on her leathery face, I may as well have flashed her my boobs. She cursed under her breath about the youth of today and left a trail of ash behind her as she stomped back inside. Hopefully, she'd think twice before bothering me the next time I binged a box sct.

"Can I come in?" Rocky asked again.

He was the last person I wanted to invade my space, but I knew Mrs. Leopard-Print-Robe would already have a glass pressed against the wall. Reluctantly, I stepped aside to let him pass. "You have two minutes."

"Looks like you've been having fun," he said, taking in the half-empty ice cream tub and spoon balanced on the coffee table.

"What do you want, *Red*?"

He smirked down at my pink fluffy feet. "I like your slippers."

Goddammit, those soft cushioned clouds really brought down my badass vibes. I'd been rocking the no make-up and messy bun look all week. Why get ready when the only plans I had involved pressing a button and eating my body weight in sugary goodness?

"My face is up here." I snapped, noticing his gaze lingering on my chest. I'm pretty sure my white vest was see-through. "Give me the fucking bag."

He cleared his throat.

"This is for you to wear at the game tomorrow." Yep, he could 100% see my nipples through this thing. "A car will pick you up at eight."

I ripped open the bag and shredded the pink rose-smelling tissue paper. Inside, a beautiful white dress had been neatly folded on top of a shoebox. It was one of the most stunning dresses I'd ever seen. Not that I'd let him know that.

I held it up and half-shrugged. "It'll do."

"Zander wants to know if it fits." Rocky planted his ass in the center of my blanket cocoon and draped his arms over the sides of the sofa like he owned the fricking place. "If it doesn't, I'll exchange it."

I checked the label. "It'll fit."

"Aren't you going to try it on?"

"And give you a private show?" I scoffed. "I don't think so."

"What about the shoes?"

I opened the lid to reveal a brand-new pair of Louboutins. *No fucking way.* I'd never been a materialistic person, but those beauties were a piece of wearable art. They were also worth more than everything I owned put together.

"They're the right size." I took great care in relaxing my facial muscles. My happy dance would have to wait until after Rocky left. "I guess they'll do too."

"Good," he said flippantly, completely oblivious to the value of the heels. Either that or becoming a Seven had completely changed his perception of money. When you'd come from a place of poverty, it was hard to leave that mindset behind.

"You've made your delivery," I said. "You don't have to stick around."

Rocky didn't move. He looked up, trying hard to keep his gaze fixed above my shoulders. "Your face looks better."

"I'm a quick healer."

The bruises had faded enough to make them easy to cover, but the cut on my lip would be harder to hide. A faux lip ring should do the job nicely. It's good I knew how to rock a disguise better than anyone.

"I see you still have a sweet tooth." Rocky picked up my spoon and took a whopping mouthful of my ice cream. If I didn't already want him dead, I would now.

I snatched the tub from his evil clutches. "Don't you know eating a girl's cookie dough without permission is the douchiest move on earth?"

"Mmm." He licked his lips to taunt me further. "My favorite!"

I threw him a filthy look. "You can go now."

"While I'm here," he went on, ignoring me, "I wanted to talk to you about something else."

"And I don't want to listen to anything you have to say."

How many times did I have to shut him down before he got the message?

"Zander has eyes in jail." He knew that would get my full attention. "Cheeks has started talking. We heard from the doc that he was drugged and beaten. The fucker wouldn't be breathing if I'd gotten my hands on him."

Well, that was one thing we agreed on.

"What else have you heard?" I probed. It wouldn't be practical to kill Rocky here but, if the cops were closing in, this could be the last chance I'd get.

"He's squealing to anyone who'll listen that it was a setup." Rocky watched me closely for a reaction. "But he's not given any names."

Cheeks cared about maintaining the image he'd created over the years. He'd never want to admit how he'd got his ass beat by a stripper, who he'd tried to assault at an underground rave. It'd be too damaging to his macho persona.

"What do the cops think?" I asked, savoring the creamy goodness on my tongue. It tasted all the sweeter to know it was Rocky's favorite and he wouldn't be getting another bite.

"It's not the cops we're worried about. They've always known Cheeks was dirty, but the bastard has always had someone else to cover his ass." Rocky's brows furrowed in concern. "I've been thinking about something Cheeks said when he was last in the club. He mentioned a video, and if he was talking about—"

"The one of me?" I cut in. "You've seen it then? Old habits die hard."

He winced, but let my comment wash over him. "Where did it come from?"

"Why does it matter?" I slammed my spoon down. If things got ugly, I needed both hands ready. "You've already added it to your wank bank, what more do you need to know? It's not like you see women as any more than objects."

"Did Hiram have anything to do with it?" he asked. "I just thought if he leaked the video, then he might have had something to do with what happened to Cheeks."

"How the hell should I know what *he* is doing?" I snapped. The mention of his name in my apartment was akin to talking about anal sex to a nun. Hiram may have leaked the footage, but messing around with law enforcement wasn't usually his style. When he wanted revenge, he'd slam a person into the trunk of a car and make sure they never saw the light of day again. "If I were you, I'd be looking closer to home."

"Forget I said anything," he said, shaking his head. "I wanted you to know the video is gone, too. I made everyone turn over their cells after Cheeks's arrest. They made no other copies. Outside of Lapland, Cheeks was the only person Bella sent it to. You don't need to worry about anyone else seeing it, okay? I didn't mention to Zander where I thought it came from…"

"Doing one good thing doesn't make up for what

you've done." I narrowed my eyes. "Do you expect me to be grateful?"

"Look, Candy." Rocky sighed. "I know you're angry with me but—"

"But, what?" I placed the Louboutins carefully back in their box. If blood was going to get spilled, the only true crime would be wrecking those babies. "I think I'm entitled to be angry."

"I know you'll never forgive me for what I did." He rose from the sofa, making the room shrink around us. "And I don't fucking deserve your forgiveness, so I'm not gonna ask for it or make any excuses. But I do want us to try to get on or... be civil, at least."

The old me would have crumbled into his arms. It was the one place where I'd felt safest. Now they spelled out danger. I didn't know whether the person I used to love had ever existed, but I *knew* I couldn't trust the man he'd turned into. Rocky had always been handsome, but he'd grown a hardened edge over the years. His eyes held the secrets of a person who had seen too much darkness, and the new scars on his body showed he hadn't gotten away unscathed.

"Be civil?" I laughed in his face. Rocky was no longer my harbor. He was the fucking storm who had sent me crashing into the rocks and taught me that no one could be trusted. "We will never get on. Ever."

"What happened to you, C?" Rocky asked. "I don't even recognize you anymore."

"You happened to me," I spat. "Now, get the fuck out of here."

He sighed. "Be ready at eight tomorrow, yeah?"

He paused on his way out and looked like he wanted to say more, but shook his head and decided against it.

All I had left for company was the melted cookie dough, which served as a reminder that all good things came to an end.

Getting ready for the poker game at Briarly Manor had been a marathon activity. After a day of taming my body fuzz and blow-drying my hair to perfection, all I had to do was the final touches. Nothing could go wrong tonight if I wanted to be in with a chance of helping the Sevens in the future.

"Come on, get in!" With one last tug and a huge inhale, I pulled it up past my ass. "Finally!"

Despite having to be a contortionist to squeeze into it, my new dress was comfortable to wear. It was long-sleeved and sat mid-thigh, but the plunging V-shaped neckline more than made up for the lack of skin coverage.

I spun around to admire my reflection. "Perfect."

I'd gone for a smoky eye and red lip to match the white dress. My tattooed skin against the white fabric combo made me look like an angel who'd got turned away at heaven's gate. Living in sin was always more fun anyway, right?

I did a few bunny hops to make sure my boobs stayed in place. I didn't need to add a nip-slip to the list of things I needed to worry about. Thankfully, the tape kept them strapped down.

Whilst my cleavage looked epic, it still surprised me whenever I looked in the mirror and saw my new breasts. Honestly, I hadn't even wanted the procedure done. A few years ago, I'd been whisked away in the middle of the night and woke up as a D-cup. I hadn't been completely flat-chested before, but going under the scalpel molded my body to meet the bullshit ideals of the men I needed to seduce. All of my experiences since had reaffirmed how men who judged girls on their bra size were grade-A assholes.

Over time, I'd grown to embrace and accept my new look. My shape may have been altered to meet other peoples' ideals, but I'd never fully be free if I allowed that to become my story. Getting ink, dying my hair, and reclaiming my body had unlocked me from an internal prison where I'd remained trapped for too long.

"Shit," I cursed, glancing at the time and grabbing my purse.

I needed to follow the instructions exactly.

Albeit breathless, I made it outside my apartment block at eight o'clock exactly. Right on cue, a black Range Rover pulled up with West glowering behind the wheel. I couldn't help feeling a little disappointed. I'd been expecting a yellow Ferrari, or something more flashy. These poker games were the perfect opportunity for the richest to show off their wealth. Why waste such a chance?

"Aren't you a little under-dressed?" I asked, slipping into the passenger seat. If it wasn't for the blood spatters up his arms, he could have come straight from the gym. Holy shit. My eyes were drawn to West's lap like a fucking magnet. Whoever designed gray sweats had to like dick because why else did they show off an asset like a fucking frame? I forced myself to look away from the obvious bulge visible in his pants.

"I had some business to attend to." He scowled. After our spin the other night, I should have known better than to wind him up. The tape wouldn't survive the whiplash. "We're swinging by the club first, so I can change."

"You've been very busy with *business* recently," I said, keeping my gaze fixed firmly ahead and clenching my thighs. I needed to distract my mind with the least sexy thing I could think of. "How is Cheeks?"

"I should be asking you the same question."

"I only broke his nose and ribs." I shrugged. "What I want to know is how you pulled it off."

"Me?" The car ground to a halt at a red light. "Getting him busted on a drug charge isn't my style, Pinkie."

"But you said you'd deal with him."

"If I had," West said, his eyes were soulless, like the very first time I saw him in the parking lot, "there would be no mess left behind."

"If you didn't do it, then who did?"

A horrible sinking feeling in my gut told me Rocky's suspicions about Hiram's involvement may have been right. It was too much of a coincidence for his arrest to happen right after being seen at the Maven with me.

"If I did know anything, which I don't, do you really think I'd tell one of our strippers?" West asked. From his snide tone, the answer was pretty fucking clear. He saw the dancers as lower-class citizens. Lucky for me, I knew my real value and didn't rely on an arrogant prick to dictate my status. "Being able to play poker and catching Zander's attention doesn't make you any better than the rest."

"Are you always this charming when you take a girl out on a proper date?" I questioned. "Because you seriously need to work on your game, if you want our act to be convincing."

"This is a one-off," he hissed. "Don't get used to it."

"Are you that delusional to think I'd actually want to get used to hanging out with someone who acts like a fucking asshole? Don't flatter yourself," I snapped. Contrary to his belief, looking hot didn't compensate for acting like a total jerk — even if it made him a whole lot easier to look at. "We've got a job to do. That's all."

West gripped the wheel hard like he wanted to tear it off, as we pulled up at the club.

"Zander is waiting."

"Well, what are *you* waiting for?" I demanded. "Are you going to open my door, or not?"

Tonight was all about business, and I was going to make sure West put in the work.

Going to Lapland in this outfit would be like lighting a stick of dynamite, but entering with West on my arm? Well, that'd be enough to blow the entire place up. Bella had already drawn up her battle lines. It was time for me to ignite the war.

Eyes raked over us from the moment we stepped inside. Shitting in a cup would have drawn less attention than this. At the other end of the bar, Scarlett burst into tears. Strike one.

"I'll be back soon," West muttered. "Try not to cause any trouble while I'm gone."

"I'll try," I replied, then added under my breath, "but I can't make any promises."

As soon as West left, Mieko bounded over like an excitable puppy and launched into my arms. I wasn't used to physical affection, but it was sweet to see how much she cared and confirmed I'd made the right decision. After striking a bargain with Zander, I'd made up my mind not to tell Mieko what I'd found out. We all had secrets we wanted to keep buried. If Zander's information was correct and Mieko had killed her father, then he must have been a monster to push her to do it. Besides, who was I to judge? I'd lost count of the number of lives I'd taken.

"Hey, go easy!" I laughed. My make-up had taken time, and I didn't want to leave here looking like I'd stepped straight outta the circus. "You know I didn't die, right?"

"I've been worried about you." She pulled away. "I would have called, but—"

"Shit, your phone…"

With everything else going on, I'd completely forgotten that Vixen's plastic girlfriend had smashed Mieko's cell into smithereens.

"Don't worry, I have a spare." She pulled another out of her bra like a magician would yank a rabbit out of a hat. "I lost all my numbers though."

"What have I missed here?" I noticed a commotion at the bar as Bella fussed around Scarlett like a mother hen. They kept glaring in my direction like I was the spawn of Satan. "Well, apart from the usual."

"Bella's been even more unbearable," Mieko groaned. "I heard Zander broke it off with her."

After seeing him in action at the Maven, she had a lucky escape — not that she'd view it that way. All Bella cared about was her crown. Zander ending their arrangement threatened her position.

"Everyone's been talking about what happened to Cheeks. Rumors have been going around that you went to the Maven with him because you were going to buy drugs," Mieko said. Being heartbroken must have really affected Bella's imagination if it was the best she could come up with. "Vixen has even banned everyone from talking about him. If she hears anyone say his name, she'll fire them on the spot."

I glanced over at Bella and crossed my fingers. "Here's hoping."

Damage control was one of Vixen's areas of expertise, and it was more important than ever. Lapland didn't need any extra attention when it was the Sevens' base for an underground illegal poker ring… and whatever other shady operations were happening.

"Enough about what's been going on here," Mieko said, then lowered her voice. "How are you feeling about tonight? Is it true you're actually going to Briarly Manor?"

"Does everyone else know about it?"

"I don't think so." She blushed. "I *may* have overheard the Sevens talking earlier."

"Even better," I said. The best way to bring down a clique started by breeding insecurity. "Have you been to the manor before?"

"Only once," she admitted, wrinkling her nose. "I didn't like it. It's one of the oldest buildings in Port V, and it has a creepy vibe. I swear it's haunted."

I winked. "Don't worry, I'll keep an eye out for the ghosts."

"It's not the ghosts you need to look out for," she warned. "The Briarly family founded this town. Bryce Briarly practically owns it, and he makes all the rules. Tonight a chance for anyone who is anyone to meet, throw away money that normal people could only dream about, and decide how the rest of us mere mortals should live."

"So, as fucking usual, it's a boy club," I summarized. Luckily for me, people who thought they ruled the world rarely saw what was right in front of them. Just like the players in Lapland's underground game, they would never see me coming.

"I don't know what you're planning, and I don't want to know. But just be careful, okay?" Mieko said. "Bryce is not someone you want to mess with."

Before I got the chance to delve deeper, Bella stomped over with a sniveling Scarlett in tow. Their expressions were murderous.

"What were you doing with West?" Bella demanded.

"What I do in my spare time is none of your business," I said.

"Wait!" Scarlett's mouth hung open. "Are those Louboutins?"

For someone with cotton candy for a brain, she could sniff out a pair of designer shoes quicker than a piranha detecting a drop of blood.

"Do you like them?" I twisted my ankle to give her a better look. If I wasn't the one wearing them, I'd have been drooling with jealousy too. Zander may not be paying me a cut for my help tonight, but these shoes cushioned the deal and came with the bonus of infuriating Bella. "They were a gift from Zander."

"Zander?" Bella put her hand to her chest like I'd shot her. "You're lying. Why would he give anything to you?"

The guys chose the perfect moment to make an appearance.

"Why don't you ask him yourself?" I suggested as they neared.

Holy shit balls. Zander looked fucking insane in a pinstripe black tux, and his sharply trimmed beard signaled he meant business. It was the first time I'd seen West dressed smartly, and he scrubbed up well. Too damn well. The buttons on his shirt strained under his massive pecks, which made me realize why some women had a thing for men in his suits.

"We're leaving," Zander said to me, nudging his head at the exit.

"Before we go," I said, knowing we had an audience, "I never got the chance to thank you for the shoes."

"I'm glad they fit." His words caused Bella's face to crumple like a wet paper bag. "The car is waiting."

"But... she…" Bella stammered, losing her ability to speak.

It wouldn't last for long, but I shot her a smug smile for good measure. "I'll see you tomorrow, Bells."

Tonight, I dropped the bomb. I would have to deal with the fallout later.

NINE

Ablack stretch limousine lay in wait for us, taking up most of the narrow dingy street.

Zander held the door open. "Ladies first."

His gentlemanly act didn't fool me. The last time we saw each other, he'd almost stroked my vagina with a gun. Zander kept a lot of things hidden under his mysterious inked exterior, but manners were not one of them.

"Sweet ride." I exhaled, leaning back into the sleek leather seats.

Plush velvet lined the walls, and it boasted a host of flashy features: a large fold-down plasma TV, sound system, mini-fridge, a disco ball, and a giant number seven spread over its ceiling. It was more like a vacation destination than a car. The lavish sheepskin rug was the only thing I didn't like... fuck knows who had rolled around on it before.

Zander grabbed an expensive champagne bottle from the icebox and poured himself a generous glass. I coughed pointedly. Like, hello? If he hadn't noticed, three of us were here.

"You two need to stay clear-headed." Zander put his feet up, almost reclining entirely. All he needed was someone feeding him grapes to complete the overall picture. "I have other matters to deal with tonight."

"I didn't know you were coming along," I said, watching with envy as he refilled and downed it like water.

"And miss a chance to go to Briarly Manor?" Zander gave a hollow laugh. "I don't think so."

West grimaced, his arms pressed to his sides. Why did I feel like I was missing part of the story?

"Are you ready for tonight, Candy?" Zander asked. "Can you handle it?"

"Handle it? Please!" I scoffed. "I'm not an amateur."

West coughed. "Bullshit."

"Listen up, asshole. Let me tell you how it's going to go down." I swung around to face him and flipped my hair over my shoulder. I meant fucking business, and I wouldn't let him ruin our chances of winning tonight because of his oversized ego. "I can read a room better than anyone. If I scratch my ear, it means fold. If I run my hands through my hair, it means to lay down more chips. If I spill my drink, it means we get the fuck outta there."

"She has you there, West." Zander let out a low whistle and tipped his glass in my direction. "I'm impressed. You've thought this through."

"As I said, I'm no fucking amateur." I shot daggers at West. "Were you taking notes, West? Or, do you need me to repeat myself?"

"How can you still think having her around is a good

idea, Zander?" West's face reddened. Healthy competition was new to him. "I told you, she's fucking reckless."

"What's wrong, West?" I fluttered my eyelashes. "Feeling threatened?"

"I don't need help from you." West pouted, balling his fists in his lap. "I can win on my own."

"Only if you don't underestimate other players again," I reminded him. I would never let him live that down. "I can help you, and you know it."

"If we're going to pull this off and walk away with fifty thousand dollars," Zander said, pausing to look between us, "then everyone needs to believe you're a real couple. Can you both do that?"

I lifted my shoulder in a half-shrug. "Depends."

"On what?" West growled.

"Whether you can behave yourself."

"You little—"

"See?" I said. Teasing him was easy, and I couldn't help myself. His moody pout was just too fucking irresistible. "We're even arguing like we're married already."

Married couples bickered, right? They did in movies, anyway. In reality, I'd known no one who had a successful marriage. Growing up, the only people I saw getting hitched were those who had knocked up a townie and super religious parents orchestrated the whole thing. Under Hiram's wing, I'd been to a few weddings, but most of those had underlying motives too. Marriages of convenience, pairing off people to call a truce between rival families, or gold-diggers seeking to land a fortune from killing their spouses. Marrying for love only existed in chick flicks.

"Enough," Zander snapped. "This isn't child's play.

You need to make it convincing, or we'll all have to face the consequences."

I peered out the window. "Holy crap."

The car climbed a steep hill to a gothic mansion looming ahead. I hadn't taken Mieko's warning about ghosts seriously enough. The place looked haunted as fuck. If the walls could speak, they would have stories to tell. When one family had sustained their grip on a town for generations, the manor had to have a bloody history. How else would the Briarlys have ruled over Port Valentine for so long? No one stayed in control by being nice.

"Welcome to Briarly Manor." Zander rubbed his hands together. "Let the games begin."

"Ready?" West laced his gigantic fingers through mine as Zander held the door open for us to follow. His huge hand completely entombed my own.

"Let's do this." I nodded. "It's showtime."

My dress was too tight to wear panties, so getting out of the limo had to be a slick maneuver. Thankfully, I avoided pulling a Britney to the gaggle of men smoking cigars. An onlooker held up eight fingers followed by nods of agreement from the others. I didn't even want to know whether he was rating me or the car, but that set the tone for what I should expect.

Rich entitled pricks. They would get what they deserved when we cleaned out their wallets by the end of the evening.

"This is how the other half live, huh?" I murmured.

I'd never seen so many expensive cars in one place: Maserati, Ferraris, Lamborghinis, and even a gold-plated Bentley. A red carpet led up a stone staircase to the entrance where butlers, who looked like they'd come straight from an English period drama, handed out flutes and canapés.

"Make the most of it," West said, guiding me towards the house. "It's the only time you'll ever come here."

"We'll see about that." If tonight went well, he may have a partner, whether he liked it or not.

Inside, a gigantic staircase split into two in the center of a hall, which was five times the size of my entire apartment. Marble floors, oak-paneled walls, oil paintings, and a chandelier made a grand statement. Whoever designed the room had spared no expense to show off how much money they had.

"Would you care for a drink?" a server offered.

"Why, thank you." I ignored West's disapproving glare. We were there to win, but that didn't mean I couldn't enjoy myself along the way. "Would you like one too, honey?"

West grunted in response. He wouldn't dare say anything to risk shattering our happy couple illusion so soon.

With my pink hair and their tattoos, the three of us stood out amongst the crowd like clowns at a funeral. Most of the guest list consisted of middle-aged and graying men, accompanied by much younger female companions who were being paid to be there. Everyone in this room had something to prove. Everything was a competition from who had the best car to who had the hottest piece on their arm.

How had we secured an invitation? This wasn't somewhere the guys would usually be seen dead at.

"Zander!" A smug young man with a British accent swanned over to greet us. He was handsome in a red-faced, boyish way and looked like he'd go for tea and scones with members of the royal family. "Good to see you. I'd almost thought you'd been avoiding me."

"I've been busy," Zander replied coolly.

"I'm surprised your little club is still open," the man said, overlooking our frosty reception. "West, it's always a pleasure. Are you ready to give the game your best shot?"

"I'll try," West snarled, although I'm pretty sure the only shot he wanted to take was a bullet straight through the obnoxious fucker's forehead.

"You do that." He clapped West on the shoulder, then turned his attention to me. "Who is this pretty thing?"

"This is Candy," West said. "She's mine."

"Giles," he said, holding out his hand for me to shake. I hated him already. "Giles Briarly."

"Sorry," I said in a sassy tone that implied the opposite. I held up my glass and my other hand interlinked with West's. "My hands are full."

"Aren't you a feisty one?" Giles wiggled his eyebrows suggestively and nudged West in the ribs. "I've always liked my girls a little less refined."

He had the Briarly name, but that didn't stop him from being one of the world's biggest douchebags. I'd met men like Giles before. Men who had come from a long line of generational wealth. They'd been born with a silver polished butt plug up their ass and expected life to be laid out on a platter. The worst thing is, it normally was…

"I told you," West growled. He tightened his grip on

me. I couldn't tell whether it was because he wanted to hold me or himself back. Either way, I'd have broken bones if Giles kept this act up. "She's all fucking mine."

Giles smirked, causing West to crush my knuckles further. "If you say so."

If we'd been anywhere else, West would have knocked him out by now. But things didn't work like that in high society. People still hated each other, but scores got settled differently. They replaced fists with cunning plans and scandals to cause financial or political ruin.

"Let's talk business, Giles," Zander said, gesturing to an adjoining room. Smart move. He needed to get him out of West's range fast. If Giles opened his mouth one more time, I'd never be able to tie my shoes again. "Somewhere more private."

Giles winked. "Don't miss me too much, Candace."

"It's Candy." I glowered as Zander steered him away.

Good fucking riddance.

West waved a server over. A few moments later, they returned with a whiskey on the rocks. He knocked it back and ordered another.

I raised an eyebrow. "I thought you wanted to have a clear head."

"That was before we ran into Giles Briarly."

"Would you mind not taking your anger out on my hand next time?" I suggested. "I can't feel my fingers."

"Shit." He loosened his grip instantly. "Giles knows how to get under my skin."

"I have a feeling he knows how to get under everyone's skin," I said. "Let's keep moving."

We followed the flow of people into a library-turned-bar. Bookshelves covered every wall from ceiling to floor. I doubted the Briarlys had even read any of the books in their vast collection. They probably used first editions to wipe their asses.

A small group gathered to admire one painting on the wall.

"Look at the technique," someone drawled.

Another nodded. "One of his finest pieces."

"You can really feel the emotion behind it," I mimicked sarcastically. Whoever painted it must be prestigious, but it looked to me like someone had vomited over the canvas after a messy night out. "When does the game start?"

"After the torture ends," West muttered, leading me away from the art snobs. "They love to stretch it out."

"You were pretty convincing back there with Giles," I said. He'd owned the whole protective boyfriend routine. "Maybe you're not such a terrible actor after all."

"I'm full of surprises." He picked up a canapé and swallowed it whole. "What's the point of these tiny things?"

"More money than sense," I answered, popping one in my mouth. The whole thing was as disappointing as premature ejaculation. It was over before I'd even had a chance to appreciate any of the flavors. "Give me a burger and fries any fucking day."

I spotted Giles and Zander re-entering with two gorgeous brunettes. It looked like they'd sorted whatever important 'business' they had to discuss.

West leaned against one of the old bookcases and gave me his undivided attention. "You look nice tonight."

"You don't have to pretend," I said. "They can't hear us from over there."

"Who says I'm pretending?" West put his hands around my waist. The heat from his fingertips radiated through the fabric and sent my heart racing. With palms the size of baseball gloves, they could almost wrap right around me. "Are you always bad at taking compliments?"

"Only fake ones."

He pulled me closer. "How do you know they're fake?"

I couldn't think straight, knowing the arms holding me had smashed skulls into dust.

"I know men like you." I ran one of my red nails down his chest. "You'll say anything to get what you want."

"What do I want, Candy?" West brushed a loose strand of hair out of my face, and I had to stop myself from dislocating his wrist. Our every move was being watched and monitored. I couldn't fuck this up. As well as blowing our cover, it'd ruin any chance I had of being part of any future schemes. "Tell me."

"You want money," I said. "And you want to win."

"I don't *want* to win," West said. His hands slid down to rest on the small arch of my back above my ass. "Winning is inevitable."

"Are you always so fucking full of yourself?" I narrowed the space between our bodies until I almost pressed my tits against him. Two could play at that game. If West wanted to give Zander a show, then who was I to let him down? "Or, are you trying to impress me?"

"Has anyone ever told you that you'd be a lot hotter if you kept your mouth shut?"

I leaned in closer, so close our lips were almost touching. "So I've been told."

"Maybe you should take the hint," he murmured, allowing his lips to gently brush against mine.

It was too bad he'd missed the memo saying I didn't give a shit what other people thought. No man would ever put me in a muzzle. And this bitch? She wasn't afraid to bite. West would learn that the hard way.

"Ouch!" West pulled away to check his lip for blood and his eyes darted around the room. I wasn't stupid enough to do it when people were watching. "You're fucking unbelievable."

"I don't kiss on the first date." I smirked, running my tongue over my sharp canines. "Now, if you'll excuse me, I'm going to reapply my lipstick."

I needed to give West time to lick his wounds. He was so used to having free rein in the candy store that he didn't like being told he couldn't have every treat on the shelf.

Three men were talking in hushed tones by the staircase, which piqued my attention.

"But they arrested him." One of them raised their voice in frustration, "Isn't there anything we can do?"

"What if someone gets to him?" another questioned. "What does that mean for us?"

"Cheeks was our man," the third cut above the rest, silencing the others the moment he opened his mouth. He was the ringleader. His tone was sharp, flippant, and oozing with the arrogance that came with a life filled with everything money can buy. Something was vaguely familiar about him, but I couldn't place it. "A move against him is a strike against us. Someone will pay for this. I will make sure of it."

It was no surprise Cheeks made his bucks sidling up to a bunch of men who thought they were Port Valentine's answer to the Illuminati. His getting locked up threatened their dominance, and they'd make sure the responsible party would suffer.

"How can we find out who did it?" one asked.

"Secrets never stay hidden for long." Their leader made a steeple with his fingers. "All we have to do is wait until the time is right."

"Are you lost?" Zander's chilling whisper in my ear sent a shiver down my spine.

I whirled around. "You shouldn't sneak up on people."

"Why aren't you with West?" he hissed. "He's looking for you."

"Relax, it's not a crime to pee." I rolled my eyes sarcastically. "Besides, I was doing some… research."

The more I learned about these people before the game, the easier it would be to squeeze cash out of their stuffed pockets later. Staying glued to West's side wouldn't help us get the right information. I needed to find their weaknesses to exploit their vulnerabilities.

"I asked you to win the game." Zander's voice was a dangerous low whisper. "Not poke around in Briarly business."

"I didn't—"

Suddenly, the leader of the group I'd overheard was headed in our direction. He was probably in his seventies but looked younger. He dressed in a smart silk suit, and his silver hair was immaculately groomed.

"Zander." The older man approached us with open arms. Instead of looking tired with age, his extra years had only made him more shrewd. "Someone told me you'd decided to show your face around here."

"What can I say?" Zander shrugged, burying his hands in his pockets. "I had nothing better to do."

"Who is this with you?" The man scanned me up and down like a fucking barcode. Every movement and look felt calculated like he was already ten steps ahead. "A girlfriend, perhaps?"

"She's with West," Zander said.

"Pity." He sniffed. "Then again, you were always a disappointment. Aren't you going to introduce us?"

"Candy, this is Bryce Briarly." Zander looked at him with utter hatred. "My father."

Wait, hold up! Zander was a motherfucking Briarly?

"It's nice to meet you, Bryce." I molded my face into an unreadable mask to hide my shock. "You have a beautiful home."

Zander being a Briarly explained our invitation to the poker night and his general my-shit-doesn't-stink attitude, but it didn't answer the other million questions rattling around my mind. Why was a Briarly running a strip joint in the worst part of town when he grew up in a fucking manor?

"I always like it when my son brings his friends home." Bryce's thin smile didn't meet his unfeeling eyes. Now, I saw the family resemblance. "Enjoy your evening, Candy."

He glided past to greet late arriving guests, stopping only briefly to whisper in Zander's ear. From

Zander's stormy expression, it didn't look like a friendly father-son conversation about their next fishing trip.

"Keep fucking walking," Zander hissed, taking my arm. "You have a job to do."

"When were you going to tell me?"

"It's not relevant," Zander dismissed. His fingers cutting off my circulation told me we wouldn't be discussing his lineage any further. "You're here for one reason only."

Back in the library, our chances of winning the poker game were dropping fast. The scene unfolding was a catastrophe waiting to happen. West was still standing where I'd left him, but he wasn't alone. He and Giles were in a heated conversation, which threatened to spill into a full-on brawl. At this rate, we wouldn't even make it to the table.

"This is what happens when you can't follow instructions," Zander said.

"It's not down to me to keep West under control," I snapped. I'd not seen West this rattled since I'd beat his ass at poker. Whatever Giles had said to provoke him was making its way through his veins like poison. "Do I look like a babysitter?"

"You said you wanted this job." Zander pushed me forwards. "Fucking prove it."

I didn't need to be a mind reader to know who would be held responsible if West unleashed The Hulk. There wouldn't only be consequences for me, but for Mieko too. I had to make sure that West didn't lose control. Not until we'd rinsed the bastards dry, anyway. Hitting them in their wallets was how we would make them pay.

"Babe, I've been looking for you." I re-joined West and put myself in between them. "I've missed you."

West had once told me he'd never hurt a woman, but now I wasn't so sure. I'd played enough computer games to know Bowser was never afraid of mowing down Princess Peach if it meant winning a race.

"Why you'd miss that gorilla is beyond me," Giles scoffed.

He knew exactly what he was doing, and how to press West's buttons. If it wasn't in my best interests to diffuse the situation, I'd be first in line to cut out his tongue with a scalpel.

"Let's go for a walk," I whispered in West's ear. His entire body shook with the power that threatened to burst free. The muscled hurricane had the potential to tear through the library and leave thousands of dollars of damage in his wake in seconds. "We can go outside?"

The dead look behind West's stare told me all I needed to know. He had already passed the point of no return. Unless I acted fast, Giles's head would be the next stuffed animal mounted above the fireplace.

"I'll kill him," West roared. "I'll—"

Before he could finish talking, I did the only thing I could to distract him… I threw my arms around his neck and brought his mouth crashing down against my own.

He responded like lightning. His arms squeezed around me like a fucking python, devouring me in his darkly delicious smell. I had instigated the kiss, but West was now in charge. His lips consumed me in a hot, explosive frenzy. His tongue slipped into my mouth, and the sweet taste of his fury engulfed all of my senses. All I could do was hold on tightly as the hurricane swept me away.

One of his hands slipped through my curls, whilst the other snaked around my waist and pulled me deeper into the storm. He kissed me like I was the very air he needed to breathe. Like I was the only way to satiate a ravenous hunger, and... I fucking hated myself for loving every second of it.

The shrill sound of a ringing bell brought us both to reality with a thwack. We sprung apart. Giles had disappeared, and Zander was smirking up at us from a red high-backed chair which gave him a front-seat row to our show. Next time, I'd remember to charge him.

West whipped his head around to look at the crowd filing through large wooden doors. "It's starting."

"Can you get your shit together?" I murmured into his shirt, leaving a red lipstick mark on the edge of his collar. Nobody would question who West belonged to. "We've got a job to do."

"Let's fucking do this." West nodded. His anger still lurked underneath the surface, but the murderous rage within him had been caged... for now. "Oh, and Pinkie?"

I kept my stare firmly fixed on the poker room. "What?"

"So much for not kissing on the first date."

"Screw you." I cracked a small smile, daring a glimpse up at his swollen lips. Well, shit. I was now the one who needed to pull myself together. This was just business, okay? I only did what I had to do. "Let's bleed them dry."

TEN

W est draped his arm around my shoulders and
strode forward with purpose. We were like two
soldiers heading into battle. Our tattoos were our armor,
our fists were our swords, and our minds? Well, I needed
to get mine out of the gutter after the kiss we'd shared.

"Remember what I said," I reminded West as we
headed towards the poker room. I played the role of
nagging girlfriend so perfectly that no one would guess
I'd never had an actual relationship before. "Don't do
anything stupid."

West scowled. "I'm not on your fucking leash."

"You are tonight," I said. "I'll even put a collar
around your neck if it'll help."

After his earlier outburst, what the hell had he
expected? I'd brought him back from the brink of erup-
tion. I hadn't thrown myself into the fire for him to ruin
things. I'd do whatever needed to be done to stop the
night from turning into a bloodbath.

"Be careful, Pinkie." West shot me a warning glare,
making me tingle in parts that should be unacceptable

in a public place. "You wouldn't want to make me angry again."

We passed through the gigantic wooden doors. A full forest would have had to be cut down to construct them. Somehow, I doubted sustainability was high on Bryce Briarly's agenda. Beyond them, an impressive room with a domed ceiling had a poker table positioned in its center.

The crowd parted for us to make our way past. West's little performance in the library hadn't gone unnoticed, and no one wanted to get on the wrong side of the scary tattooed beast. Hell, I didn't blame them. Those people may have seven zeroes after their bank balance, but they couldn't buy a backbone.

At the table, players had already taken their seats. A black rope barrier around its edges separated them from the swarm of onlookers.

"Right this way, Mr. Parker." A guard manning the border opened the gap for West to pass.

Before he went up and over the front, I caught West's arm.

"Don't do anything I wouldn't do, honey," I simpered for the benefit of the guard, but my stare was laser-focused. Hopefully, West could read me well enough to understand the underlying threat behind my words. "Good luck."

"Don't miss me too much." West bent down to kiss me roughly on the cheek. He almost had me convinced until he added menacingly under his breath, "I don't need your fucking luck."

West spoke too soon. As soon as he took his designated seat at the table, Giles pulled up a chair opposite. The two of them sat eye to fucking eye with locked jaws. All I could do was hope for the best because we were past the point of a make-out session saving the day. From here on, I needed to trust West to keep his cool. We had a plan, and we needed to stick to it.

As we'd agreed, I circled the table to get a read on the nine other players like a shark planning a strike. The men came from all walks of life, from stuffy politicians to obnoxious business executives. They were all powerful people Bryce had collected over the years, who influenced the town in some capacity. None of them would be seen dead in a place like Lapland. If they wanted to see a girl undress, they had enough money stored in offshore accounts to hire an entire penthouse to rival the Playboy mansion.

Whilst West battled to keep his anger in check, I had a more pressing challenge ahead. I needed to look like I was trying to blend in and socialize. The thought of mixing with these assholes was even more torturous than staring at Giles's smug grin. Even though I could talk the talk, I'd never felt comfortable rubbing shoulders with people who'd never done a day of washing up in their lives. How can you trust someone who had never scraped grease from a pan? They lived in their ivory towers with no clue about what went on in the real world.

The game was just another evening of light entertainment for them. Sure, they wanted to see who'd win, but the outcome didn't matter when they were all loaded and could afford to throw dollars to the wind. None of them understood how this amount of money had the power to transform lives.

Bryce Briarly rose from the poker table and chimed

on a glass to get everyone's attention. A hush swept over the room like he'd cast a fucking spell.

"Welcome, ladies and gentlemen!" Bryce extended his arms in the air like he was some kind of prophet. From the round of applause that followed, he may as well have turned water into whiskey. "This is our biggest prize yet."

West caught my eye, and we exchanged a look of mutual understanding. A quarter of a million dollars was on the line. We were not leaving empty-handed.

As the clapping died down, Bryce's chest had visibly inflated like he'd fed off their admiration.

"Let the game begin," Bryce declared.

Daddy Briarly would not miss the opportunity to crush his minions in a game. Losing was not in his nature. He was used to other people rolling over to give him what he wanted, which would make navigating a win even more difficult. It was one thing coming here to screw over rich strangers, but it was another to know that we were trying to dupe Zander's fucking family. When we got through it, Zander had some serious explaining to do.

As the dealer shuffled, a voice with a familiar New Jersey accent crept up behind me. "You and West are together, huh?"

I spun around to face Vinny. The last time I'd seen him, he'd been pass-out drunk from celebrating his big win… after he'd given me half his winnings for being his lucky charm.

"It's so nice to see you again." I adjusted my pitch to the same high-pitched whine I'd used at the Lapland underground game. "It's been too long."

His previously friendly demeanor had crumbled,

and the cogs in his brain were turning. Shit. We hadn't planned for this. With all the drama this evening, we'd fucked up by allowing him to slip underneath our radar. While I was trying to stop West from murdering Giles, Vinny had been watching from the shadows all along and jumping to the wrong conclusions.

"So, it was all a fix?" he demanded.

Come on, Candy. Channel your inner ditzy gold-digger!

"You've got it all wrong, Vinny." I swatted his arm playfully, hoping charm alone would be enough to diffuse the situation. "We didn't start dating until after the game."

"You owe me money." Vinny put his hands on his hips in a power stance. Now, I was getting a glimpse of his mob boss alter ego. "I want it back."

On the plus side, his assertion that we were a proper couple meant we'd put on an Oscar-winning perfor-mance. It's a shame that it also threatened to tear down the house before the dealer laid a card. All it would take is for Vinny to sound the alarm for others to suspect there was more to West and I's 'relationship' than staged sexual chemistry.

"You heard me." Vinny advanced forwards. "I want it back, or I'll tell everyone how the Sevens run a rigged ring."

Before I could reply, two suited men swooped down on Vinny like vultures. Each of them grabbed one of his arms.

"Hey!" Vinny tried to shake them off, but they held on fast. "What do you think you're doing? You know who I am!"

"You're not on the guest list," one sneered.

"There's been a mistake. I was invited!" Vinny's

raised voice drew the room's attention. From the poker table, Bryce watched the unfolding scene in bemusement. "Ask Bryce. He'll tell you."

Bryce raised his watch to his mouth to communicate with his men through their earpieces. It's a damn good thing that I could lip-read. "Take him outside," he ordered.

Vinny looked between the men and Bryce in confusion, then realization set in as Bryce's lips curled into a cruel snarl. All the color drained from Vinny's face as their grips tightened. He may have been invited to the game, but that didn't mean the host intended on him staying until the end.

"No!" Vinny shook his head wildly. "You can't do this!"

Vinny tried to thrash around, but it was hopeless. He wasn't as young as he used to be. His resistance was futile against the strength of the two trolls. It had only been a matter of time before someone took him out. He may have been important once upon a time, but it was inevitable someone would make a move to replace him eventually. The screech of his shoes against the newly polished floor made me cringe. If Vinny hadn't threatened to blow the lid on the Seven's illicit operations, then maybe I'd have intervened. Instead, I stood by and watched as they dragged him out of the room like a bag of garbage.

His cries of objection slowly faded. A few moments later, the sound of a muffled gunshot rang through the building.

"Someone needs to get their car to the shop," an idiot guffawed over his caviar, mistaking the noise for an exhaust backfiring. It was easier to dismiss anything that threatened his perfect rose-tinted view of the world than face the brutal reality of Bryce Briarly being a cold-blooded murderer.

He may have been able to fool some people in the room, but I noticed who stood a little straighter. Those were the ones who knew exactly why Bryce had lured Vinny to the game. Those were the people we had to watch out for.

"Don't even think about causing a scene," Zander hissed in my ear.

"It's nice of you to finally show up." Where had he been all this time, anyway? With West and I busy doing his dirty work, he'd probably been busy hooking up with a leggy brunette on a four-poster bed. "Vinny almost blew our cover. Your father has done us a favor."

We both watched as another player slid a thick envelope across the table to Bryce. The content of the envelope was the price of Vinny's life.

"My father's favors usually come at a high price," Zander said drily. If Bryce could orchestrate a brazen murder in the middle of a party, what else was he capable of?

"Now that outstanding business has been taken care of," Bryce said, clapping his hands together. I could see where Zander had inherited his ruthlessness from. Growing up in this house of horrors with a beast of a father would be enough to screw up any child. "It's time to play."

Zander whispered, "You know what you have to do, Candy…"

"I do," I snapped, "and I don't need you fucking reminding me."

Zander chuckled to himself as I stomped away. If he

thought Vinny's death would distract me from our mission, then he was wrong. I knew exactly what I had to do. The game was on, and there was only one thing on my mind. Winning.

I started by doing a few laps of the room and engaging in mindless small talk to blend in. All the while, I gave West the right signals and watched from the corners. My initial assessment confirmed most players were mediocre. Only three of them posed actual competition, including Giles and Bryce. Although, the cards were the least of my worries. I couldn't hear what was being said from behind the barrier, but West's shaking arms were enough of an indicator that trouble was brewing. We couldn't afford any more fuck-ups.

"It's almost time for the interval," Zander said, re-joining me.

"An interval?" My mouth fell open. What happened to playing a simple game of poker without the bullshit theatrics? "This is poker, not fucking Broadway."

"My father enjoys putting on a show." Zander downed another shot. In the past hour, I'd lost track of how many he'd ordered. It was impressive how little of an impact hard liquor had on him. "It's what he does best."

"Clearly." I pressed my lips together to stop myself from saying something I'd regret. "Giles looks like he's enjoying himself."

"My cousin has always enjoyed causing trouble…"

"It must run in the family." I narrowed my eyes. "Didn't Vixen want to come along to the family reunion?"

"Don't mention her name here." He grabbed my wrist, and his cool gray eyes turned into burning hot coals. The monotonous drone of a pianist playing didn't even break Zander's furious stare. His fingers pressed hard into my wrists as a warning. "Not now. Not ever."

"What's going on?" West's question broke up the moment.

"Nothing." I ignored West's frown and yanked my wrist from Zander's grasp. If Zander wanted to censor what came out of my mouth, he should have given me the full story before throwing me into a snake pit. "I'm going to the bathroom."

"I'll come with—"

"I don't need a fucking bodyguard to pee, okay?" I jabbed a finger into West's chest to silence him. "Try not to kill anyone when I'm gone."

"Don't wander too far," Zander called after me. "If you get lost, you might not be able to find your way back."

There may be ghosts haunting these corridors, but none of them could scare me. When you've already looked death straight in the face and laughed, you had nothing left to lose.

———

A helpful server pointed me toward the nearest 'powder room'. I wove through the manor's corridors, passing several locked doors. Behind one of them, Bryce's men would be busy zipping Vinny's corpse into a body bag. They extinguished everything Vinny had built over the years the moment they pulled the trigger. In his final moments, would Vinny have thought it had all been worth it? It's a question I asked myself.

The grand sweeping staircases of Briarly Manor

reminded me of a place I'd been to six months before. A place where I had slashed Giovanni Romano's throat for my freedom.

I was never naïve enough to think Hiram would let me go willingly, but I knew he'd strike a deal if he thought it'd be impossible for me to win. Our terms were simple: I kill Romano, and he permits me to leave his service, or I stay his Kitten forever. Giovanni was the oldest brother in a family who had controlled the drug scene of half the country for years. He had recently taken over as the kingpin; his house was a fucking fortress, and his entourage made him virtually untouchable. Hiram knew killing him was basically a suicide mission, but he'd underestimated how much I'd wanted to get away… and it'd cost him.

Getting into the Romano house was easy, seducing him was a breeze, and killing him was even quicker. Getting out undetected posed more of a challenge, but Hiram had trained me well. He'd created the perfect weapon in me. It kept me up at night wondering whether my freedom had been worth the final cost. Romano may be dead and not able to hurt anyone else, but Hiram had taken over part of their business. I may have gotten away, but it'd come at the expense of expanding Hiram's empire.

Pull yourself together. I reminded myself, pushing thoughts of Giovanni Romano's dead body from my mind. *You have a fucking job to do.*

As I turned a corner, an open door caught my attention. I pressed myself against the wall and shimmied to get a closer look. My first reaction was to vomit in my mouth and get the fuck away. The sight of Giles Briarly plowing a blonde over a marble sink was enough to put me off eating any more canapés. Her high-pitched, grating moans made me want to rip my ears off… well, shit. It looked like the Briarlys had the same taste in women.

"Have you missed me?" Giles panted between thrusts.

Vixen wouldn't be too pleased to find out what her girl was doing at a gathering they'd banned her from attending. Being cheated on was bad enough, but finding out it was with a member of your fucking family? Not even she deserved that, especially if your cousin was a bastard like Giles balls-deep Briarly.

"Yes," Charlene squealed. "So much!"

Despite the urge to rinse my eyes with rubbing alcohol, I forced myself to stay rooted to the spot. The pair knew each other, and the fact I hadn't seen her downstairs amongst the rest of the party seemed even more suspicious.

I pulled out my phone and hit record. Karma was about to come around and bite her on the fucking ass. Seeing them fuck for thirty seconds would be enough evidence, right? Vixen didn't need to watch him finish too.

"When I win tonight, we'll fuck on a bed of money." Giles took a break to check out his reflection in the mirror. "They won't even see it coming."

"But you can't know you'll win, right?"

"Oh, but I do. Let's just say I've called in a favor," Giles said, then winked. "I'm unbeatable."

Of course, the bastard had resorted to fixing the whole fucking game! Giles knew West would thrash him with his eyes closed if they were playing based on skill. I needed to get to West and Zander before the game started. We needed to get the hell outta Briarly Manor before Giles cleaned us out… unless, I came up with a better idea.

Out of the corner of my eye, I spotted the dealer loitering in the hall. If Giles wanted to play dirty, then I could play him at his own fucking game. With each step, I swayed my hips to draw attention to my curves and painted a sultry pout over my lips.

"Do you have a minute?" I put a gentle hand on the dealer's arm and stroked it gently. He gulped as I bit my lip and looked up at him through my lashes. "There's something I want to show you. Giles sent me."

"Sure!" The idiot grinned like he'd won the jackpot. He'd been too busy working out how to bend to Giles's demands to notice that I'd arrived on West's arm. "But I have to get back to the game in a few—"

"It won't take long," I insisted, taking his arm to lead him in the opposite direction from the party. I had to act fast before Giles returned downstairs. "You don't want to upset Giles, do you? It's something he thinks you'll really like."

The first door I tried was unlocked, and we stepped into a study. I clicked the door shut behind us and twisted the lock. We couldn't be disturbed.

"What do you want to show me?" The dealer loosened his tie. "Giles said nothing about—"

His voice trailed off as I stepped forward to run my hands up this thigh. His erection caused a tiny tent in his pants. Unfortunately, I was no fucking gift from Giles.

I leaned forwards to whisper in his ear, "How much is Giles paying you to cut him the winning cards?"

"I don't know w-w-what you're talking about," he stammered. "Is this some kind of weird foreplay?"

"Oh, I think you know exactly what I'm talking about." I grabbed his balls. "How much is he giving you?"

"YOWCH!"

"If you want to have children, I'd suggest you answer the question." I tightened my hold and dug my nails into his scrotum. "Tell me what I want to know."

"Three," he gasped as tears ran down his face. "Three percent, okay?"

"I'll tell you what…" I relaxed my grip a little. "You can walk away from this room on two legs if you play it straight for the next half."

Giles may be a fucking cheat, but that didn't mean we had to lower ourselves to his level. If we won fairly, there was no way anyone could question the integrity of the win.

"What about the money?"

"Would you rather have a little more cash in the bank or be able to walk?" I asked. "Or, would you rather I tell Bryce Briarly how you were trying to con his son's business partner out of money? I think he'd do a lot worse than break your legs if he found out."

All the color drained from his face. Thankfully, he seemed to know even less about the Briarly family than I did, as the mention of Bryce's name alone was enough to spook him.

"Okay, I get it," he whimpered. "Fine, I'll do it! Just let go, please!"

"Good." I released my hold, and he fell to the floor.

"You can tell Giles you made a mistake when dealing the cards. Understood?"

He nodded meekly, rolling around and cradling his balls like they were wounded animals. Hopefully, he'd be able to get up and handle the rest of the game.

"And don't even think about crossing us," I warned. "Or, you'll face the consequences."

Zander and West immediately stopped talking the moment I returned.

"Don't let me interrupt," I muttered sarcastically.

"We'll talk later," Zander said to West before marching in the direction of the bar. The longer we stayed here, the worse his mood seemed to get.

We were supposed to be a team, but these guys didn't seem to know the definition of the word. Rule number one of working together was not to leave a person in the dark. If they wouldn't let me in on their plans, then I was going to keep my little conversation with the dealer quiet... for now.

"You took your time," West grumbled.

"What's wrong?" I asked. West had made it perfectly clear he didn't want my help, so I'd have thought he'd have been happy if I didn't return. "Were you scared they dragged me off to shoot me like they did to Vinny?"

"That's not funny."

"Are these nights always so eventful?" I snagged a miniature cheesecake from a server's tray. Holy shit, vanilla and blueberry goodness exploded over my tongue. One bite wouldn't cut it. "You can leave them with me."

The server frowned. "The whole tray?"

"You heard the lady." West took it from their shaking hands. It was easy to forget how intimidating he must be to strangers. "If my girl wants the tray, she's getting the whole fucking tray."

I crammed two more in, and a moan escaped my lips. What more could a girl want? A muscled man holding twenty mini cheesecakes? This was as close to heaven as you could get.

West grinned down at me wickedly. "How much more can you fit in?"

"Fuck you," I retorted, sending cream dripping down my chin. West wiped it off with a swipe of one finger, then popped it into his mouth to lick it clean.

"You're right." He nodded in approval. "These do taste good."

"Hey," I objected as he grabbed the last one. The entire lot had only lasted a few minutes between us. God damn him for making me share. "No fair."

He demolished the bite-size dessert in seconds. "I'm the one playing, remember?"

"You don't need the extra energy." I scowled. "If you're sitting across the table from Giles, we don't want you tearing his head off."

"Speaking of the bastard, where is he?" West looked around the sea of jerks. "It's not like him to miss an opportunity to work the room."

I snorted. "He's busy working on other things..."

West eyed me with suspicion, but I didn't elaborate. It wasn't fair to tell him about catching Giles with his pants around his ankles before I told Vixen. She may be a bitch but, if it was the other way around, I wouldn't want to be the last person to find out that my cousin had been fucking my girlfriend.

"Incoming," West muttered, right in time for me to put on my fake smile.

"West, Candy, how nice to see you together," Bryce acknowledged us with a smooth demeanor. He'd spent years putting on a polished front to hide who he really was. He reminded me of a politician who shook hands with the poor, only to make their lives even more unbearable. "Are you enjoying your evening?"

"Very much," I lied. Spending time with a load of rich assholes and listening to someone get shot was hardly my idea of a fun night out, but I'd never let it show. "They were some great, um…. canapés."

"My son's friends are always welcome here," Bryce said. From his tone, it sounded like Zander's friends were about as welcome as a pack of rabid dogs. "Where is Zander? I was hoping to catch up with him this evening."

"He had to take a call," West replied smoothly.

"Always business before pleasure. Later then." Bryce motioned for someone to join us. "Have you met my nephew, Candy?"

Giles swanned over, still busy fastening his shirt buttons. Charlene, Vixen's girlfriend, was nowhere in sight. After watching one too many movies set in England, I'd thought British men were sweet and charming. Giles had completely shattered that illusion and dashed any hopes I had of finding my Mr. Darcy across the sea.

"We've already met," I sniffed.

"He studied economics at Oxford before moving to the States," Bryce bragged.

Formal education didn't impress me. Books can teach you a lot of things, but they don't tell you what you need to know to survive. How does understanding the theory of relativity help when four men corner you on your walk home? How does memorizing the periodic table assist if you have to create a new identity and start over? The knowledge I needed to stay alive couldn't be found in the lecture theatre of a fancy college. I learned all I needed to know from the streets.

"I'm sure Candy doesn't want to hear about my history, Uncle." Giles tutted. What I wanted to know was why he'd moved over here and how he'd got his feet firmly under the Briarly table. "She's not used to being around such civilized company."

"I think we have very different definitions of civilized," I replied. I put my hand on West's arm to steady him, hoping the sugary cheesecake bites of dreams weren't like spinach to Popeye. "I know exactly what kind of company I like to keep."

"I like this one." Giles laughed. "She must be a tough one to handle, isn't that right, West?"

Every word coming out of his mouth only made me hate him more. Nothing was more terrifying to a man than a woman who knew her power and wasn't afraid to use it. Giles was about to find that out in the next half of the game.

"I like a woman who knows what she wants," West said through gritted teeth.

"If this is the type of woman you're offering, maybe I should pay your little club a visit?" Giles winked. He saw strip joints like shopping malls, where he could take his pick and buy whatever he wanted. No matter what the media says, society still isn't an equal place for women. In elite circles and old institutions, gender differences are even more pronounced. Wrinkly men still sat around tables making the big decisions, which made it easier for pond scum like Giles to bring women down. "I'm sure you have quite the selection."

I bit my tongue so hard that the taste of blood filled my mouth. Some feminists argued stripping helped to support the patriarchy, but screw that. Dancers worked damn hard pulling tricks to make their money. Customers didn't exploit us. If anything, it was the other way around. We'd bat our eyelashes to get what we wanted, which gave us a power that men like Giles could only dream about.

"Our girls dance," West growled. "They're not for fucking sale."

Bryce glanced down at the gold Rolex on his wrist. "Let's take our seats, gentleman."

I caught West's eye. "Have fun."

If this conversation was a prelude to the type of shit Giles was going to spout over the next half of the game, West had deserved the last cheesecake.

"I don't know much about poker." I giggled along with a boring aristocrat, watching the game unfolding over his shoulder. "What can you tell me about it?"

We were almost on the last hand.

"It's all very exciting," the man replied, then launched into a lengthy explanation about the rules. I nodded along animatedly as he talked. It turned out he knew fuck all about poker but loved chatting with anyone who made the mistake of listening to him.

I had hoped Zander may have been able to save me from the company of the rich and entitled, but he'd disappeared. From the amount he'd been drinking, he'd probably passed out in a shadowy corner somewhere. I didn't blame him. As a child, having a family seemed like the best thing in the world. After meeting the Briarlys, I wasn't so sure. What was worse: having no family at all, or one filled with fucking monsters?

I'd been on my own from the start. Abandoned on the steps of Evergreen in the depths of winter, wrapped in a blanket at only a few weeks old. If I hadn't been screaming at the top of my lungs to draw attention to myself, I wouldn't have lived until morning. That night set the precedent for the rest of my life.

Fighting to survive was all I'd ever known. The only two people who had promised to protect me had let me down. First, Rocky had shattered my hopes for a future by handing me over to a vicious crime lord. Next, Hiram had sworn to take care of me. It'd been his way of manipulating me into staying under his control forever. Before Blackthorne Towers, I'd thought I might have had a chance of an ordinary life: college, marriage, kids... but I'd been stupid to think that would even be possible for someone like me. Whatever the future had in store, I'd come to expect nothing.

The aristocrat broke me out of my reverie. "This is the last turn."

A hushed silence swept over the room as the tension mounted — even the gossiping crowds broke up their conversations to watch. The winner was going to take all.

"I'm going all in," West said, sliding his entire mountain of chips into the center of the table.

His hand was mediocre, but he was doing all he could. The only chance he had was by trying to bluff his way through. I raked my hands through my hair and shook out my curls. He needed to pile on the pressure to shake the others.

West's confidence caused three of the remaining players to fold and cash in what they had left. They were all financiers who spent their days calculating risk. West's smug smirk had them all fooled. Their small-minded analytical brains wouldn't expect to be outsmarted by a tattooed thug. Quitting whilst they were ahead would save face and a lecture from their wives later.

Bryce was up next.

"And we're down to the last two," he declared, folding in a surprise twist.

I'd already calculated Bryce had the best hand on the table. The fucker wasn't quitting because he was afraid to lose. Bryce got his kicks from pushing two opponents together and sitting back to watch them fight to the death — or, in this case, to win a quarter of a million dollars. That was where the real entertainment was for him.

It was now between West and Giles. I caught the dealer's eye, and he winced. The poor guy still wasn't able to stand upright.

"I'll match you." Giles pushed his pile into the middle and unclipped his diamond-studded watch. "I'll even throw this in."

"Giles loves his watch." Zander suddenly materialized by my side, watching and calculating every move. "He wouldn't risk it, unless—"

I raised one eyebrow. "Unless, what?"

It wouldn't be long until the house of cards shattered Giles's gigantic ego. He'd be coming into paper tissues instead of fucking cash at the end of the night.

Everything came down to this moment.

This was it.

Giles and West laid their cards in front of them.

The smug smile on Giles's face turned to fury as his eyes flitted from the dealer to the table.

"We won?" I covered my hand over my mouth in mock disbelief. And the best part? We hadn't had to cheat our way to the top either. "I can't believe it."

I followed Zander to join West at the barrier.

"How the fuck did you do that?" Zander murmured. If I didn't know better, I'd say he sounded impressed.

"I don't know what you mean," I replied coyly. Giles was used to getting what he wanted, but this victory was something he would never have won. "It was a *fair* game."

The dealer busied himself counting the chips and lining a black leather briefcase with stacks of cash. Charlene would be disappointed about not getting the happy ending she was waiting for.

"Now I can treat you to the vacation I promised, Candy," West said, wrapping his arm around my waist. He was going the extra mile to make our act convincing. "Just point at the map and tell me where you want to go."

Giles's cheeks turned a deeper shade of red with every passing second like he was about to throw a tantrum. *Boo-fucking-hoo.* Was diddums unhappy because he didn't get his way?

"Good game, Giles," Zander addressed his cousin. "But not good enough."

"Why don't you try the watch on, West?" I suggested. It was worth almost as much as the winnings. "It'll make you look so much more civilized."

"Nothing can make an animal seem civilized," Giles hissed. He looked like he wanted to rip the watch straight out of my hands. "You should use the money towards that business of yours. Charities are always looking for donations."

"We're leaving." Zander's vicious tone could have cut through steel bars. "Now."

"Going so soon, son?" Bryce asked.

Zander drew himself up to full height. "We have other business to attend to."

Bryce's lips pressed into a firm, disapproving line, but he didn't argue.

If we were in a movie, this would be the moment when the credits rolled. The camera would follow the three of us walking side-by-side down the manor steps in slow motion. Then it would zoom into the case, swinging in West's hand.

As soon as we got into the back of the limo, Zander popped another champagne cork. He didn't care that the foam sprayed all over his suit; in fact, it was the happiest I'd seen him all evening.

"Our win calls for a celebration."

"So, we're allowed to drink now?" I grinned and

watched Briarly Manor fade into the horizon. I was in no rush to return.

"Tell me," Zander said, "how did you know Giles was cheating?"

"Does it really matter?" I raised my glass in a toast. I hadn't forgotten what Zander said to me in his office. He may be trying to figure me out, but he was still no closer to discovering my secrets. If I had anything to do with it, they would stay hidden. "I handled it."

West clinked his glass against mine. "Cheers to that."

My rumbling stomach caused the two of them to stare at me like I'd dropped a massive fart.

"Hello? What are you both staring at?" I demanded. "All we had to eat were those tiny canapés."

Zander pressed the button to lower the screen through to the driver and gave him hushed instructions. Within no time, we'd pulled up outside a fast-food joint where Zander ordered three of everything on the menu. When we pulled up outside my apartment, I'd eaten a lifetime's worth of mozzarella dippers and the guys looked at me like a monster who'd devoured an entire village. It's like they'd never seen a girl eat before.

West cleared his throat. "We'll see you tomorrow."

"Yeah." I wiped my mouth on the back of my hand. "I guess you will."

The night may have ended on a high, but real life was no movie. This wouldn't be the end. In fact, this might only be the beginning…

ELEVEN

After the hive watched me leave with West and Zander, my next shift at Lapland would be as pleasant as walking naked into a wasp's nest. Girls like Bella did anything to protect what they had. They stung when they felt threatened. But I wasn't going to wear a fucking beekeeper suit; instead, I wore my gorgeous pair of new shoes. Confrontation didn't scare me and, if I had to face the swarm, I wanted to look damn good doing it.

As soon as I stepped into the club, the sight of Vixen gnawing on the face of her melted Barbie girlfriend welcomed me.

"Oh, it's you." Charlene tore her face away from Vixen's long enough to look me up and down like a piece of roadkill she'd scraped off the sidewalk. It's a wonder she could even sit down after seeing how hard Giles pounded into her last night. "Have you come over to add to your porn collection?"

The only collection she was getting added to was the list of people who'd crossed me and got what was coming to them. I'd been deliberating over whether it was worth telling Vixen what I'd seen last night, but now? There was no doubt in my mind. Hopefully, she'd learn to lock the door before banging in a bathroom next time.

"I need to speak to you, Vixen," I said. "Alone."

"This better be fucking good," she snarled, giving Charlene a parting kiss, which I'm sure would be their last. "I'll be right back."

"Don't get too close to her, babe." Charlene smiled smugly. "You don't know what you'll catch."

The tunnel between Charlene's legs was the only thing around here that Vixen would catch something from, but I held my tongue. I already had the ammunition to wipe the smirk off her rubbery face without getting my hands dirty.

I led us away from any prying ears. "I don't think you'll want this to be overheard…"

"You can't tell me anything that I don't already know," Vixen said. "Zander and West told me what happened last night."

"Not everything." I held out my cell and pressed play. Vixen's eyes widened momentarily, as she realized who was on the screen. There were no mistaking Charlene's wails and Giles slapping against her like a wet fish. Sure, I could have used this information to blackmail Charlene, but... exposing her as a cheat was the right thing to do. Plus, I'd be pleased to never have to hear her fake orgasm again. "I thought you should see it."

Vixen snatched it from me and watched it again. Then again.

"Why show me this?" she asked. Like me, Vixen had trained herself to keep her emotions under control.

Hiding your feelings was a way of protecting yourself. It stopped other people from seeing your weaknesses. The only problem was when you kept them buried for years, you started to question whether you had any feelings left at all. "You didn't have to."

"No one deserves to be cheated on," I said. "Not like that."

"Who else knows? West? Zander?"

"Nobody," I confirmed. "I came to you first. I thought you'd want to handle it personally."

For the first time, a look of understanding passed between us. Maybe we weren't so different after all.

"Get back to work, Candy." Okay, I was wrong... that bitch and I were nothing alike. I guess expecting a thank you was a little too much to ask. "You were ten minutes late today, so you can make up the time by cleaning the stage at the end of the night."

I headed to the dressing room to leave Vixen to ponder her next move when Rocky called me over. He sat slumped over a table by the bar with an array of empty glasses around him. He looked like he'd fall straight off the stool if someone poked him with a straw.

"Did you enjoy yourself last night?" he asked.

As soon as I was within a six-foot radius of him, the lingering smell of pot hit me. "It looks like you're starting early."

"Congratulations," he slurred. His bloodshot eyes confirmed he was high… and drunk. "You won the game."

"You're a mess." I sniffed the air. "Have you even showered today?"

"Who needs to shower?" He took a swig straight

from the bottle. "You didn't listen. I told you to get outta here when you had the chance."

When we were teenagers, Rocky had been the life and soul of any party. He was the funny joker who could make anyone laugh, but he'd never gotten out of control. The person in front of me was nothing more than a shell of a human. What had happened to him over the last five years to be in this fucking mess?

"It looks like you've had enough," I said. "Maybe you should sleep it off?"

"No!" He slammed the bottle down on the table and poured another glass. The liquid sloshed over the sides, but he didn't notice. "It's only enough when I say it's enough."

I went to take his drink away, then stopped myself. Why was I allowing myself to feel sorry for him? What Rocky had done to me was unforgivable. The only thing I should be thinking about was how I was going to kill him.

"Fine," I hissed. "See if I give a shit if you drink yourself into oblivion."

The truth was, I did care. But only because it would be too fucking easy for him to die from alcohol poisoning. He needed to suffer. Just like he'd made me suffer.

"You should have listened to me." He shook his head. "You don't... you don't know what it's like here."

West slapped him on the back. "Hitting the hard stuff already, Red?"

"Join me, bro," Rocky said. "Le'ss party…"

West sat down without looking in my direction. A small part of me was disappointed, but I had no reason to expect any more. The poker game was purely trans-actional. Everything had been an act, including the kiss we'd shared. Now, it was back to business as usual and treating me like a piece of furniture.

"Enjoy your night," I snapped. "Some of us actually have work to—"

Over on the dance floor, a woman's cry drowned out the deep bass and the rest of my sentence. It sounded like a demented chicken trapped in a metal box.

"No, babe," Charlene wailed. Her anguish almost sounded believable. If it wasn't for the hard evidence I'd shown Vixen, Charlene's blubbering may have resembled heartbreak convincingly enough. Instead, she was digging her own grave with every shoulder-wracking sob. "You've got it wrong!"

Mieko emerged from the dressing room in a sexy black latex dress to see what all the fuss was about. She must have used an unthinkable amount of baby powder to slip into it.

"What's going on?" Mieko joined me and followed my gaze. "Oh, shit."

"It looks like Charlene isn't going to win the most faithful girlfriend of the year award."

"But I love you!" Charlene desperately tried to cling to Vixen. "You can't leave me! You love me!"

"Get the fuck outta here," Vixen spat. The fake tears and performance had no effect on her. "And tell my cousin I said hello."

"How did you…" Charlene's mouth opened and closed like a drowning roach gasping for air. I may be a little late to start my shift, but having a front-row seat to this was something I had to see.

"I have eyes and ears everywhere." Vixen shot her a filthy glare. "Don't even think about stepping foot in here again. Or else."

Charlene grabbed her purse and nearly tripped over her feet to get to the door. What was the sense in hanging around now her cover was blown?

"Oh, and Charlene?" Vixen called after her. "Lock the fucking door next time."

"Good fucking riddance," I mumbled under my breath.

Mieko's jaw dropped. "Did she mean Zander?"

"Her *other* cousin," I said. "Trust me, the less you know about him the better."

In the last twenty-four hours, Giles had lost his undercover mole and his prized Rolex. It wouldn't take him long to work out who might be responsible and, when he did, he wouldn't take losing lightly. Briarly blood ran through his veins and the desire to win was engrained in his DNA... no matter the cost.

"Poor Vixen." Mieko fiddled with her earring. "Do you think she'll be okay?"

I didn't like cheaters as much as the next person, but this was Vixen we were talking about. While I wasn't going to stick on a party hat and do the conga, I wouldn't lose any sleep over someone who'd spent the past month trying to make my life hell.

"She seems fine to me," I said. We watched on as Vixen barked an order at a security guard. Some girls got knocked down and cried into their pillows after a breakup, but Vixen? She was the type who came back swinging. "See? She's just peachy."

"Don't you feel sorry for her?"

"Has anyone ever told you that you're too fucking nice for your own good?" It was easier to feel sympathy for a dog gnawing on a corpse than it was to pity Vixen, who tore down everyone to make herself feel better. "Vixen's a big girl. She can take care of herself."

Mieko sighed. "She deserves better."

I shook my head in disbelief. "Whoever ends up with her will deserve a fucking medal."

"She's not *that* bad…"

"Are you sure?" I asked. At that moment, Vixen spun around in our direction. The look of pure anger could have turned us into stone. "Now, seems like the perfect time for me to change."

There was no way I was risking getting my ankles snapped under her massive New Rock boots. If Mieko thought something was redeeming about her, that was her prerogative.

"Don't leave me alone with her," Mieko squeaked as Vixen charged forward.

"I thought you said she's not that bad." I laughed and slipped away. "Good luck."

***

Bella lay in wait. She'd been building up for this moment all night. I could practically smell her frothing at the mouth and ready to attack.

"Why did Zander give you those shoes?" Bella demanded.

"These old things?" I flaunted the heels from every angle. "I guess he thinks I'm a really hard worker."

"You've been fucking him, haven't you?" She rose from her seat. Up close, her make-up wasn't as flawless as usual. Her foundation was cakey and sat in her skin's creases, which drew extra attention to all her fine lines and blemishes. "Tell me!"

I inspected my nails. "Not all of us have to fuck the boss to get what we want."

"You think you're better than the rest of us, don't you?" Bella edged closer. "Because you're not. You're not special."

"You have a little something under your nose." I pointed at the hint of lingering white powder. After a week off, I had better things to do than waste time arguing with a paranoid cokehead. "You might want to look in the mirror."

She scowled and wiped it away, but she wouldn't let it hold her back. "Zander was going to take me on a date."

As if on cue, Scarlett stepped inside, flanked by two more of Bella's closest minions. An ambush? How interesting. It was like being back in high school around the popular girls who thought they were God's gift because they had the bounciest hair. No one ever taught them beauty was only skin-deep.

"West was going to take me out too," Scarlett chipped in.

"If I wanted to hear both of your dating histories," I said, "then I'd have booked the night off."

Bella's nostrils flared. "You're a fucking slut."

"If you want to hurt me." I looked her up and down. "Then I'd think again."

These girls fought with their words, but they'd be no match for my fists. I didn't want to resort to violence, but if I had to yank out a few hair extensions to make a point, then I'd do what I had to do.

"Oh, we're not here to hurt you." Bella threw back her head and cackled like a possessed banshee. She looked to the girls with trained precision and nodded. "Take them."

A second later, two of the bitches dived to the floor to knock me off balance like human fucking bowling balls. I fell on my ass like a stack of skittles, whilst Scarlett was perfectly positioned to wrench the shoes straight off my feet. It felt like we were in a Cinderella retelling gone wrong.

Bella clapped her hands. "Bring them here!"

Scarlett held the shoes as if they were a crown ahead of a coronation. Meanwhile, another accomplice disappeared and returned with a trash can. The smell of gasoline filled the room.

"Put them in," Bella ordered.

A flash of pain crossed over Scarlett's features, but she bowed her head and dropped my Louboutins in with a tinny crash. All I could do was watch on in horror as Bella gleefully lit a match and threw it in. The flames engulfed my only prized possession. They may as well have destroyed the fucking Mona Lisa. As much as I wanted to, I didn't retaliate. One wrong move and the entire club could go up in smoke.

Suddenly, someone charged the door open.

"What the hell is going on in here?" Vixen barged in and sent Scarlett tumbling to the floor. Bella should have known better than to leave the weakest link guarding the door. "Is that a fire?"

Vixen stared into the smoldering pile of leather, and then at my toes. She took a sharp intake of breath. "Are those fucking Louboutins?"

Vixen seemed more horrified at the charred remains of my shoes than when I showed her the video of Charlene fucking Giles — perhaps she was human, after all.

Bella threw her hands in the air and dropped the matches from her shaking claws. "I c-c-can explain."

"You don't have to." Vixen took one look at them and back at Bella. "You're fired."

"Wait, what?" Bella spluttered. "It was only a joke!"

"Well, I'm not joking." Vixen advanced towards her. "Find a new fucking job."

"Vixen, please!" Bella's eyes filled with tears. No amount of begging would save her now. She'd got caught red-handed with a smoking bin. Her fate was already sealed. "I need this. You know I'm the best dancer here. It won't happen again."

"It won't, because if you don't get the fuck outta here in the next thirty seconds, then those shoes won't be the only thing on fire," Vixen threatened. If she didn't already have a job, she'd make a shit tonne of cash as a dominatrix. She'd have grown men crying like babies in minutes. "Don't fucking push me."

Mascara ran down Bella's cheeks as she grabbed her coat. She took one last pleading glance at Vixen and opened her mouth to grovel more, but hastily shut it again. Who knew she could make smart decisions? With that, she rushed out sobbing with snot dripping down her face. My shoes may be a pile of burnt ash, but it had been worth it to bring Bella's reign to an end. Every war has casualties. She'd blown up her own fucking crown, and things were going to change.

"Going somewhere?" Vixen whirled around to face Bella's minions, who were slowly edging backward. After watching their monarch get dethroned, none of them wanted to be next on the guillotine. Vixen stared at them, one by one. "The rest of you should consider this a warning. Now, get the fuck out of my sight."

They all nodded furiously. I didn't know anything about Vixen's past, but her threat alone looked enough to make the girls shit their pants in fear. As they filed out, Vixen offered her hand to help me up.

I took it. "I was all down for burning her on the stake."

A trace of a smile fluttered over her lips. Then it vanished.

"This changes nothing," she spat. "We're even."

"Got it," I said, wiping myself down. Hell, I'd take what I could get at this stage. We may be a long way off from a truce, but I respected someone who paid back their favors.

Mieko rushed over to me. "I've been looking for you everywhere."

"I had to find a spare pair of shoes." I grimaced. The drab pair of stilettos on my feet were the only things that fit me, and a blister was already forming over my heel.

"I heard what happened." From the serious expression on her face, you'd have thought a family member had died. "I'm sorry about the shoes."

"They can be replaced," I said. Well, not on my wages... but I'd already allowed myself a two-minute silence to mourn for their loss and then strapped on my big girl panties. Like people, it was pointless getting attached to material possessions when everything could be taken away at a moment's notice. "Plus, Bella getting fired was a real consolation."

"Speaking of replacements…" Mieko shifted

nervously from one foot to the other, as she tried her damnedest not to smile. "I've just spoken to Vixen, and she's offered me Bella's spot."

"No way, congratulations!" Mieko was the most flexible of all the dancers and deserved recognition. If she wanted to, she could join the circus or be part of a theatre show but, if she had to stick it out here, I wanted her to be the rightful star of the show. "You've earned it."

"I feel like I should thank you."

"You don't need to." I held up a hand to silence her, then winked. "Thank Bella. She's the one who dug her own grave."

"Not because of that," Mieko said. "Things have been different around here since you started. You don't take any shit. You've made me see that I don't have to be a doormat."

Compliments weren't something I was used to, especially from other women. Girls were always so quick to bring each other down but, with Mieko, she wore her heart on her sleeve. We couldn't be more opposite. Whilst I'd mow down anyone who stood in my way, she preferred to be invisible.

"You've never been a doormat," I said. "You're a survivor."

"You think so?" She looked up at me through watery eyes. Goddammit, I'd purposefully not wanted to make any real friendships, but I couldn't help feeling protective over her. "If you knew some of the things I'd done…"

"I know you've always done what you had to do," I interrupted, noticing her retreating into the safety of her head. We didn't need to talk about her past. Not if she didn't want to. "Why don't we focus on celebrating tonight, huh? You've gotta kick ass on stage."

Mieko beamed. "You got it."

"Do you think it's too soon to sing Ding Dong the Wicked Witch is Dead?"

Mieko collapsed in laughter, then groaned and clutched her sides. "This dress is too tight to laugh this hard."

"How the hell do you pee in that thing, anyway?"

She shook her head. "You don't want to know."

Making enemies came naturally, but making friends? It was still an unfamiliar territory, but it felt fucking good to have fun and act like a normal twenty-one-year-old for a change.

My voice was hoarse from cheering so loud. Mieko's performance was an incredible success — even Vixen didn't offer any criticism. Bella's prior minions had scurried around like headless chickens trying to stay out of my way, which suited me just fine. Now the monster's head had been cut off, they didn't know which way to turn.

"Are you sure you don't want me to wait?" Mieko paused at the entrance. "I can help?"

"It's fine," I insisted. Vixen needed to find a way to way to punish me for my late arrival, which had landed me extra cleaning duties. It made no sense for both of us to suffer through it. "I'll see you tomorrow night, okay?"

"If you're sure?"

"You're running up the cab fare." I pointed the

brush toward the noisy engine running outside. She couldn't argue with my logic. "Go!"

I swept up the explosion of gold confetti over the stage; it looked like a fairy had jizzed all over the place. Luckily, I was no stranger to cleaning up messy scenes. I'd take cleaning up the glitter to entrails any day. The club felt strangely empty. Vixen was somewhere in the back, working on the books, and the guys had left earlier. Rocky picking fights with the customers hadn't gone down too well, so Zander and West had taken him elsewhere to cool off.

The sound system was still on, and I hit play. The song 'Gasoline' by Halsey whirred into life.

How could I resist such a tune?

Whenever I danced in front of a crowd, I was hyper-aware of needing to put on a show. Everything was an act to make the audience happy; a combination of conscious movements and flattering angles to make guys reach into their wallets. When I danced for myself, it became something else entirely.

As a teenager, I'd used my beloved CD Walkman to drown out the arguments from the surrounding corridors in Evergreen. It had been a hot summer evening when I'd first discovered the power of dance. The police had raided the room directly below mine. I'd locked my door and drew the curtains to seal out the chaos. All I wanted to do was take out my frustration, and dance gave me a way to do it.

Dancing could make even prisoners feel free. During the months trapped in my apartment in Blackthorne Towers, music became my lifeline again. It helped time pass quicker and made it easier to forget where I was, and the person I'd become.

In Lapland, the bright lines shone down over me. Performing on an empty stage had an unsettling, almost ironic, beauty. Dancing for no other reason than pure pleasure. I embraced the cool metal of the pole and pirouetted around it. Instead of grinding, I climbed up, then slowly twirled back down. As a treat, Hiram had once taken me to see an Italian ballet. I didn't understand what was happening, but it was still the most beautiful thing I'd ever seen. Sure, dancing on a pole could be sexy… but it could be a graceful art form too.

The song faded to a close, and slow applause broke out from the back of the room. I snapped my head up into the shadows to see Zander step forwards and approach the stage.

"You gave quite a performance."

In seconds, I'd gone from feeling like I was flying to being stuck in a police interrogation room with nowhere to hide. I couldn't bring myself to meet his gaze and quickly returned to sweeping up the remaining pieces of confetti. "I'll be done in a sec."

"You don't have to stop on my account."

"I need to get home."

Zander had watched me strip back my layers of armor and let myself go. Knowing he had watched the video of me giving head was one thing, but seeing me in my most raw, vulnerable state was an even deeper violation. No one got to see that. Ever. Letting my guard down around him, or anyone, was something that couldn't happen. I wouldn't allow it.

"Why don't you join me for a drink?" He inclined his head towards the bar. "We could call it a tip for an exclusive show."

"I wasn't giving *you* a show."

"Have a drink with me, Candy."

"Is that one of your rules?" I challenged. "If I say no, will there be consequences?"

He paused, and my heart thundered at the sight of the sly smile spreading over his lips. Whatever made Zander grin meant trouble. "Would you like there to be consequences?"

"Fine," I snapped. Giving in would be less hassle all around, and it's not like I had any other plans. "Just one."

He pulled out a chair for me to sit down. "Espresso martini?"

"Sure." I shrugged. "Why not?"

Zander moved with purpose behind the counter. Watching him work was mesmerizing. Every flourish and pour was deliberate and calculated. He spun the shaker around in his hands better than any bartender. As he shook it, the sleeves of his shirt rode up to expose more inked skin. I forced myself to look away. Unfortunately, that didn't stop my mind from straying to what was lingering underneath.

"Why didn't you tell me you were a Briarly?" I asked.

He raised one eyebrow as he expertly poured the cocktails. "Would it have changed anything?"

"It'd have been nice to know what I was walking into," I quipped.

"Think of it as a test." He pushed the glass towards me. Holy hell, one sip was enough to tempt any angel down to the gates of hell. It tasted of fucking creamy coffee perfection. "When people hear the Briarly name, there are certain expectations."

"Do I strike you as someone who gives a shit about

expectations?" I questioned. "I told you I'd help you win, and I did. Even if it meant fucking over your own family."

"I may have been born into the Briarly bloodline, but that doesn't make them my family." Zander tensed. I'd hit a nerve. "A name is nothing. It's just empty letters. The Sevens are my real family. I got to choose them myself."

"So, you wanted to start over?" I probed. He had gotten the chance to see me open up on stage. Now it was his turn to answer some of my questions. There was more to him than the face-tattooed womanizer who acted like he had everything figured out, even if he didn't like to show it. "Why here? Why Lapland?"

"You mean, why did Bryce Briarly's son choose to open a strip club and not join the family business?" Zander laughed coldly. "You've met my father. What do you think?"

"Fair point," I murmured, recalling Vinny being dragged into the hidden depths of the manor. "Has he always been like that?"

"We've talked enough about the Briarlys." Zander circled the bar and pulled up a chair next to me. "Why don't you tell me how you learned to dance?"

"I'm self-taught."

"That's not what I asked." Zander brushed a loose hair off my collarbone. The feel of his skin on mine sent a shot of adrenaline racing through me. Either that or the caffeine was kicking in. "You can't hide from me, Candy."

"You have your secrets." I drained my glass. "And I have mine."

"For now." He leaned back, resting his arms behind

his head. Confidence oozed from every pore of his body. He'd be able to convince someone that signing over all their worldly possessions to him would be a good idea. "I was wrong to pair you with West last night."

"Wait, what?" I crossed my arms. Without my input, West would have never made it onto the fucking table, and Briarly Manor's library would resemble a bomb site. They needed me. "We won the game."

"You did." Zander looked at me like I was lying naked on a plate, ready for him to devour. "But I didn't like sharing you."

"I'm not a piece of fucking property you can put your claim on."

"You agreed to play by my rules," he said. "That makes you all mine, Candy. No other man can touch you without my permission."

"That was never the deal." My body shook with anger. "No man tells me what to do."

"You've never met a man like me before," Zander said. "Besides, I think you like it."

He reached out to stroke my cheek, but I grabbed his wrist before he got too close.

"I've finished my drink," I snapped. "You can clean the rest of the fucking mess up yourself."

I didn't know what scared me more: Zander thinking I was his, or how he was right... a small part of me liked it.

TWELVE

Z ander got under my skin. Just as he had wanted to.
He'd caught a glimpse of a part of me that I kept
hidden from the world, and I fucking hated it. Every
time I thought about him watching me dance, my collar
bone seared like a fresh scar where his finger brushed
against me. It could have been worse, though…

I stroked the hidden scar on my thigh, a memento
from the darkest period of my life. It was shaped like the
letter 'R'. When I arrived in Blackthorne Towers,
Raphael tortured me to make me more pliable to
Hiram's future demands. As his final sadistic act,
Raphael tied me down and took great pleasure in
branding me with his initial. It was his signature mark.
The sick bastard.

When I killed him, he'd known exactly what was
coming when I lowered my stockings. I'd never forget
the look of pure disbelief in his eyes. Raphael couldn't
understand how someone so broken could put themselves back together enough to bury his twisted ass. His
initial was no longer the mark of a victim; it was the sign

HOLLY BLOOM

of a warrior. I'd covered it with a beautiful piece of ink, but the raised skin underneath still provided a daily reminder of what could happen if you found yourself out of control. Something I wouldn't allow to happen in Lapland.

'That makes you all mine.' Zander's words floated back to me. Even remembering them sent a shiver down my spine. 'No other man can touch you without my permission.'

Zander was a control freak who liked to have everything his way, so I needed to be careful. I had to play by his rules to stay in Lapland until I dealt with Rocky, but there was another problem. Zander's touch may have seared my skin, but it had left me wanting more, which made me even angrier. How was it fair he looked like a fucking angel? Every fiber of my being knew he was a monster, exactly the type I'd sworn to avoid. Yet, my body betrayed me whenever he was around. Why couldn't I be attracted to stable men who held down boring office jobs? Seemingly, even my hormones were programmed to self-destruct mode.

The doorman nodded at me as I stepped into the neon lights with my head held high. "Evening."

Being attracted to someone was different from acting on it, I reminded myself. Rocky was smoking hot, but it didn't stop me from wanting to kill him. West had the body of a God, but an ego bigger than his fucking biceps. Attraction meant nothing. Besides, Zander already had enough women throwing themselves at his feet. I wouldn't fall for his high cheekbones and smoldering smile. He needed to get it through his head that I'd never become one of his fucking groupies. Instead, I wanted to know more about the man behind the rose tattoo and his family of the Sevens.

Mieko hurried over to greet me. "You don't want to go into the back."

I raised my eyebrows. "Oh, really?"

Mieko should know telling me not to do something would have the opposite effect. The raised voices of Lapland's management team in a stand-off were coming from behind the door leading to the back corridor. I positioned myself at an angle to listen in and get a sense of what was going on through the frosted pane.

"What do you mean they're working together, Red?" Zander spat out each word like an angry bullet. "It was your job to make sure this didn't happen."

"Calm down!" Vixen positioned herself in the middle of the two men. Everyone knew telling someone to calm down was the equivalent of splashing accelerant on a fucking fire. If Vixen had any sense, she'd back out of the way before Zander took her down as collateral. "Look, it's not his fault."

"You know as well as I do what this means. Now, we've got to fix this fucking mess," Zander snarled. "Don't defend him."

Vixen sighed and reluctantly stepped aside. Water was already up to her knees, and the Sevens were sinking faster than the Titanic. Like Rose, she knew this was a losing battle. She had to cut Rocky loose and leave him for the sharks.

"They were taking time to think about it. I thought we had them," Rocky explained. "How was I supposed to know they'd get a better offer?"

West shook his head. "This is all because of the fucking watch, isn't it?"

"It's more than that," Vixen said. "We all know that it was only a matter of time before they reached out to one of the local gangs, after what happened with Cheeks."

"I'll try to talk to the Razors again?" Rocky offered. "See what they—"

"The deal's already done," West dismissed. "It's too late for negotiations."

"This is on you, Red," Zander growled, giving a glimpse of the devil lurking underneath the perfectly pressed suit. "The Razors were ours, and you lost them. Now, the Briarlys have control over the whole fucking town."

Zander stormed past the others. He marched into his office and slammed the door behind him, making the frame rattle. Maybe it's not a bad thing that the room was sound-proofed after all.

Mieko tapped my shoulder, making me jump out of my skin.

"Told you so." She smirked, then her expression turned to worry as she grabbed my arm and pulled me away in time for the Sevens to storm back into the club. "That was close."

"Care to fill me in on who the Razors are?" I asked.

I'd heard their gang name thrown around casually, but didn't know where they fit into Port Valentine's criminal eco-system. Wherever you went, there was a hierarchy in the streets. It started at the bottom with petty thugs and runners, then went all the way up to the whales at the top of the food chain who could swallow everyone else whole. Whoever the Razors were, they were now at the center of the latest shit storm.

"They think the name makes them sound tough, but

they're only kids," Mieko said. "Most of them skip school or have already dropped out. They hang out on the project on the edge of town in Bayside Heights thinking they're gangsters. They steal cars, set fires, the usual stuff, you know?"

When people had nothing to live for, they did stupid shit. It wasn't hard to risk everything if you had nothing to lose and, sometimes, crime was the only way for kids like them to make a living. Most of the people Rocky and I had grown up with were now behind bars for making those same decisions. It had started when they were young and now; they bounced in and out of facilities like human pinball machines.

"I've heard things." Mieko looked over her shoulder to check the coast was clear. "Apparently, Zander wanted to bring the Razors in on some of his operations to help them get up on their feet."

"Zander doesn't exactly strike me as the charitable type." If Zander wanted the Razors to work for him, then he must have had a hidden agenda. As someone who had grown up with everything, he had no reason to care about what happened to a group of down-and-outs from the wrong side of the tracks. "What would happen if, say, the Briarlys had the Razors in their pocket?"

"The Razors may be kids, but there are a lot of them." Mieko's eyes widened. "They have the numbers and manpower to do serious damage. If the Briarlys have control of them, then they'll be wanting to prove themselves and there will be no going back. They'll be running heavy drugs in no time."

"The Briarlys are big in the drugs scene, huh?"

If the Razors were young and impressionable, they'd be easy to manipulate by a puppet master, especially one as experienced as Bryce Briarly. What's another wayward kid getting wrapped in drugs to him? With control of the Razors, Bryce would have an army of young men at his disposal who were eager to prove themselves and stupid enough to die trying.

"The Briarlys are big in a lot of scenes." She played with her skirt hem, then nudged her head toward Vixen approaching. "We shouldn't talk about this here."

I nodded and grabbed my tray of shots. If Bryce was drawing up battle lines against his son, then any customer could be one of his spies.

Filling in as a shot girl officially sucked. No one was interested in buying anything from me, without expecting something in return, and my cheeks ached from smiling. To make matters worse, a group of businessmen had come to town for a conference, so the club was even busier than normal. Thankfully, most of the suited newcomers were being entertained by a group of blonde dancers. They seemed to favor the ex-cheerleader type, which I certainly was not. Thank fuck, even listening to snatches of their conversations about stock options made me want to tear out their tongues.

As I patrolled the dance floor, doing my best to dodge any wandering hands, I recognized a face in the crowds. Sandy hair, flannel shirt, ripped jeans, baseball cap. I blinked to make sure I wasn't seeing things. Yep, it was definitely him. *Q.*

I'd thought seeing me again at the Maven would have chased him away, and it would be the last time we'd ever see each other. Relief washed over me. The fact he didn't run had to count for something, right? It showed he trusted what I'd said. If he believed I was still working with Hiram, he'd already be on the other side of the country by now.

As I pushed my way through the crowds to get to him, someone else blocked my path. West strolled over to Q and shook his hand. What the fuck? There was an easiness to their body language that came from familiarity. How did they know each other?

I wasn't the only one who looked shocked. Q's eyes landed on me. He froze on the spot. Shit, I needed to speak to him. To explain. Before he got the chance to ruin everything I'd been building by telling West what he knew.

I charged forwards, almost sloshing the entire tray over them both. "Drink?"

"Not now." West scowled down at me like an annoying fly he wanted to swat and made a shooing motion. "Go."

"Maybe I could interest your guest in a private dance?" I wasn't about to give up. West's flexing muscles didn't intimidate me. Too much was at stake. My eyes burned into Q's, hoping he'd take my bait. "What do you say?"

"A dance sounds great," Q said. His stare didn't leave mine. This was not a conversation we could have in the middle of the dance floor. "I'll catch you later, West."

"Fine." West gritted his teeth as if it was anything but fine. My interruption may have annoyed him, but I was in full-on damage control mode.

"Why don't you follow me?" I tried to keep my tone light, but my smile faltered. Hopefully, West wouldn't be able to tell anything was amiss. I needed to keep calm, at least on the outside, anyway. "This way."

I led Q into a booth and drew the curtain behind us.

"Why are you still here?" Q asked. He remained standing. I didn't blame him — just being in here made me feel like I needed to get checked out at a sex clinic. "I thought you were passing through on business?"

"I could ask you the same question," I said. "If you hadn't noticed from the tray of shots, I work here."

"I thought you were at the Maven for…" He paused. "Other business. I know you said you left Hiram, but—"

"Don't talk about him here," I snapped. Now it was his turn to look on edge. Q had never been someone who engaged in physical combat, and he knew exactly what I was capable of. I softened my voice to put him at ease. "I meant it when I said I was trying to start over, okay? I'm not working for him anymore. I've cut ties."

"How do I know you're not lying?"

"You don't," I replied. I didn't blame him for being suspicious. Hell, he'd be stupid not to be. Knowing what he knew about my time at Blackthorne Towers, it's a miracle he even agreed to come into a booth alone with me at all. "But do you really think Hiram would have let me work here?"

He mulled things over in a long silence.

"I never thought he'd set you free, Kitty." Q shook his head eventually. "How did you do it?"

"That's a story for another time." One no one else could find out about. Knowing I was the one who killed Giovanni Romano wouldn't just be a death sentence for me, but for them, too. "And I go by Candy now. My real name, remember?"

I always hated it when Hiram called me Kitty, but I wasn't the only one with a nickname. Everyone in Hiram's circle went by a code name. Including Q. In fact, I didn't even know what his real name was.

"What are the chances we both end up in the same town?" Q asked. He was a maths genius. It came with the territory of money laundering. He would already be running through the stats in his head and calculating the low probability. "Two people on the run from the same person."

"Coincidence? Fate? The pull of Port Valentine on people like us? Whatever it was, we're here now." I exhaled. I couldn't do anything to prove to him I wasn't lying, even if I wanted to. "And I'm not leaving. Not yet."

"I wonder why," he muttered sarcastically. The way he looked at me made my skin squirm like he could see right into the inner workings of my mind where revenge plans were forming. Was I being paranoid? Q had no way of knowing Rocky and I used to know each other, did he? It was hard to hide from someone who knew the darkness I was capable of. "I thought you'd left that life behind."

"I have," I insisted. Well, I'd left behind the part about following other people's orders at least. "That's why I want to talk to you about what happened the last time we met."

When I was younger, I believed everyone made their own luck. Life had proved me wrong. No one who grew up in Evergreen got out unscathed, and I'd been no exception. My upbringing set me up for failure. It didn't matter how hard I'd tried, or the dreams I used to have, I couldn't escape it. It's rare to get the chance in life for a second chance. This town offered me the chance to right Rocky's wrongs, but maybe it also offered something else… the chance to make amends with Q.

"We don't have to talk about it." He stood up straighter and cleared his throat. "Crystal knew the risks."

Crystal was my confidant during my year in captivity under Hiram's control. She did other jobs for him, mainly involving entertaining his guests on their visits. As I started doing more work of my own, Crystal helped me master my disguises. All she needed was a make-up bag and a wig to turn you into a different person. Over time, we slowly became friends. Unluckily for her, Crystal didn't know it would be the biggest mistake she'd ever make.

"It didn't have to happen," I murmured. Crystal knew what Hiram was capable of, but she also showed me that there was more to life than killing on command. "It's my fault. I want you to know that if I could go back and switch places with her, then I would."

As I'd spent more time with Crystal, Hiram felt threatened by another influence in my life. His hunger to control me overshadowed everything, and everyone, else. There was no level he wasn't afraid to sink to, and the worst thing of all? I didn't even see it coming…

"You didn't kill her, Candy." Q placed a gentle hand on my arm. "It wasn't on you."

Crystal was a one-off. She was my sunshine in a place filled with darkness. She taught me to laugh again and reminded me of a world outside of my prison… and she was the love of Q's life.

"How can you say that?" My voice trembled. I took a deep breath to regain control of my emotions. If I let them out, they'd hurtle from me like a train. "He killed her because of me."

The night she'd died, we'd been working in a casino seeking intelligence on one of Hiram's competitors. It'd become a regular fixture in my calendar after Hiram trusted me enough to leave the tower. Crystal and Q had planned to make their escape that evening. I'd never forgotten how happy she was, talking about how they were going to start a new life together. Hiram had other ideas.

"You don't know that," Q said.

"If it wasn't for the stupid tattoo, it'd never have happened."

Not long before it happened, Crystal had snuck me into a tattoo studio with Q's help. I got a tiny inked diamond on my ribs, and she got a tiny candy cane on her hip. It was our way of signifying our friendship forever. Wherever we were in the world, we would have always had each other. Somehow Hiram found out about it. Permanently changing my body without his permission was a punishable offense. Crystal paid the ultimate price for my wanting to do something for myself…

"Who helped get you into the studio?" His face contorted in pain as if he'd ripped off a bandaid. A year may have passed, but the pain was still raw. "You're not the only one who Hiram wanted to punish. What if Hiram found out that I was going to skip town?"

"He had no way of knowing," I said. Neither of them had shared their plans with anyone but me. The only thing worse than Crystal's death was believing Q had blamed me for it. "I swear I never said anything. I'd never have done that to you, either of you. It's what she wanted. I wanted you both to get away and be happy."

"We both know Hiram has other ways of finding information," Q said. "Maybe I got sloppy? He could have caught a trail of what I was planning."

"This wasn't your fault, Q," I whispered. "You didn't pull the… you didn't kill her."

We both stood in silence, remembering those last moments. Crystal and I had been walking to meet Q, where we were going to say our last goodbye. Before we reached him, an unmarked car pulled up alongside us. One minute, we were talking about her future. The next, she was lying lifeless in a pool of blood. Losing Crystal shattered us both and changed our lives in so many ways.

Q refusing to let go of her body, as the ambulance arrived, was the moment I decided I was going to leave Hiram. In the past, I'd believed he was tough on me because he cared. Killing Crystal finally broke his spell.

"Maybe not." He avoided my gaze. "But that doesn't make it any easier. I still think about what I could have done. If I got there earlier, would things have been different?"

"You can't think like that," I said. "She wouldn't have wanted you to. She'd have tried to kick your ass if she heard you talking now."

"You're right." Q laughed and wiped his eyes. "She'd have been proud of you, you know. For what you're doing."

"She's the one who made me believe it was possible, even when I didn't." I managed a half-smile. "I only wish she was around to see it."

"Me too." We shared a watery look of understanding. We may not be working for Hiram anymore, but we shared a bond. We both missed Crystal and, even though it was bittersweet, it felt good to talk about her again. "I think she'd have liked this place."

"She'd have loved the costumes…"

"I better be getting back." Q nudged his head. "West isn't someone who likes to be kept waiting."

"Wait!" I stopped him. After our conversation, I'd almost forgotten why I'd dragged him into this disease-ridden booth. "How do you know him?"

"Around here," he said, "I'm known as Cupid."

Cupid? Hang on a fucking minute! I'd heard that name before. Then it hit me.

"You run the escort agency?"

"That's where my nickname came from. It kinda goes with the whole town's vibe, doesn't it? People have expectations when they come to a place like Port Valentine." He shrugged. "Girls have always worked these streets, but I give them a safe place to come to. If I can get them out, I try. It's what she would have wanted."

Crystal was a sex worker when they first met. Running Cupid's was his way of trying to make sure no one else would end up in the place she did. Finding herself as part of Hiram's entourage.

"So, why do you need to speak to West?"

"We have a mutual agreement," he explained. "The Sevens help me with security. I help them with… other matters. Running a business has its uses."

It made sense. Q needed some kind of business for the money to run through. The Sevens had struck lucky in finding him. They wouldn't get a better launderer anywhere.

"Does that mean I'll be seeing you around more?" I asked.

"I swing by from time to time, but I keep my distance," he said. "Don't worry, kid. You have your past, and I have mine. Let's keep it that way, huh?"

"Deal."

As soon as we left the booth, West was lying in wait, prowling around like an animal in heat.

"Well…" Q shot a nervous look at West, then fished out two fifty-dollar bills and handed them over. "Thanks for the dance."

"I'm here anytime," I said. "You know where to find me."

West glared at me in fury. What the hell had got his balls caught in knots? He wasn't to know I hadn't given Q a dance. Shouldn't he be happy that I delivered fantastic customer service? Lapland was supposed to make them money after all.

Q nodded his cap. "I'll see you around, *Candy*."

"We're one dancer down because of you." West scowled. I resisted the temptation to remind him that it was Vixen who had fired Bella. I should be flattered he thought a lowly dancer like me would have such responsibilities. "You're on the late-night cleaning shift again tonight, got it?"

"Got it," I chirped back. "No problem."

West's eyes widened in surprise. Let's face it, obedience wasn't exactly one of my biggest strengths. Usually, I wasn't one to disappoint, but working an extra hour wouldn't bring my mood down.

"Good," West growled, turning on his heel with Q in tow.

Nothing would bring Crystal back. But, wherever

she was looking down on us, she'd be happy that Q and I had found each other again. For the first time in a long time, I felt a little lighter. There was only one other thing I had to do to make this happy feeling complete. It'd only be a matter of time before I got my chance.

THIRTEEN

A part from scrubbing the urinals, the biggest downside to working the late shift was trying to catch a cab home. I'd already been standing outside for twenty minutes. Where was my ride? What was the point in ordering something for a specific time when it didn't show? I began walking to see whether the car was at the end of the road. If not, I'd already resigned myself to having to walk the hour across town in heels. Blisters beat shivering out in the cold, right?

Suddenly, the sound of crunching metal and muffled shouts drew my attention. Usually, this wasn't the type of street where people stopped to see what was happening. Everyone knew keeping your head down and minding your own business were the unspoken rules of the street.

However, something compelled me to investigate. Trouble drew me in, like a vampire compelled to drink from an open wound. I knew I shouldn't, but I couldn't help myself. More than likely, it'd only be a few drunken guys in a brawl who I'd be able to take out with my eyes closed.

I peered around the side of an abandoned building into the alley. It was a thin street, narrow enough for only one car to fit through. Halfway down, a group of five men in balaclavas loomed over a groaning body. They drove their feet into the curled up figure like they were playing a game of soccer.

"Hey, assholes," I called out. "It doesn't exactly look like a fair fight."

I slipped my fingers underneath my waistband to feel the reassuring coolness of my trusty knife as I made my way toward them. I didn't need a blade to win a fight, but when it was five against one? It wouldn't hurt to have it ready to grab at a moment's notice.

"Turn around and go the other way, princess." One of the masked attackers, who was twice my size, looked me over. He seemed to be the leader of the group. "We're not playing games."

"I can see that," I said, continuing my advance. "But isn't it a bit of a coward's move to jump someone who can't defend themselves?"

They had bound their victims' hands behind his back, making it almost impossible to escape. It didn't look like kicking was the only damage they'd inflicted from the pool of blood. As I got closer, the man lying on the concrete twisted around to look up. It was hard to make out his features because his face was so swollen, but I'd recognize those dark brown eyes anywhere.

"Get out of here, C." Rocky rasped, trying to heave himself up but failing miserably. "Go!"

It'd be easy to turn away and leave them to beat him to a pulp, but… this wasn't how I wanted Rocky to go.

"Is this your girlfriend, Red?" another taunted, kicking him again. "How do you think she'll enjoy seeing your brains spill outta your head? Will she like that?"

I was close enough for my nostrils to be assaulted by the smell of overpowering body odor. Had these oafs not heard of deodorant? It was worse than standing in a guy's locker room.

"Maybe we'll play with her before finishing you off?" another leered. "How would you like to see me fuck her before you die, Red? We'll show her how cowards can fuck."

"Don't fucking touch her," Rocky threatened. He gritted his teeth to fight against the pain as he maneuvered himself to his knees. As soon as he was up, one of his attackers delivered a sharp blow to his jaw, which sent him slamming backward.

"What're you gonna do, Red?" they mocked. "Let's see how brave you are now."

Rocky wrestled to get up again. The bindings and his injuries made it too difficult. At the rate the blood was coming out of his wounds, it was surprising that he hadn't already lost consciousness.

"Kill me." Rocky spat blood at their feet. "But leave her out of this."

I crossed my arms. He couldn't be serious. Even after being beaten to a pulp, he still thought I was a damsel in distress. From where I stood, he was the only one who needed saving. His begging was about as useful as waving a burger in front of someone who hadn't eaten in days and expecting them not to eat it. Showing weakness would only encourage them more.

"Do you want to have fun with us, princess? You

should have listened to your boyfriend when you had the chance." The leader talked down to me like I was a child, then nodded at one of his henchmen. "Take her while we finish him."

"I wouldn't do that if I were you," I warned as a thug stepped forward.

"What're you gonna do?" He lunged, but his reactions were slow. I easily stepped out of his reach. He may be a wall of fat and brute strength, but he wasn't quick on his feet. "You little—"

The ogre charged again, but I dodged him and stuck out my foot. The lump of lard fell face-first into the wall. *Eat a fucking brick.* Before he had the chance to retaliate, I grabbed the metal lid of a trash can and sent it crashing into the side of his head.

"What the—" The sound of his skull shattering drew the attention of one of his cronies. "You bitch."

"Bring it on," I mumbled under my breath, as he abandoned his attack on Rocky. It's a good thing I'd tied my hair up tonight. Things were about to get messy, and it was a pain to wash blood out my lengths.

"We're going to have some fun with you," he sneered. "Then, we'll cut your throat and let your boyfriend watch."

"Is that supposed to scare me?" I narrowed my eyes, channeling my inner animal and bringing her to the surface. "If you want me, you'll have to catch me."

He dove and pinned me to the wall. His sweaty hand closed around my throat.

"You weren't that hard to catch." He smirked. That's right. I'd give him a moment to enjoy his perceived victory before I snatched it out from under him. I had always enjoyed that part. The part where they thought they had the upper hand. His breath reeked of cheap beer, which made me want to heave as he pawed at my shirt. "How about we see what's under these clothes?"

Perfect. He was right where I wanted him. The man was of a short and stocky build. His height gave me the right angle to lean in, and... I went straight for his ear, tearing it off the side of his head with my teeth. His skin ripping sounded as satisfying as whipping off a wax strip after a few months of regrowth.

"Fuck," he wailed, letting me go and dropping to roll around in pain like a kid who'd been told they had to leave a playdate. "Help! Someone help!"

Looking to his leader for assistance was his second mistake. Didn't anyone ever tell him it's a rookie error to lose sight of an opponent? I spat his ear into his lap and plunged my knife into his neck. The fountain of blood spraying up my arm let me know I'd hit the major artery. Bullseye! The sound of him choking would make a sweet lullaby.

"Holy shit!" Another turned their attention to me. "What did you do?"

Becoming a killer didn't happen overnight. It was something you built up an appetite for. The first time I'd killed a man, I'd expected to feel something. Remorse, guilt, and sadness, but... those feelings never came. It was easier to live with the thought of taking someone evil out of the world than letting them live. There was no reason to fear evil when I'd become someone who could destroy it.

"What's the matter?" I wiped the blood dripping down my chin with the back of my hand. "Don't you want to play anymore?"

The leader laughed. "Do you really think we're scared of you?"

"You should be," I said. The bodies of their two friends lay motionless in my wake, like tombstones displaying the magnitude of my destruction. They were going to be next to meet the monster who lived inside me. "This is your last chance to run."

"You're a crazy bitch!" The taller of the three cast a telling glance at their getaway car. I had to take him out first because he was the only one smart enough to start to plan their escape route.

"So I've been told." I grinned, flashing them my canines. "But I'm the last crazy bitch you'll ever meet. Say hello to the creature from your fucking nightmares, boys."

The next five minutes passed in a blur. My body went into autopilot as I worked like an artist, focused on creating a masterpiece. Their lives were my canvasses to toy with. Every slash, stab, punch and kick added an extra stroke to the perfect picture. By the time I'd finished, it looked like a pack of starving lions had gone wild. Someone needed to award me a public service medal for taking those assholes off the streets. Now, I had only one thing left to do.

I kicked a body out of the way to get to Rocky, who was curled up in the fetal position. He was still alive… just.

"I've been waiting years for this." I knelt at his side and listened to his shallow breathing. My shaking hand held the bloody knife to his throat. It'd only take a few seconds to slit it open and watch the life drain from him. "You betrayed me and now you're going to pay."

"Do it then," he gasped. His voice was rough with

pain, but he didn't move or resist as the blade dug into his skin. "Kill me."

This wasn't how I'd imagined it going down. I'd played the scenario through in my head so many times that it felt like a movie I'd watched on repeat. I had wanted to make him understand how much he'd hurt me and let him plead for mercy — not beg to fucking die!

"Before I do, there's just one thing I want to know," I hissed. After all these years of wondering, it was time to get the answers he owed me. "I want to know why you did it."

Rocky's gaze found mine in the dark. He was now a stranger, but he still had those same brown eyes. The eyes of the boy who'd smuggled me candy, who'd taught me how to blow smoke rings, who'd watched the stars at my side, and who'd convinced me I had a chance of a normal life… only to burn those hopes to the ground.

"If I didn't do it, they'd have killed you," he said. His body went rigid from the agony, but he didn't look away. "I knew what Hiram was, but I couldn't… couldn't… lose you."

"You're lying." My hand gripped the hilt tighter, hovering before making the last cut. He would say anything to save his skin, but I wouldn't fall for his lies again. "Tell me the truth."

"I did what I did because I loved you, C," he murmured. "I still do. I've… always loved you. It's only ever been you."

His eyes flickered shut as his voice trailed off.

"Rocky?" I shook him, but his limbs slackened under my grasp. His body didn't want to fight anymore. "Rocky!"

This wasn't how it was supposed to happen. I'd been looking forward to my moment of redemption for years, but why did it suddenly feel so wrong? If he died, I'd never know if there was any truth in what he was saying. Did he really have no choice at all?

"What the fuck happened here?" Zander's voice behind me sent the knife slipping through my fingers. "Is he alive?"

I fumbled around, trying to find Rocky's pulse. "It's slowing."

"Go back to the club." Zander threw me a set of keys. What would the scene have looked like through his eyes? "Get Vixen and go to the bunker. Now."

"Don't you want to know what—"

"There's no time. Get out of here," Zander ordered. Five dead guys surrounded me, but Zander didn't even blink as he took in every detail. He may as well have just walked into a kid's birthday party. "I'll fix this."

My head nodded along, but it didn't feel like it was attached to my body. The only thing I could focus on was Rocky's last words.

'It's only ever been you.'

FOURTEEN

I tore off my shoes and raced to the club. A rogue glass shard dug into my foot, but pure adrenaline stopped me from registering the pain.

"Fuck," I swore as I grappled with Zander's keys. Why the hell were there so many? How did he even fit them all in a pocket? "Stupid fucking-fuckety-fuck keys!"

I struck lucky. It only took the third try for it to click open. A light whirred on like I'd breached a prison alarm, and Vixen's shrill cry echoed through the building. "Who the fuck gave you a key?"

"I don't have time to explain." I dragged a table behind the door. The barrier wouldn't be enough to stop someone if they wanted to come in, but it'd slow them down and the noise would give us enough of a warning to act. "We need to hide now."

It might only be a matter of minutes before someone came looking for the five masked men. This would be the first place they'd check. Hopefully, Zander could clean up against the clock, because whoever they were taking orders from would not be happy when they

218

discovered they were missing… or what I'd done to them.

"Hang on—" Vixen began. As soon as I spun to face her, she looked like she was staring into the face of a resurrected corpse. "Holy fucking shit."

If she couldn't force out a bitchy remark, then I must look like hell.

"Where's the bunker?"

Her eyebrows raised in surprise. "How do you know about that?"

"We don't have time for one of your fucking interrogations." I waved the keys under her nose. We both need to get to a place of safety. "It's Zander's orders, okay?"

Vixen eyed me suspiciously but nodded. "Follow me."

We cut through the private booth and headed down the secret staircase into Lapland's underbelly, where the Seven's secrets lurked. I recognized the room where we played poker games, but we pushed on. Vixen stormed ahead. I had to half-run to keep up with her pace. Eventually, we came to a stop outside a door that looked like a janitor's closet.

"This is it," she said, holding out her hand for the keys. She didn't even flinch at the sight of my bloody arms and the slick metal. "Let me."

Once inside, there was hardly enough space for the two of us to stand next to each other. The only other thing in the room was a shit tonne of spiders and an ancient-looking filing cabinet, which had been pushed against the wall.

"Are you sure this is the right place?" I asked, swatting a cobweb.

She scowled and pushed me out of the way. "Move."

Vixen pulled open the third drawer and ruffled around amongst a ream of paperwork. A few seconds later, a mechanical clicking noise caused the entire cabinet to slide to the right to reveal a hidden passage.

"That's some serious Batman shit," I murmured, following her through the concealed entrance.

Vixen sealed the opening behind us by pressing a button on a control panel. The Sevens seriously valued their security to put those measures in place. We then went down a further set of narrow stairs to join an underground tunnel. Emergency lighting buzzed into life overhead to illuminate the way. Like the Maven, Lapland's hidden depths went even further beneath the surface than I'd first thought. What was it with this town and underground bunkers?

"Here we are," Vixen said, as we came to another sealed door that required a code to open. Vixen punched it in too quickly for me to make it out, but it beeped in agreement and swung open. "Welcome to the bunker."

It wasn't a large room, but thought had been put into its design to make the most of the space. There were two comfy-looking sofas, an armchair, a television, a dartboard, and a well-stocked drinks fridge. Imagine a doomsday bunker for bachelors, and you'd hit the jackpot. It'd be a great place to kick back and unwind away from the chaos of the strip club above.

I sunk into a chair. Who cares about blood stains, when the Sevens had won a quarter of a million at the poker game? They could afford to get it reupholstered. Vixen sat down opposite. She stared at me with an intensity that made me squirm; I couldn't tell whether it signaled concern or the fact she didn't trust me.

"So, are you going to tell me what the fuck is going on?" she asked.

"Roc-Red got jumped."

"How bad was it?" Vixen's guarded expression didn't change, but the slight edge to her tone told me what she really wanted to know.

"He was still breathing when I left… just." I looked away. "It didn't look good. It was one against five."

She stood up and kicked the vending machine hard enough to rattle its contents. "What happened to you? Why're you covered in blood?"

"I'm not one to run away from a fight," I said. Vixen didn't need to know the full story, but Zander? He'd want to know how those five men ended up dead, and I needed to get my story straight. "Let's just say, they got what was coming to them."

"You're a psycho, you know that?" From Vixen, I'd take that as a compliment. "Who even are you?"

"Do you have any pain relief?" I needed to change the subject before we got into dangerous territory. Plus, the initial adrenaline was wearing off. A dull pain shot down my shoulder, from where a fucker had got a nasty right hook in before I buried a blade in his gut.

"Here." She passed me a pack of pills and a cold can of beer to wash them down. "Your feet are cut."

I shrugged. "It looks worse than it is."

She frowned, rummaging around in the cupboard and retrieving a first aid kit. "I'll clean them."

"Now, there's a sight I never thought I'd see."

"I'm not doing it for you. I'm doing this for Red," she snarled. "The Sevens don't owe anyone anything. They don't need your help."

I snorted. Vixen had no idea. Helping dab my

wounds didn't come close to making up for the massive five-year hole in my life that Rocky owed me. How would she go about repaying that favor? Feed me fucking grapes whilst wearing a toga?

"Maybe I should have left him to die then?" I snapped. "He wasn't doing a good job of fighting his battles when his hands were tied behind his back."

"Hold still," she ordered, then yanked the shard of glass out of my heel with a pair of tweezers. "Done."

"Motherfucker!"

Vixen smirked as she rubbed the wound roughly with disinfectant. She was about as gentle as fucking Godzilla. The bitch was taking way too much pleasure in my suffering.

"I saw you two together, remember?" Vixen continued. "Don't get your hopes up. Red doesn't do girlfriends. Never has. Never will."

I took another swig of beer to drown out the stinging pain and winced. "Should I be touched you care about my feelings?"

"I don't," she retorted. "I'm telling you how it is. In the four years I've known him, girls have tried and failed. He's not interested. Red won't tie himself down."

I did the math in my head. For so long, I'd believed Rocky's and I's connection had been built on a lie. But if he hadn't had a girlfriend during our time apart, could there have been an ounce of truth in what he'd said? Part of me wanted to believe I'd been wrong, but that was a fool's way of thinking. It didn't matter whether our feelings were real. It changed nothing.

If Rocky had thought he was saving my life by handing me over to Hiram, he'd have been better off killing me himself. Hell, at the bare minimum, he could have given me some warning to help me understand, instead of luring me to my fate. How he treated me is not how you treated someone you loved.

"Don't worry, I have zero interest in being a Seven groupie."

"That makes you one of the only ones." Vixen rolled her eyes, then wrapped my foot. "All done."

"Thanks," I muttered. To her credit, she'd done a good job. It clearly wasn't her first rodeo. "So, what do we do now?"

"We wait." She pulled out a metal tin from under the sofa and opened the lid to reveal sweet green buds which filled the room with a distinct earthy smell. "Do you smoke?"

"Sometimes."

Well, not since the days I'd spent with Rocky back in Evergreen. Our favorite spot to hang out used to be on the roof of an abandoned warehouse. I pushed the memories of our time together away and coughed to clear the lump forming in my throat. Rocky's life hanging in the balance should be a celebration. Why did it feel like the opposite?

"Red always keeps an emergency stash." Vixen ground the buds into a powder and carefully rolled out a perfect joint. "Smoking it will teach him a lesson. Stupid fucker is always getting into shit."

She lit up and inhaled deeply, then passed it over. Why the fuck not? Getting stoned may not be the answer to my problems, but it'd help me relax long enough to answer any questions Zander threw my way upon his return.

I let the smoke fill my lungs and embraced the heady feeling. Neither of us said another word as we passed the joint between us. Smoke hung above our heads with the questions we didn't know the answers to. The swirling mist morphed into shapes and faces, but there was no more we could do. It was a waiting game.

The weed, or pure exhaustion, must have taken over because loud thumping interrupted my dozy haze. I shot bolt upright like someone had given me an electric shock. Vixen was even quicker. She was already up on her feet and swinging the vending machine away from the wall. If I hadn't pulled my legs back fast enough, she'd have decapitated my ankles.

"Another one?" My mouth fell open. "This place has more secrets than a fucking carnival house."

The new passageway led away from the club, which meant it must connect to a wider network of tunnels that sprawled underneath the town. It was a smugglers' dream.

"How is he?" Vixen asked.

Zander and West stepped into the bunker from the outside. Considering they'd spent their evening disposing of five bodies, the pair looked unscathed. If it wasn't for the flecks of blood over West's brow and the scuffs on Zander's shoes, the pair wouldn't have looked out of place at Briarly Manor.

"Alive," West said. His eyebrows raised as he looked me over. I'd almost forgotten I looked like a fucking butcher. Blood had congealed and dried hard on my clothes. "He's stable."

"Thank fuck!" Vixen's shoulders slackened. She may

be frosty on the surface, but she couldn't hide how much she cared about the guys. "Who's with him now?"

"Our best men are on it," West replied. "No one will get close to him."

I'm not sure how I'd expected to feel at hearing the news. One of the main reasons I wanted to stay in town was to kill Rocky. Despite that, I let out a breath I didn't realize I'd been holding onto.

Zander sniffed the air, and his expression turned to fury. "Are you both fucking stoned?"

I suppressed the urge to collapse in a fit of giggles. The two of them had cleaned up five dead bodies for me tonight. The least I could do was try to show some courtesy.

"How else could we entertain ourselves down here?" Vixen asked. "You were the one who wanted to fucking seal us away."

"For your own protection," Zander snapped, starting to pace the room. "And for good reason. We found out who was behind the hit."

"Who?" she asked.

"The Briarly heavies came for Red." West winced. The Briarlys were even more fucked up than I'd first thought. What kind of father orders a hit on one of his son's friends? "They were some of Bryce's best."

"Red went against my orders and approached the Razors again to make them change their mind. The hit on him was my father's way of sending a message to stay out of Briarly business. They were only meant to scare him," Zander explained. His unfaltering stare lingered on my bloody clothes, making me shift uncomfortably in my chair. How was I to know they didn't intend on killing him? They sure sounded set on the idea. "Now, they're dead. All five of them."

"Jesus…" Vixen dropped to the sofa and ran a hand through her short hair. "When this gets back to Bryce, he won't let this go. How?"

"We've dealt with it. There's no proof," Zander said. "But secrets in this town never stay buried for long."

"This is the start of a fucking war." West pressed his lips together in a determined line and cracked his knuckles. "We have to be ready."

"And we will be," Zander said. "But, for now, West is going to take you back to the hotel."

"This is our home," she objected. "Why should we run away scared? We don't want to show weakness."

"This isn't open for discussion, Vixen," Zander shut her down.

"Zander is right, Vix," West said. She opened her mouth to argue but stopped herself. They already had enough enemies without turning on each other, too. "It's better we don't stay here for a while."

"Fine." She bowed her head, and the two of them made to leave.

I stood to follow them out. What I needed more than anything was a shower. There'd be no hot water left, but it'd beat having a heart-to-heart with Briarly Junior, who looked like he wanted to burn a hole through my head with his glare.

"Where are you going?" Zander blocked my path. Well, it'd been worth a try. "You're not going anywhere."

"I can give Candy a ride to her apartment?" West suggested. He looked even more uneasy about leaving me alone with Zander than I felt. If Zander killed me down here, no one would ever find my remains. "It's on the way."

"I said, she's not going anywhere," Zander snarled. "Candy and I need to talk. I'll see she gets home."

"Whatever you say, boss."

Their footsteps faded down the tunnel, and Zander sealed the tunnel behind them, leaving us alone.

Zander studied me from across the bunker.

"Will this take long?" I crossed my arms. "In case you haven't noticed, I need to wash, and I'm not in the mood for an inquisition."

"I don't care what you're in the mood for." He took a step closer. "Care to explain why I had to dump five bodies in the lake tonight?"

"The lake? Really?" I sighed in an exaggerated way. "Is that the best you could do?"

My head still felt weird, like it was floating in the clouds. If it wasn't for that, maybe I'd have held back my bitchy remarks. As much as it pained me to admit it, Zander had saved my ass. I didn't have the resources to make one person disappear with a click of my fingers — let alone five. Still, it was disappointing he couldn't have been more imaginative. It wouldn't be long before the bloated blobs floated to the surface or washed ashore.

"I improvised." Zander's nostrils flared in a don't-fucking-push-me way. "What would you have suggested?"

"Burning them? Dissolving them in acid?" I started counting them on my fingers. "Digging a mass grave in the middle of nowhere? Pigs? Take your pick."

"How did a girl like you learn how to do such terrible things?"

I gulped. "There's a lot you don't know about me."

"I'll find out, eventually." His lips curled into a smile as he took a strand of my hair and twisted it around his finger. The way he looked at me sent a lightning bolt shooting down between my legs. Even though I looked like I'd stepped out of a slasher movie, he made me feel like a piece of meat he wanted to sink his teeth into. Now, I needed a cold shower for other reasons. "But, for now, why don't we make a deal?"

"I'm listening."

"You can tell me exactly what happened tonight. Divulge every gruesome dirty detail, or..." He leaned in closer to whisper in my ear, making me shiver as if someone had twerked all over my grave. "You can do a job for me."

"Let me guess. I'll get no payment for that too?"

"What price would you put on keeping your secrets a little longer?" Damn, he could see right through me like my skin was fucking glass. He had me by the nipples, and he fucking knew it. "I've done you a favor tonight. Now it's your turn to do one for me. You want us to be friends, don't you?"

Friends? *Fucking please.* There was nothing friendly about the way he looked like he wanted to crawl under my skin and eat his way out.

"What's the job?"

"West is going on a debt collection trip tomorrow," he said. "With Red in the hospital, you can accompany him. We'll call it a trial."

"A trial, for what?"

"You'll see." A smug smirk spread over his face. "What do you say?"

"I'll do it," I agreed. If I had to go on an excursion with the big man to get Zander off my back, it'd be better than the alternative. How hard could it be? Besides, it'd been too long since I'd seen West's sulky pout. "But I don't think your golden boy is going to be happy with me tagging along."

"You seemed to enjoy yourself last time," he said. "You know how to put on a good show, remember?"

"I-I-I don't know what you mean," I stammered. "It was just business."

Thankfully, the blood spatters covered the blush spreading over my cheeks at the memory of kissing West. How could I still be lusting after a kiss from someone who regarded me as highly as a cigarette butt in the gutter? I'd never smoke a joint again if it turned me into a pathetic mess.

"Tomorrow will be strictly business, too," Zander said. "You're all mine, remember?"

"You've seen what I can do." I stared him down. "Don't you realize that no man can own me now? I don't need someone else's protection."

Zander's chilling laugh echoed around the empty room, drawing attention to the fact we were the only two people in a room under layers of dirt.

"What's so funny?"

"Oh, I know you don't need my protection, little one." He put his hand under my chin and forced me to look at him. "But I think you know as well as I do, I get what I want. When I say you're mine, that means I own you."

"Well, you can't fucking have me."

I wouldn't be afraid to take him out if I had to, but Zander was a worthier opponent than the apes outside. He had already employed his most dangerous weapon against me. His brain. I wouldn't make the mistake of underestimating him.

"Can't I?" Zander grabbed my waist and pulled me closer. How was it possible for someone to smell so good after dumping five bodies? The heat from his palms made my sides tingle. "What's stopping me from having you right now?"

"You mean, apart from me ripping your balls off?" I pushed him away, ignoring every primal urge in my body begging for inked hands to explore me. "You're an arrogant bastard. I'm not your plaything, Zander."

"No, you're not like the others," Zander said. "But I will find out what you're hiding sooner or later."

"I need to go home. Now."

Zander opened the vending machine passageway and stepped aside. "A car is waiting at the end of the tunnel."

"Aren't you a gentleman?" I murmured sarcastically under my breath.

"Don't play games you can't win, Candy." He held out a flashlight. As I went to snatch it, he caught my wrist. "You don't want to see me when I'm angry."

"Likewise," I hissed. "Or, didn't five dead guys already prove that?"

When we were together, the two of us drew darkness out of each other. Breathing in the same air was fucking intoxicating like an outside force pulling us into a black hole. The harder I fought against it, the more it felt like I was drowning, but letting go? That was even more terrifying. I marched straight into the blackness and didn't look back. I wouldn't let him win. Ever.

"Remember what I said, Candy," Zander's voice echoed after me. "I always get what I want."

The darkness may be my fucking home, but I wasn't the only one used to living in the shadows. Being alone was one thing, but it was another to know Zander was right by my side. Ready to consume me.

FIFTEEN

For a change, the sunlight slipping through the threadbare curtains didn't wake me. Instead, the sound of someone hammering on my front door like they were trying to knock it off the hinges did.

"What the fuck?" I murmured, rolling over to check the time and see it was only eleven am.

Whoever was ruining my sleep was going to get a piece of my fucking mind. I'd only had three hours of sleep after my return from the bunker. It'd taken an hour to scrub off the blood, and my skin resembled hamburger meat after the ordeal.

The pounding on the door continued. If they knocked any harder, their entire fist would burst straight through the wood. I slipped out of bed and winced from the sharp pain in my heel. I'd have to walk on my tip-toes to avoid the worst of it. I peered through the keyhole to see West huffing like a dragon trying to breathe fire from his nose. He needed training.

I yanked it open as he rose his hand once more. "Are you trying to break down the fucking door?"

"I thought you were expecting me," West said. "When you didn't answer, I thought—"

"I overslept, okay?" I noticed my nosey neighbor's door squeak open and ushered him in before she made any rude remarks. "You can wait inside."

West's eyes strayed downwards. In my groggy state, I hadn't realized my oversized T-shirt flashed the bottom of my ass. Before my overtired brain could bark out a comment about clawing his eyeballs, a flicker of concern passed over his strong features. For someone with a poker face, I'd already worked out one of West's tells. His brows scrunched up slightly when something worried him. I recognized the minute movement from the time he'd left me alone in Zander's office after Cheeks's arrest and, again, last night.

"Are you sure you're okay, Pinkie?"

He frowned at my cut knees and the gnarly bruises decorating my thighs. You'd think I'd have learned that hot pants weren't the best thing to wear when fighting in the streets. Apart from the pain in my foot, I didn't register any other discomfort. I remember a time when my entire body had been a tapestry of different colored bruises in various stages of healing. It was something you got used to.

I wasn't ashamed of my battle scars, but West's pitying looks would drive me insane. The sooner he realized I wasn't a pretty princess who feared breaking a nail, the better. I'm the type of girl who ripped fingernails clean off to get what I wanted.

"I'm fine," I snapped, turning on my heel and not caring whether he saw my ass cheeks. "I'll be five minutes."

I got dressed quicker than the Flash; throwing on a

pair of leggings and a comfy hoodie. As I returned, West jumped. I'd caught the fucker red-handed rooting around the papers on my table. Did he honestly think I'd be stupid enough to leave anything compromising lying around for anyone to find?

I cleared my throat. "Looking for something?"

"What really happened last night?"

I raised one eyebrow. "D'you think you're going to find the answer on my table?"

If he wanted to find out more about me, he'd have to dig a little deeper. The only thing he'd find in my apartment were local takeout menus, too many empty ice cream cartons, and overdue bills.

"You could have got seriously fucking hurt," he said. "Zander said he stepped in—"

"Oh, yeah." I laughed. It was typical of Zander to take all the credit and play the fucking hero. "I don't know what I'd have done without Zander to save me..."

"Why did you get involved?"

"Why do you care?" I countered, pocketing my trusty chapstick. You couldn't kick ass when your lips felt like a two-hundred-year-old women's shriveled labia after soaking in a five-hour bath. "Don't we have a job to do? You seemed pretty eager to get going when you woke up the undead with your banging."

"You're only coming along for the ride." West may have dropped it for now, but our conversation was far from over. "Leave me to handle it."

"Have it your way," I said. "I'll be around to supervise."

He shot me his famous pout and stomped off. What a diva. As we left, my neighbor's scathing remarks stalked us down the stairwell. "That's her second gentleman caller, you know. Waking up the entire block!"

"Do you cause trouble everywhere you go?" West asked.

"I don't cause it," I replied. "Trouble finds me."

We were traveling in a slick black Mercedes. How many vehicles did West own? I didn't think I'd ever seen him in the same set of wheels.

"What do you think?" West admired it like he was reviewing his mail-order bride. Men's relationships with cars would always be a mystery. "She's a beauty, huh?"

"When you're done jerking off over the paint job, let's get this over with." I slammed the door shut and killed a little piece of West's soul. It served him right for my rude awakening.

As I slid inside, the smell of fresh coffee and hot cinnamon sugary goodness hit me instantly. It reminded me of a fairground that used to come to town every year when I was a kid, not that I ever went on the rides or bought any food. Evergreen kids didn't get those kinds of privileges. But I'd never forgotten lusting after the cotton candy, popcorn, and corn dogs.

"I didn't have you down as a morning person." West shoved a paper bag of mother-freaking goodness into my hands. Now, I felt a little bad about shutting his baby's door so hard. "I thought you might be hungry."

"You got me donuts?"

"Hey, I can always take them back," he grumbled. "If you don't want them."

"I didn't say that," I said, clutching onto the devil's food. No one would take them from me if they wanted to keep their hands.

West grinned and turned on the ignition. "That's what I thought."

Goddammit, he'd found my kryptonite.

On the outside, West came across as a tough as nails brick wall of muscle who could crush you harder than a plastic bottle underneath a bus. But maybe he had a softer side. Any guy who greeted me with coffee and donuts couldn't be a total monster, right?

"Where are we heading?" I took a bite and let out a small moan. Who cares where we were going? The only thing I needed to know was where the hell he had bought these from. Every bite felt like an orgasm exploding on my tongue. "These are so freaking good."

Back in Blackthorne Towers, Hiram put great emphasis on the importance of maintaining my figure. I followed a strict diet of shakes, salads, and other boring-as-shit foods that made wood shavings look appetizing. Keeping chocolate away from me had been a big mistake. My first rebellious act, in opposing Hiram's regime, was eating a bar Q smuggled in. I hid it under my duvet and savored every mouthful. It felt like someone had given me the key to Willy Wonka's factory.

"They're the best in town," he said, swinging a right onto the highway. "We're heading out to Shade Vale."

I groaned. "I didn't realize this was going to be a road trip."

It'd be a five-hour round-trip easy. After my actions the night before, this had to be another way for Zander to punish me. He may have put me on a 'trial', but the only thing he was trialing was my fucking patience, which was diminishing the closer I got to finishing the donuts.

The stark ringing of a phone bursting through the

speakers almost made me spill coffee over myself. The in-built fancy display showed who was ringing. It was no surprise who was on the other end of the line.

Zander's voice filled the car. "How is Sleeping Beauty this morning?"

The bastard knew how to wind me up.

"Screw you," I mumbled.

Zander laughed. "As charming as ever, I see."

"How's Red?" West asked. "Any news?"

"He's still out cold," Zander said. "Vix's staying at the hospital today..."

The rest of his words washed over me. Rocky had been my metaphorical voodoo doll for the past five years. Him lying comatose in a hospital bed was something I'd dreamed about when my mind escaped to the darkest places. Why did it no longer feel like a victory?

After a few minutes, the line went dead.

"Buckle up, Pinkie," West said. "You're in for a bumpy ride."

"Tell me something I don't already know."

I'd moved to Port Valentine to start over, but old faces lurked around every corner. First, there was Rocky, then Q... it wouldn't be long until my past caught up with me, but for the time being? All that spanned ahead of us was the open road and the likelihood of having to watch West beat the shit out of someone at the end. I couldn't allow myself to think about anything else.

"Why buy me a coffee if you didn't want to stop to pee?" I returned to the car after he'd finally agreed to pull over at a rest stop. "You're the one who loves your leather seats so much."

Our honeymoon donut period had officially ended. We'd been bickering for the past hour. It started with who should pick the radio station. I wanted to listen to rock, whilst he wanted to listen to jazz. Next, we argued over his need to hit the gas like we were in a formula one race when there was no fucking need for it. My bladder, almost bursting, was the final straw. If I got a UTI after this trip, then he'd be paying the fucking bill.

"You could have gone behind a tree…"

"I'm not an animal like you." I glowered at him. "That wasn't a fucking compliment, either. How much further is this place?"

"Not far," he said, checking his beloved sat nav. He was especially fond of the machine's smooth accent, which made me want to throw it out the window. I wouldn't be surprised if he got off to her purring dulcet tones: continue on, take a sharp right, and you'll cum in your fucking pants.

"Are you even going to tell me about what we're here to do?" I asked for what felt like the millionth time.

"I already told you," he said. "You won't be doing anything."

"You're fucking impossible," I said, cranking up the music which he'd switched back to his station in my absence.

After a long frosty silence, the car approached an old junkyard and ground to a halt outside the rusty gates.

"Is this the place?" I asked.

"Yes, but—"

I'd already unbuckled my seat belt and jumped out before West could lock me inside. He may want me to stay behind, but Zander had given both of us this job. We were in it together, whether or not his pouty ass liked it.

"I thought I told you to stay in the car," West growled, driving along slowly at my side. "I made myself clear."

"I was feeling travel sick," I replied. He'd be the first to complain if I vomited over his pristine dashboard. "You really need to get the suspension sorted."

West's fists clenched on the wheel. Any word said against his car was akin to preaching about satanism to a priest.

"If you're coming in," he hissed, pulling to a stop, "keep your mouth shut and let me do the talking."

"Me? Talk out of turn?" I held my hand to my chest. "I wouldn't dream of it."

We made our way through the yard. It was the kind of place where you walked in constant fear of getting your skull crushed by an ancient television falling from a precariously piled stack. What kind of business could the guys have here? Comparing this place to Briarly Manor was like comparing a juicy rare steak to a burger that had been half-eaten by a rabid dog.

"Don't touch anything," West warned.

"No shit." I rolled my eyes. "I'm not a total idiot, and being squashed by an eighties sofa isn't exactly the way I want to die."

He snorted and strode forwards with purpose. His tight black T-shirt left little to the imagination, and I noticed a bulge tucked into his waistband. I had to do a double-take before realizing it was a gun. Out of the piles of scrap, a grimy trailer came into view.

"This is it," West said, rapping on the tin door. I

squinted through the dirty window, but a build-up of grease, dead flies, and yellowing blinds made me give up any hope of seeing anything useful. Although, the radio playing suggested someone was inside. West knocked even harder. "I know you're in there, Eddie."

A moment later, the door creaked open to reveal a sniveling man. He wore a gray oil-smeared vest, which may have been white once upon a time. He looked to be in his forties, with a bulging beer belly, bloodshot eyes, and an unshaven face. Before he even had the chance to speak, I immediately disliked him.

After working with Hiram and mixing with his associates, I'd honed my instincts. My bad vibe detector could pick creeps out of a crowd easier than a metal detector could find a can. It didn't matter what walk of life they came from; they all had one thing in common. A distinct aura that made my skin crawl.

"Long time no see." The man wiped his nose with his hand, then held it out. When he realized West had no intention of shaking it, he awkwardly shoved it back into his pocket. "What kind of business can I do you for today, West? I've got some things you might be interested in."

"I'm not here for business today." West put a foot in the doorway. "I'm here to collect."

The little color in Eddie's cheeks drained away in a blind panic. The spineless rat attempted to grab the handle, but his body couldn't move quick enough and West's leg was one mighty doorstop.

"I didn't do it," Eddie wailed. One of the first signs someone was lying was how quick they were to beg. "Come on, West. We're friends, aren't we? How long have we known each other?"

West barged inside and pressed his gun into the middle of Eddie's chest. We had no time to listen to his bullshit.

"Please!" Eddie raised his hands. "It wasn't me, I swear!"

This was a textbook case. Now he was trying to shift the blame to someone else. Yet another pointless attempt to avoid a beating. Not taking accountability usually only ensured you got hit five times harder.

"We can do this the easy way or the hard way." West pressed the barrel of the gun harder into him. "It's your choice."

"What about your girl? She doesn't want you to hurt me." Eddie looked at me through his piggy eyes for support. Unfortunately, he was looking in the wrong fucking place. He wouldn't find any sympathy there. "A nice girl like you doesn't want to see him hurt me, do you?"

"Actually," I said, "I don't mind at all."

"You fucking whore!" Eddie screeched. Well, he turned quicker than I thought.

West struck him across the face with the gun with a smack. "Don't fucking call her that."

"Sorry, I'm sorry," Eddie whimpered, clutching his cheek, which was puffing up like he was sucking a gobstopper. "I don't know what you want, okay? I'd help you if I could, you know I would."

"You know why I'm here," West said slowly. "Give me what I want."

"I don't know. Please, I swear!"

West ignored his begging and delivered another blow. One after the other. Two of Eddie's last remaining teeth flew out of his mouth and landed at my feet, but I didn't make a move. I stood back in the shadows and watched West's beast erupt. Unlike most fighters, West didn't tire. The relentless beating only seemed to amplify his energy.

"Stop, please! You win!" Eddie wheezed. He'd curled into a shaking mess, lying in his feces and smearing the brown stain over the floor as he rolled around in pain. "Fine, I'll give it back. I'll give you what you want."

I expected West to stop, but he didn't. Pounding the guy with his fists had silenced his rational brain into submission. He'd entered the zone. The zone in which the power of another life lay at your mercy.

"Enough, West." I stepped in against my better judgment. "He'll give us what we want."

As much as this creep deserved to die, it wasn't the job we'd been given. We were there to collect. After having to clean up my mess yesterday, Zander would lose his shit over another bloodbath. Eddie spluttered blood over the floor — at least he wasn't dead, yet.

"West!" I shouted as he delivered another bone-shattering punch. "You're going to kill him!"

West's eyes were devoid of all emotion. He looked at me like he'd never seen me before. The supposed gentle giant who'd bought me donuts had vanished. In his place, the monster staring right through me wasn't even a human being anymore. The only thing it craved was blood.

For fuck's sake! West had been the one who insisted he didn't want me to be involved, but what other choice did I have? I launched forward to catch West's wrist. His whole body resisted and shuddered. The sheer force of his rejection sent me crashing into a pile of junk stacked in the trailer's corner. The bang must have stirred something in the depths of West's subconscious as he froze and turned to face me.

I staggered to my feet and brushed myself off. "Get out of here, West."

West looked from me to Eddie like he'd woken from a sleep and didn't know how he'd got there.

"Go," I repeated.

He turned and stormed out, pulling the door clean off its hinges.

"Listen here, you useless sack of shit." I ducked down next to Eddie and yanked his head upright by his thinning hair. "Tell me where it is, or I'll call West back in here to end your miserable existence."

"Under the chair," he rasped. "Tube..."

"A tube?" I pressed. "Eddie?"

Damn it, the bastard had lost consciousness. I dropped my hold and stepped aside as the growing puddle seeping through his pants got dangerously close to my sneakers.

Fantastic. A tube? What the hell did that even mean? The chances of finding anything in this hoarder's paradise were slim, and it didn't help that West hadn't told me what we were looking for. My nose wrinkled at the smell coming from the empty food cartons surrounding the mangy armchair. As I knelt to peer underneath it, I expected a demon to pull me under and drag me into the depths of hell. Thankfully, a half-eaten rotten sandwich was the worst I had to deal with.

You can do it. I took a deep breath and shoved my arm underneath to disturb the piles of wrappers. West owed me a manicure after this. Amongst the trash, a small cardboard tube around six inches in size nestled between empty chip bags. This had to be it, right? After all, it'd taken Eddie a few snapped fingers and broken ribs to reveal its location.

"It's been a pleasure doing business with you, Eddie," I said, stepping over his unmoving body and out into the fresh air with the package safely in my pocket.

All I had to do was tame the beast long enough for us to get the fuck outta there. Finding West wasn't difficult when I could follow the sound of smashing metal.

"Feeling better?" I called. He kicked a massive dent in a refrigerator with the force of a steamroller in response. "I'll take that as a no?"

Sweat dripped down his face from exertion. "Don't come near me," he panted.

When I first saw West outside Lapland, I wondered why he'd chosen to shoot the guy. Now I understood. When West loses control, he can't stop himself. He would keep going until he tore everything in sight to shreds… or until someone was dead.

"West?" I ignored him and picked my way through the rubble. "Look at me."

"I can't," he grunted through gritted teeth.

He pummeled the fridge so hard that the skin over his knuckles split open — even the blood trickling down his arm didn't stop him. He kept going and going, delivering blow after blow, like a car hurtling full speed towards a cliff's edge.

"I said, look at me," I repeated.

"You shouldn't see me like this." He didn't look angry anymore; instead, his face contorted in excruciating agony. "Stay back."

"I'm right here." I took a step forward with my hands raised in the air. "Come back to me, West."

He gulped. "Don't come any closer."

"It's okay," I soothed, reaching out to him slowly. His eyes followed my every move, but his body stayed frozen in place as if he feared what he might do. "I'm not going anywhere."

The seconds stretched into eternity as I took his gigantic hands in mine. His blood slipped between my fingers like we were entering a binding pact. I knew how it felt to lose control when your body spiraled into a place of no return. You needed something to ground you and bring you back to reality to stop you from drowning in a sea of your own making.

His hand eclipsed mine and held on tightly. "Aren't you scared I'll hurt you?"

I shook my head. Him asking the question told me all I needed to know.

"You shouldn't have seen me like this," he murmured. "I'm a monster."

"I think everyone can be a monster sometimes," I said, squeezing his hand. "Let's get back to Port Valentine, okay? I can drive."

West looked at me like I'd just stepped out of an alien spaceship. From his horrified expression, you'd think I'd decapitated Eddie and offered him his head mounted on a stick. He may lose control of his temper, but he'd rather die than give someone else control of his car.

"I'm driving," he said, grabbing his keys and marching to the car. "That's final."

"Do you have to walk so fast?" I had to run to keep up. "I'm not going to hot-wire it."

"I wouldn't put it past you," he said, pausing and peeling off his T-shirt.

Fuck, how was it even possible for someone to be so defined? His body was a freaking work of art. From his sharply defined pecks to the tattoos which spread from his neck onto his torso like a delicious trail. His ink was an intricate mix of black and gray images telling a story, which I could stare at all day… but shouldn't.

Get a grip on yourself, Candy!

West tore the fabric apart with his bare hands, then used the strips to wrap his knuckles and clean up some of the blood with the rest. Nothing suppressed a murderous rage more than the threat of wrecking your car's interior. If he was back to worrying about his precious seats, the beast inside him must have slinked back into its cave to hibernate once more.

What the fuck is wrong with you, brain? Under the sun, sweat glistened in every crease of his muscles — those big, bulging muscles. *I'm telling you to look away, can't you read my signals?*

I tried the car door.

"You're not getting in like that," West growled, throwing me the bloody tatters to wipe my own hands.

It would never be perfect, but it'd do.

Back in the car, a half-naked West seemed to take up twice the amount of space. Had it really been so cramped on the drive over? Hopefully, the rolling scenery would be a distraction from the literal Adonis sitting a few inches away.

"Fuck!" West slammed his hands against the wheel. His fury still lurked in the danger zone like a town sat on the edge of a forest fire. All it would take is for the wind to change direction, for the blaze to spread and burn your house down. "The package…"

"You mean this?" I pulled out the tube quickly,

extinguishing any further risk. "I mean, you didn't exactly let me in on what we were here to collect."

West's eyes widened. "How did you—"

"It doesn't matter." I handed it over. "Now, are you going to tell me what's inside it?"

"You're telling me you didn't look?"

"I didn't exactly have the time," I reminded him. Funnily enough, making sure he didn't kill anyone or hurt himself was higher on my list of priorities.

West flicked the lid open and slipped out a rolled-up painting of a woman. From the discolored edges, it looked old. The subject was strangely familiar, but I couldn't place her. She looked to be in her late twenties or early thirties, and she could have easily been a model. Pretty blonde curled hair, red lipstick, a pearl necklace, and a beaming smile... whoever had painted her had captured her spirit.

"Who is she?" I craned my neck to get a closer look. "She's beautiful."

"You've already seen enough." West rolled it up carefully and sealed it back inside, then slammed it into the glove box. "Let's get outta here."

Minutes passed by, and my unanswered question still hung in the air. Whoever the woman was, she must have meant something to someone for us to come out to the sticks to pick it up. What was so special about it to make it worth beating the shit out of someone for?

West was the first one to break the silence. "Zander can't know you've seen the painting."

"Then why did you show me?" I challenged. "I thought the Sevens weren't supposed to keep things from each other?"

West wrenched the wheel to the right, causing the car to swerve off-road.

"What the fuck is wrong with you?" I screeched as he slammed on the brake. My heart skipped a beat like someone had thrown me off the edge of a building. "Why do you always have to do that? You—"

Before I could say anything else, West's mouth was on top of mine. The warmth of his lips was both intoxicating and suffocating at the same time. We'd already kissed before at the manor. But this? This set my entire freaking body on fire.

Candy! A distant voice in the back of my head tried to jolt me to see reason. *You shouldn't be doing this! You should know better!* I mean, I should… but why couldn't I stop?

Knowing what West was capable of didn't frighten me. It only strengthened the irresistible draw I felt toward a man who could rip me apart. I knew exactly what kind of demon lurked beneath West's muscled surface, but I couldn't think straight as his tongue explored my mouth and penetrated my fucking soul.

The heat radiating off his skin ensnared all my senses, rendering me powerless under his touch. I didn't resist when his blood-smeared hands cupped my face and pulled me closer. I kissed him back hungrily like he was my favorite snack that I hadn't eaten for weeks. I slid my hand over his tatted chest and caught his lip between my teeth, then…

BEEEEEEEEEEEEEEEEEEEEEEEEEEEEEP!

The sound of a passing car brought us both thudding back to reality.

"Fuck," West pulled away, breathless. "This shouldn't—"

"—have happened." I finished his sentence and adjusted my top, trying to muster what I hoped to be a business-like tone. Instead, I sounded like a sultry porno actress.

"Zander can't know about this," West said. For someone under Zander's thumb, he did a pretty good job of breaking his orders. "Not ever."

"Agreed. It was a mistake." A big stupid head-fuck-ingly wonderful mistake that would bring down the wrath of Zander's consequences, if he ever found out about it. "It can't happen again."

In my defense, it wasn't like I'd been the one to insti-gate it. How else was any sane person supposed to react in that situation? Demons attracted demons, and a girl's willpower could only stretch so far. What I didn't under-stand is why West kissed me. The two of us were alone, and he had nothing to prove. Or did he?

"I'll take you home." West's gaze lingered on my swollen lips and swallowed hard. "Then I need to take over at the hospital."

The sound of the engine drowned out my racing pulse. We'd completed the job and picked up the paint-ing, but I didn't feel victorious. The men in Lapland had infiltrated my life in more ways than one. Rocky had broken me, Zander wanted to own me, and West? Well, who knew what game he was playing…

SIXTEEN

"Have you heard about what happened to Red?" Mieko asked. "Apparently, it happened right outside the club. It makes me not want to stand outside at the end of the night. It gives me the creeps."

I hadn't seen her since the night the Briarlys put a hit on Rocky, which seemed like a lifetime ago. After my collection job with West, Zander permitted me the rest of the day off before returning for my next shift. Pfft, I deserved a vacation after saving Rocky's ass and stopping West from killing Eddie at the junkyard. Although West must have relayed a censored account of our collection trip, otherwise Zander's reaction wouldn't have been so friendly.

"Maybe he had it coming?" I pointed out. "Good people don't get jumped for no reason."

She didn't know how close Rocky had come to dying, and I wasn't about to fill her in. I had Vixen to thank for the fact my involvement in the event had been erased.

"You have a strange sense of humor." Mieko shook

her head. "Talk of the devil, I heard he only got out today."

Rocky strode over to the bar with a slight limp. If he noticed everyone staring, he didn't let on. His facial swelling had gone down, but he sported an assortment of bruises and cuts. I didn't miss the micro-flinches he made with each breath. Bruised ribs and a stab wound hurt like a bitch. It was the least he deserved. The fucker should feel lucky he could breathe at all.

"Good for him," I muttered, looking away. The other dancers may want to treat him like an injured soldier, but I wasn't about to pander to him.

"Look!" Mieko nudged me. "He's coming this way."

The theme tune to the movie Jaws played in my head as Rocky headed in our direction. Flouncing off was an option, but what would it achieve? It'd only postpone the inevitable. We'd have to face each other at some point.

"Can I steal Candy from you, Mieko?" Rocky asked. "We need to talk."

"Sure thing," she squeaked and hurried away.

"What is it?" I demanded, planting my hands on my hips. If he expected me to ask how he was healing, then he'd be waiting for an eternity. "I'm busy."

People watching our every move made my skin prickle. Being the center of another Lapland scandal wouldn't do my popularity any favors. All of Bella's ex-minions may have learned it wasn't worth getting on the wrong side of me, but it didn't stop bitchy rumors following me around like toxic gas. I didn't need to invite any more bad karma into my life.

"Let's talk somewhere private," Rocky suggested,

nudging his head away from the prying eyes. "Zander's office is free. Meet me in there?"

"Okay," I agreed reluctantly. "But you only have five minutes."

"That's all I need."

I slipped into Zander's office, where Rocky was already waiting. When I looked at him, it was like staring into the face of a ghost.

"Well?" I tapped my heel against the floor. The awkward silence stretching out made me regret not killing him when I had the chance. "You dragged me in here to talk, so talk."

"Where do I start?" He sighed. "Life didn't turn out how we expected, did it? I never thought we'd be standing here like this."

"You shouldn't even be standing here at all."

When someone defied death, they joined an elusive club of the walking dead. Rocky owed his membership to my weakness. A weakness I should never have shown.

"I've got you to thank for that," he said. "Zander told me the fake bullshit story, but I know you were there. I know what really happened."

"You had a nasty fall." I flicked my hair over my shoulder. "Your mind is playing tricks on you."

"I remember you coming into the alleyway, and then..." Rocky's voice drifted away, then returned stronger. "You killed them. All of them."

"Do you realize how crazy you sound?"

"You should have killed me, C," Rocky said. "After everything I've done to you. I'd have killed me too."

"If you're trying to say thank you," I spat. "Save your breath."

"You don't get it. I wanted you to do it. It's what I deserved!" He kicked Zander's desk with a bang, forgetting about his injuries, then stumbled towards me. He grabbed my shoulders with both of his hands and stared into my eyes with a wild intensity. "How do you think it feels to know I'm only alive because you fucking spared me?"

"The only reason I spared you was because you caught me off guard," I sneered, meeting his gaze with fury and trying to ignore how his hard grip burned through my shirt. "Even on your deathbed, you were lying."

He dropped his arms to his sides. "It wasn't a lie."

"You expect me to believe you had no choice?" I laughed coldly. "That there was nothing you could have done?"

"I was a selfish fucking kid, okay?" he said. "I know it's my fault. All of it. Don't you think I've hated myself for it every fucking day? If I hadn't got wrapped up in that gang, then taken you to the fucking clubhouse, none of this would have happened..."

Sometimes people can pinpoint a time in their life when everything changed. They don't realize it at the time but, after that moment, nothing would ever be the same again. That night was mine, and I remembered it well.

It'd been a hot summer evening. Rocky was close to graduating. We'd spent most of the night sitting at our spot on the warehouse roof, sharing a spliff and talking about how we couldn't wait to get away from this dump. On our way back to Evergreen, Rocky got a text to swing by a place they called 'the clubhouse' to pick up drugs. He'd been working for a local gang and dealing to save money for college. I didn't like it, but it was the only way for him to make enough money to get away… which is what we both wanted more than anything.

When we arrived at the clubhouse, there was a party going on. Everyone was wasted, so Rocky made me wait for him across the street whilst he picked up the goods. The first flutter of the butterfly's wings altered everything. If I had stuck with him, maybe things would have been different. He'd been trying to protect me from the assholes inside, but neither of us knew who else was prowling the streets. That's when I met Hiram for the first time.

Back in the present, Rocky paced the room.

"If I could go back and change it, I would," he continued. "I'd have stopped us from going. He'd never have seen you. He'd never have taken you away!"

"When Hiram wants something, he'll do anything to get it."

"He said he'd kill you, C." Tears pooled in Rocky's eyes as he choked out his words. "If I didn't hand you over, he said he'd slit your throat. I was a selfish fucking kid stuck in a messed-up world, and I didn't know what to do. I couldn't think of another way."

"You could have fought for me!" I shouted. "You didn't have to hand me over!"

"What would have happened if I said no?" Rocky pressed. He would have known a man like Hiram didn't make empty threats. Hiram would do whatever it took and, if someone didn't give in, he'd have no problem taking them out of the equation. "Come on, C. What chance did a seventeen-year-old dealer, like me, stand against the state's biggest crime lord?"

A bitter twang of pain twisted my gut. Deep down, I knew he was right. Rocky's resistance would have been futile, but it still didn't make it hurt any less.

"You could have warned me," I whispered; my voice cracked. "You could have explained what was going on."

"I didn't want you to know what I'd done. I couldn't face it until it was too late…" He sniffed and wiped his eyes. "After he took you, I didn't give up. I tried to find you, I—"

"Wait," I interrupted him. "You tried to find me?"

"A few weeks after they took you, I went to Black-thorne Towers and saw the prison they were keeping you in," Rocky said. Then his expression darkened. "Hiram made sure I wouldn't come sniffing around again. The bastard set me up."

I racked my brain to think of anything that happened in my early days of captivity that could have hinted at Rocky trying to find me, but nothing jumped out. Back then, I'd been kept in the dungeons without sunlight. The days passed in a blur when you were in a living nightmare you couldn't wake up from.

"When I tried to break into one of the back entrances, the guards warned me away," Rocky explained. "A few days later, the cops picked me up. I got two years in juvie on drug charges. That's where I met Vixen."

For Hiram, getting sent to prison was a relatively light punishment. Rocky's earlier compliance in handing me over must be the only reason Hiram didn't plant a bullet between his eyes.

"So, you joined the Sevens after you got out?"

Slowly, I started to piece together the timeline of what had happened since we last saw each other.

"Vix told me her cousin could give me a job, so we both came here," he said. It made sense now why the two of them were so close. "But I didn't give up on finding you. I'd go away for weekends to trail around the city, following whispers about what Hiram was up to. I heard nothing about you. I had to be careful. I knew if he caught me next time, then I wouldn't so lucky. Then Cupid showed up in town…"

I exhaled deeply. "Shit."

"I recognized him as soon as I saw him," Rocky continued. "He was there the day I went to Blackthorne Towers. I made a deal with him. He'd tell me everything he knew about you, and I wouldn't share his past with anyone else."

"Then you gave up on me again, right?"

"What would you have done, C?" he asked. "I didn't know if you'd even remember me after all of Hiram's brainwashing. Q told me how Hiram would kill anyone who got close to you, and how you followed his orders. I thought you were under his spell. If I'd found you, how would you have reacted?"

I ignored his question. Both of us already knew the answer. If Rocky had tracked me down, I wouldn't have needed to get Hiram involved. I'd have killed himself.

I changed the subject. "Why didn't you tell the Sevens about me?"

"I was fucking ashamed, okay?" Rocky hung his head. "Telling them wouldn't change anything. None of them could hate me more than I hated myself."

Seeing him like this should make me want to rub my

hands in glee like a supervillain, but all I felt was empti-
ness. Both of us had spent time behind bars over the
years. The only difference between us was that I'd been
freed from my shackles. Rocky's guilt kept him locked up
in his mind. No amount of bodily pain I could inflict
would ever come close to the mental torture he'd put
himself through. My time with Hiram had made me
stronger, but Rocky? It had shattered his soul into a
thousand pieces.

"I wanted things to be different in Lapland," Rocky
went on. "Zander values loyalty more than anything. I
vowed to never make the same mistake again. And I
won't. Ever."

I shrugged. "Talk is cheap."

Rocky's explanation made his actions easier to
understand, but it didn't change what had happened.
Turning off the contempt in my brain wasn't as simple
as flipping a switch. How could I ever trust a word that
came out of his mouth? He'd deceived me once before;
he could do it again.

"I know words mean shit, but I'll prove it to you,"
Rocky vowed. He held my gaze, reminding me of the
fierce protector I thought he used to be. "I don't expect
you to forgive me, but I'll spend my life trying to make it
up to you. If you'll let me."

My snarky ass mouth found itself speechless. An
apology couldn't erase the past. It didn't magically take
away the scars or memories. It didn't scrub out the
terrible things I'd done or change the person I'd
become. But if nothing had changed, then why did
everything suddenly feel so different?

"I need to get back to work," I mumbled, feeling
around for the door handle. Hell, I needed to get as

far away from him as possible. "Your five minutes are up."

Back on the dance floor, my head reeled from Rocky's revelation. What was I supposed to do with the information? It'd always been easy to blame him for putting me in a terrible situation. I hated Hiram for who he was, but I hated Rocky even more for who he had pretended to be. His betrayal had hurt more than anything Hiram had done.

If Rocky was telling the truth, then he was also a victim. His name could be added to the growing list of people whose lives Hiram had destroyed. But could I forgive him for the part he had to play in how my life turned into a fucking horror movie overnight? The old me believed in second chances, but was that something I was still capable of? Becoming the Kitten had changed me beyond recognition. Protecting myself had to be my number one priority.

"What did Red want to talk to you about?" Mieko asked. "I just watched him leave."

"Nothing," I lied. She didn't need to know about the tangled web of trouble I was caught up in. "Damn, is that the time? I'm up next."

I performed my pole routine with the same level of enthusiasm as a professional chef tasked with boiling an egg. No one seemed to notice. Everyone was too busy drooling over my tits to care if I was smiling — well, apart from West, who didn't even glance in my direction at all. He and Zander sat in their usual booth donning grave expressions; whatever plan they were concocting hinted another storm was rolling in.

It wasn't a shock that West couldn't bear to look at me. Why would he want to be reminded of his dirty little slip-up? I'd already rationalized what had happened on our way back from the junkyard and drawn the only viable conclusion. He'd kissed me because of the adrenaline rush that came from beating Eddie to a pulp. People did crazy shit when they were buzzed, right?

West didn't have to worry about me telling Zander, though. He wasn't the only one who was ashamed of their actions. I should have punched him in the mouth, regardless of whether an inked six-pack was on full display. With Rocky back on his feet, the last thing I needed was to create more drama with another member of the Sevens. Kissing West is a secret that needed to stay buried… alongside how fucking good it'd felt.

"Your performance looks like torture," Vixen barked, and broke my reverie. That made at least one person who hadn't been staring at my tits. "Would it fucking kill you to smile?"

"Maybe I don't want to fucking smile all the time."

"I thought I was the miserable bitch around here," she said. "You can help me clean up tonight. Someone's called in sick."

"Do I have a choice?" I asked, even though I already knew what her response would be. If an awful job needed doing, she'd put me at the top of the list without hesitation.

"Do you want to keep your job?"

"I'll help," Mieko piped up. She was so light on her

feet that I hadn't even realized she'd been listening in. "I really don't mind."

"You don't have to—" Vixen began.

"It's okay, I want to," Mieko insisted.

Vixen and I looked at her like she'd declared she wanted to lick a homeless man's asshole. Who would volunteer to wipe down those disgusting urinals with a smile on their face?

"Suit yourself," Vixen said, scouting out the joint for any signs of trouble. *Bingo*. Her eyes locked on a customer who looked ready to vomit all over the expensive sound system, and she gritted her teeth. "I'll catch you both later."

She stomped away to crucify her next target. The poor guy didn't know what was coming…

"She's going to eat him alive."

"She was right about your performance, though," Mieko said. Fine, make that two people who looked above my cleavage. "Are you really sure everything is okay?"

My phone buzzed in my pocket, and I checked the screen. It was an unknown caller. Getting a new phone and number was never going to keep him away for long.

"It will be," I murmured grimly. "I'm gonna get some fresh air."

This wasn't a conversation that I wanted to be overheard.

I had three choices: hang up, leave town, or speak to a man who'd make Lucifer break out in a sweat. The choice was simple. I let it ring a few more times — just long enough to piss him off, then held the cell to my ear.

"Hello, Kitty."

"Hiram," I replied, keeping my tone even and level. "This is unexpected."

Texting me was one thing, but calling meant Hiram was advancing. His urge to infringe on my life and invade was an itch he needed to scratch.

"You haven't replied to my messages." Hearing the contempt in his voice put me on edge. Hiram hated being kept waiting. The old me would have never dared leave him in the lurch, but I didn't follow his orders anymore. I was in control of my own life, even if he hadn't accepted it yet. "I was beginning to think you were avoiding me."

"I've been busy."

"I know all about that." His bitter laugh made the hairs on the back of my neck stand on end. He wanted me to feel like he was watching me. Another of his classic manipulation techniques. "I hear you've made quite a statement in Port Valentine, Kitty."

"No thanks to you." Anger built inside me like hot molten lava. "Care to explain how a certain home movie got sent around my place of work?"

"Think of it as a reminder of the good times," Hiram said. "Besides, you should be thanking me."

"Thanking you?" I snorted. "For what?"

"You owe me a favor for taking care of your little police problem," he said. "You wouldn't want me to think you're ungrateful now, do you? You know I'd never let anyone hurt you, Kitty. I'm always watching."

Fuck… *Cheeks.*

Rocky's suspicions had been right. My fucking ego

had come back to bite me. Going to the Maven with Cheeks may have annoyed my new bosses, but it'd come at an even bigger cost. Hiram's favors had a hefty price tag.

"I didn't need your help," I said. At the Maven, I'd kicked the hell outta Cheeks and taught him a lesson. The only thing locking him up achieved was starting a bigger war between the Sevens and the Briarlys. Knowing Hiram, that was no fucking accident. "I had it under control."

"I'd be careful what you say next," Hiram warned. "You know I don't like it when my work is unappreciated."

"What do you want, Hiram?" I demanded. "You didn't call me to gloat, did you?"

"How long are you going to carry on with this act, Kitten?" he asked. "You need me. We both know you're going to come back home where you belong."

"That's never going to happen. We had a deal, remember?" My entire body trembled with rage. "No matter how many fucking favors you do for me."

"Remember, Kitten," he hissed, slamming a fist down on a hard surface. "Favors can be undone."

The line went dead.

Cheeks getting out of prison didn't scare me. I could make a pathetic weasel like him cower by raising a pinkie finger. But it wouldn't be long until Hiram decided he was done with playing games at a distance. When he came for me, I needed to be ready. Death would be the only way to stop him and, even though I was one of the best, I didn't have the resources to match him.

I took a deep breath and headed back into the pink

lights of Lapland. I'd spent years working solo, but I would have to form alliances to stand any chance at defeating Hiram. The problem was, being a bitch hadn't exactly won me a lot of friends. Right now, Rocky's promise to make amends and whatever weird connection I had with the Sevens may be my only hope. But first, I needed to find out whether they could be trusted…

SEVENTEEN

"This is fucking gross." I grimaced at Mieko as I peeled a used rubber from the sticky booth floor. This was supposed to be a strip joint reserved for dancing, but some dancers didn't mind giving a little extra shimmy for cash. "Remind me why you volunteered for this again?"

"We can share a cab home this way. After what happened with Red, I don't think anyone should travel alone," Mieko said. If she knew the full story, then she'd have no qualms about leaving me to fend for myself. "Besides, I won't be able to sleep for ages. Not after the show."

"You were amazing." She truly was. The girl was crazy talented. If strip tease ever got recognized as a sport, Mieko would be a world champion. "I don't know why you're still working at this dive."

Her cheeks flushed. "I like it here."

"Where do you think you're going?" Vixen's shrill voice hit us from the other side of the building, like a foghorn.

"Out," Zander shot back. Mieko and I kept our heads down. We knew better than to stand between Vixen and the guys. "We have a job to do."

Zander, West, and Rocky were dressed head-to-toe in black. They looked like they were about to conduct a bank heist. A balaclava hung out of Rocky's back pocket, and my imagination ran wild about what West might be hiding inside his bulky backpack.

Vixen put her hands on her hips. "Why didn't you tell me about it?"

"I've been busy," Zander dismissed. "And I'm the boss around here, remember?"

"We'll be back by sunrise," West said, then winked. "Don't wait up."

"Hey, you two!" Rocky called over to us. "I'll leave money here for your cab."

"They're not charity cases," Vixen snapped. "This is their fucking job!"

"They're staying late, aren't they?" He placed down more cash than we needed. "It's the least we can do."

"Thanks, Red." Mieko smiled brightly and waved. "Have a good night."

"Anytime, Mieko." His gaze met mine. "Get home safe."

I scowled and turned my back on him to mop the floor furiously. It'd take a lot more than a few bucks to prove he truly wanted to make amends.

"Clean up when you get in." Vixen looked at all three of them. "And bring me breakfast from the place that does good pancakes."

Rocky bowed. "Will that be all, Your Highness?"

"For now," she said, cracking a rare small smile. As much as she tried to be a bitch, she thawed considerably when Rocky was around. After finding out they were in juvie together, it made me question what must have happened for them to have created such a close bond.

Zander checked his watch and nodded. "Let's move."

The men exchanged looks like were telepathically communicating in a secret language. It was strange seeing how they worked together as a unit. Whenever Hiram gave me a job, the success rested entirely on my shoulders. As did the risk. With the Sevens, they worked like a well-oiled machine. Each of them had their role and part to play.

A blustery gust of cold air ripped through the club as the trio departed. What were the Sevens planning this evening?

"Come on," Mieko whispered as soon as they'd left. "You can't lie to me and say nothing is going on between you two now."

"Who?" I played dumb. Now didn't seem the right time to bring up the secret kiss I'd shared with West or Zander's desire to lay claim on me.

"You and Red, obviously."

I sighed. "Look, it's complicated..."

"Most things are," she said.

"It's not what you think, okay?"

"Whatever you say!'" She smirked, then wiggled her eyebrows. "But I can see the way he looks at you."

"We're in a strip club, not a rendition of The Notebook," I snapped. The only male attention I attracted fell into three distinct categories: those paying me to take off my clothes, those I lulled into a false sense of security before I killed them, or those with the power to destroy me. "Real life isn't like the movies."

"You can deny it all you want, but you can't fool me," she said. "I can see what's going on."

"Maybe you should focus a little more on sweeping and less on making up imaginary theories about my love life?" I grumbled. "Then we'd finish up faster."

Mieko stuck her tongue out. "Only because you know I'm right."

She couldn't be any more wrong, but it was easier to let her believe the only thing I had to worry about in my life was whether a guy liked me.

"What do you think?" Mieko held up a lipstick. We had almost done cleaning and working together had made the late shift bearable for a change. "Do you like this shade?"

I waited until the moment she was about to try the color on. "I wouldn't use it unless you want to catch herpes…"

She dropped it on the floor, and I snorted with laughter at the look of horror on her face. The cosmetics left in the dressing room by the bimbo army should come with a fricking warning label. I'd seen the state of the men they sucked face with.

Suddenly, a crash from the other room startled us.

Mieko looked around nervously. "Maybe the guys forgot something?"

They'd only left an hour ago. Zander would never leave for a job unprepared. Precision and organization weren't just skills to add to a resume, they helped you to survive in our world. The amateurs didn't last in this game. I may not have superhero senses, but my intuition told me when something didn't feel right.

A few seconds later, a glass smashed.

Something was wrong.

"Wait here," I instructed Mieko. "I'll go check it out."

"I'm coming with you!"

We had no time to argue about why that wasn't a good idea; instead, I shoved a bottle of hairspray into her hands and said, "Spray first, questions later, got it?"

"Got it." Mieko nodded, wielding it like a weapon. At least she could spray someone in the eyes and incapacitate them long enough to escape.

"You don't want to do this." Vixen's voice floated down the corridor as we edged closer. I put a finger to my lips and pushed the door to the club floor open gently, gesturing for Mieko to follow. "The Briarlys sent you, didn't they?"

"You took out five of their men," the squeaky-voiced intruder replied. He'd pulled his hoodie over his face and stood with his back to us. His clothes hung off him in an awkward teenage way. "Now, someone has to p-p-pay."

Mieko dropped the hairspray bottle with a bang. Well, there goes our cover...

He spun around to face us and confirmed my suspicions. He couldn't have been older than sixteen. I knew Bryce Briarly had recruited the Razors, but sending someone so inexperienced into a situation like this without supervision was a fucking disaster waiting to happen. You wouldn't let a toddler loose with a chainsaw for the same reason.

"Stand back." He pulled a gun out of his pocket

with a shaking hand. "Stand back or I'll sh-sh-shoot her!"

"Get outta here," Vixen hissed at Mieko and me. The chick had more guts than most men I'd seen in the same position. "I'll handle this."

"We're not leaving," I said, standing firm. Zander would never forgive me for it. "We're staying with you."

"I'll d-do it," the boy stammered. "I'll bl-blow her brains out."

"If you were going to do it," I rebutted, taking a step forward, "you'd have done it already."

He pointed the gun at the bottles behind the bar and gently squeezed on the trigger. Then nothing.

"You've still got the safety on," I pointed out. Clearly, he'd never shot a gun in his life. "Why don't you put it down?"

"You don't want to kill anyone, do you? We can talk this through." Vixen tried to reason with him in an uncharacteristically soothing tone. "This isn't what you signed up for. We can help you and the rest of the Razors get out."

"I have n-n-no choice," he yelped. "If I do this, I'm in. If I don't, he'll k-k-kill me."

This only confirmed what we already knew: Bryce Briarly was a motherfucking monster right down to the core. This boy soldier's life meant nothing to him.

"There's always another way." I took another step closer to him and Vixen. "You don't have to do this."

"Don't move!" He pointed the gun at my face. "I'll do it, I will! I'll shoot you all!"

"You don't even want to murder one person," I responded, not breaking a sweat. "Do you seriously think you could kill two? Or, three?"

"I have to!" His bottom lip quivered. "He said I had to do it…"

"Why do you think Bryce Briarly would send one of his newest recruits to do such an important job?" I probed. This guy was nothing more than walking target practice. "He knows you won't succeed. Even if you kill all three of us, do you think Zander Briarly would let that go?"

I watched my words sink in. If he didn't kill Vixen, Bryce would kill him. If he killed us, Zander would kill him. Either way, the poor kid was fucked. Bryce had already sealed his fate. One way or the other, Bryce planned for the boy to end up dead. His death would be nothing more than a statement to prove a point about who was really in charge in this town.

"We can help you get out of this," Vixen said. "It's the only way."

"No one can help me," he screamed. His eyes darted around the room in panic and he flapped his arms around wildly. "I have to do this!"

The situation was escalating. I caught Vixen's eye and gave her a micro-nod. People did stupid things when they panicked. We needed to shut this down. Right fucking now.

I grabbed a glass from a nearby table and threw it at the wall. His momentary surprise gave Vixen an opportunity. She shot forwards like a cannonball, rivaling a star football player, and knocked the gun from his hands. The weapon slid across the shiny floor. I dove to retrieve it… but the kid was closer.

He'd recovered from the shock of being tackled faster than expected and skidded toward the gun. Then he picked it up the wrong way and…

"No!" I didn't realize the scream was coming from the back of my throat until it was too late.

A single gunshot fired straight through his chin, ripping through his flesh like it was made of butter. He hadn't even noticed the safety switch got knocked off in the fall. Now, he lay dead in the middle of the floor with a bloody mess where his head had been a few seconds earlier.

Bullets are no joke. They don't discriminate. That's why children should never play with guns.

———

"Fuck!" Vixen clutched her stomach. She'd got caught in the spray zone and splatters of brain covered her clothes. It's a good thing she only wore black. "I think I'm going to be sick."

She turned her back on the body and retched.

Tonight should never have happened. His life had meant nothing to the powerful older man who'd played with it. What happened may have been an accident, but Bryce had sentenced him to death before he'd even had the chance to live. Hell, he could have been any of the Evergreen kids I'd grown up with. When you had no family, you became an easy target for exploitation. Isn't that where it all went wrong for me too?

I took a deep breath and thought back to my earlier conversation with Rocky. Would he have ended up lying dead in a pool of blood if he'd resisted luring me to my fate? Hiram had also put him in an impossible situation where he saw no way out.

"Mieko?" I turned back. Her thin frame shook

madly like someone had doused her in ice water. "Mieko? Can you hear me?"

Silent tears fell from her eyes, leaving black mascara smudges streaming down her cheeks.

"Go sit in the back," I said. "We'll take care of it."

My automatic reflexes were kicking in. It wasn't the type of neighborhood where people called the cops whenever they heard a gunshot, but who knows what else Bryce could have in store? This could be a warm-up. There was no time to think about why the boy was sent to Lapland. Or whether I was to blame because I'd killed five of Bryce Briarly's men to save Rocky. We needed to focus on clearing up the mess left behind.

"No." Mieko sniffed, wiping her eyes and meeting my gaze with a newfound determination. "I'll help."

"Vixen, do you have any guys you can call?" I asked. "What about the club security?"

"We can't call them!" Rising panic grew in her voice. "Not with this. They can't be trusted when it comes to Briarly business."

"It looks like this we'll have to sort this ourselves then." I sighed. What was the point in having stooges if they couldn't do the jobs you needed them for? "Do you have any garbage bags? Duct tape?"

"I mean, yeah," she murmured, wiping the vomit from her mouth, "I think so… somewhere…"

"Get them," I ordered. "We need to move. Fast."

Vixen nodded and disappeared without saying a word. She needed to draw her attention away from the dead body before she went into shock.

"What are we going to do?" Mieko asked, avoiding looking anywhere above the boy's shoulders.

"Clean up," I said. "Are you sure you can do this?"

Mieko nodded grimly as Vixen returned with the materials. This wasn't the type of cleaning we'd expected to be doing, but I was no stranger to body disposal. I had Hiram's lessons to thank. Any idiot could kill another person, but not everyone could get away with it. Covering your tracks was the most important part.

I remembered the first time I'd watched someone die. It'd been a messy scene, not dissimilar to this one. Hiram wouldn't let me look away as he tortured and killed a so-called traitor. Listening to the man beg and watching his life explode before my eyes changed me as a person. The man lost his life, but I also lost a part of my soul that day. It blew apart my belief that everyone had something redeeming about them and let me see the truth. Some people were born evil, and nothing could change it.

"We need to move him before rigor mortis sets in," I said. "Vixen? Are you ready?"

"I… I…" Vixen shook her head. "I don't think I can do this."

Her chest heaved and her breathing came out in short bursts as she gasped for air.

Fuck.

I slapped her hard across the face before a full-blown panic attack took over. She'd thank me later.

"I need you to be in this," I said, placing my hands on her shoulders. "You can freak out later, okay? But, right now, we need you."

"Okay." Vixen gulped as my red handprint spread over her cheek and brought her back to her senses. Underneath the tough girl act, she had a sensitive stomach. I'd always assumed she'd played an active role in Zander's schemes, but her behavior proved me wrong. Was it possible Zander tried to protect her from the violent parts of his life? "Tell me what I need to do."

"Both of you start at the legs," I instructed, like a drill sergeant. "I'll take the head... or what's left of it."

Together, we wrapped and taped the body in black bags like an oversized present. Vixen kept gagging but, as soon as we covered his face, she regained some of her self-control. I made a mental reminder to never take her to see a gore movie.

"What now?" Mieko asked.

We were all sweating from the exertion but couldn't stop. We couldn't afford to take a break. We had to finish this. I surveyed the scene to see what we were working with. Usually, I preferred to be prepared, but we'd have to improvise…

"Get the curtain," I said. "We can roll the body onto it and slide it across the floor to the exit."

"But that's the stage curtain," Vixen objected. "It's velvet!"

"If you haven't noticed, we have a dead body in the middle of the fucking dance floor," I pointed out. "Is having to buy a new curtain really your biggest problem right now?"

"I guess it needed replacing anyway," she mumbled, as Mieko scampered away to unhook it.

Next, we needed to get the body off the premises. With the security staff unavailable and the other Sevens out on a mission of their own, we would have to do this ourselves.

"How many cars do you have?" I asked Vixen.

"I've got the keys to West's entire collection," Vixen

said. Well, who'd have guessed West's love of cars would come in handy? "His garage is at the end of the block."

"We'll take two," I decided. "Pull them up at the side."

Meanwhile, I'd do a rough clean to remove the chunks of flesh and the huge blood splatters. We could do a deep clean after we'd disposed of the body, but getting rid of the most obvious signs that a crime had taken place would help if anyone came looking whilst we were gone.

The three of us were panting after we'd dragged the body over to the open door. Vixen had already opened the trunk of the car, which concealed us from view, so all we needed to do was get the wrapped package from the floor into the back. It was easier said than done. For a skinny guy, he weighed more than he looked. Talk about dead weight...

"Three, two, one," I counted down. After heaving and pulling, we managed to bundle him in. Our muscles would ache tomorrow. Who needs to lift at the gym when shifting a dead body gives you an intense workout?

Mieko wiped away the hair stuck to her head. "Why do we need two cars?"

"Because," I said, patting the hood, "we're going to light this baby on fire."

Vixen let out a low whistle. "West is not going to be happy."

"Shit happens." I'd originally planned on pushing the car into a ravine, but I changed my mind after seeing the spare can of gas in the trunk. It was West's fault for keeping his cars so well-maintained. "Now, all we need is a screwdriver and clean clothes."

"Already done." Vixen nodded at a bag thrown into the front seat.

I raised an eyebrow. "How did you pull that together?"

"Zander insists on keeping one in every car." Well, I had to give Zander credit when it was due. Damn, he really was a professional. I respected someone who planned for every eventuality. "Where are we heading?"

"We can drive around until we find somewhere?" I suggested. "Unless either of you—"

"I know a place," Mieko said quickly.

In an ideal world, I'd have preferred to scope out the location first, but we didn't have that luxury. We needed to get this done before the sun came up.

"Lead the way." I threw Mieko the keys to the escape car. Vixen couldn't be trusted behind a wheel, after her panic earlier. "We'll follow."

"Wow!" Mieko's eyes widened at the red Jaguar. "I've never driven one of these before."

"Go easy on the gas," I said. "The last thing we need is the cops pulling us over."

We didn't need to add any other bodies to our pile to burn…

"How did you learn all this?" Vixen asked, wincing as the car went over a bump in the road and the body lurched inside the trunk with a smack.

"Learn, what?"

"Strippers don't usually know how to clean up dead bodies."

"It doesn't matter." I kept my stare locked on Mieko's headlights ahead. We'd been driving for a while, and the neon lights were far behind us. "All that matters is we clean up this mess before one of us is framed for murder."

"Why didn't you leave when I told you to?" Vixen pressed. "He could have killed you both."

"We may not be best friends," I said, "but I wasn't about to stand by and let him shoot you."

If the situation was reversed, I doubt Vixen would have shown us the same level of courtesy.

"I thought I could deal with it," she murmured. "I thought he only wanted to scare me. I didn't think—"

"It was an accident," I interjected. No amount of over-analyzing the situation would bring him back. The only thing it would do was fuck with her head. "There's nothing you could have done. He was a dead man walking. It was better he choked on his own bullet than whatever Bryce would have put him through."

"But we could have pushed the Razors harder." Vixen wrung her hands over and over. Seeing a dead body was as normal to me as seeing a dog in the street. It was easy to forget not everyone was used to being surrounded by violence, and they'd need more than a quick breather to recover after a traumatic event. "They never should have made a deal with the fucking Briarlys. We were trying to help them."

"Why were you trying to help them, anyway?" I asked. "Don't take this the wrong way, but the Sevens don't exactly come across like a soup-kitchen type of gang."

"We're not complete assholes." She scowled. Well, they could have fooled me. "All of us know how easy it is to go down the wrong path."

"Too fucking easy," I agreed. I squinted down the open stretch ahead. I hadn't seen another car for the last twenty miles. Abandoned farms crumbling by the road-side were the only sign people had been here before. "Any idea where Mieko is taking us?"

"Beats me." Vixen shrugged, wrinkling her nose. "I'm not exactly a country girl."

Mieko's car suddenly made a sharp turn to the right, into a patch of overgrown woodland. Even in the daylight, the dirt road would have been impossible to spot if you didn't know it was there.

"Oh, fuck!" Vixen retched at the noise of the body thumping against the metal. Riding alongside a cadaver wasn't exactly first-class travel. "I'm going to—"

"If you're gonna hurl, do it in the footwell." What difference would it make if the car was about to turn into a burning wreck? She could vomit all she wanted over West's precious upholstery, but I didn't want to be picking it out of my hair for the rest of the night. The smell had a way of lingering even after you washed it. "Aim it away from me, okay?"

We continued until we were deep in a thicket of trees, which opened up to reveal a clearing. As we turned the next corner, Mieko pulled to a stop. Vixen managed to keep herself together long enough to stagger out of the car before I'd even pulled on the brakes.

I looked around. Up ahead, a ramshackle cabin stood nestled between the trees. It didn't look like a cute gingerbread house; instead, it resembled the scene of a horror movie. If anyone camped here, they were asking to be woken up by a crazy axe-wielding lunatic.

"What is this place?" Vixen asked.

"My dad used to bring me down here when I was a kid. No one else knows about it. He left it to me," Mieko said, her voice devoid of all emotion. This place didn't hold happy memories for her. "I've not been back for years."

"After tonight, you won't have a reason to come back again," I said gently, then returned to the task at hand. We could be sentimental later. "Now, let's get to fucking work."

I started by removing the registration plates to lessen the chances of the wreckage being linked back to us, then we worked together to splash petrol throughout the car's interior. The chemical fumes made my eyes water, but they beat the smell of decomposing flesh any day.

"We need to take our clothes off," I prompted.

We had spares to change into from Zander's bug-out bag. If there was ever a doomsday apocalypse, I knew who to come to.

"What?" Vixen stuttered. "Why?"

"Don't tell me you're shy. You've seen us half-naked a hundred times." I rolled my eyes and pulled down my shorts. "We need to get rid of the evidence. You're covered in brains."

"Fine," Vixen relinquished, adding her clothes to the pile to burn.

Mieko froze.

"Mieko?" I asked. Maybe this place was getting to her. I don't know how I'd cope if I had to return to my old cell in Blackthorne Towers. "You good?"

She flushed, pulling off her clothes and putting on the clean ones quickly. "Yep, all good."

"Great," I grumbled, looking down at myself. The shirt I'd pulled over my head hung down past my knees like a dress. I looked like a fucking house-elf. "Looks like I got West's."

A giggle escaped from Vixen's lips. I'd never heard her laugh before — not like a girlish schoolgirl, anyway. She slapped a hand over her mouth like she couldn't believe she made such a sound. We were basically holding a funeral, and she may as well have just burped the alphabet.

The guilty look on Vixen's face set Mieko off. Before we knew it, the three of us collapsed into hysterical laughter until we were cackling like witches. Emotions came out in unexpected ways. My stomach and face ached as Vixen handed me a lighter.

"Should we say a few words first?" Mieko paused. "It doesn't feel right to just… you know."

She was right. The least we could do was try to honor him in some way. The kid may have tried to kill Vixen, but he was desperate. If he'd been able to get the right help and support, none of this would have happened. Bryce was the real one to blame… and he wouldn't get away with it.

"I'll do it," Vixen volunteered.

She cleared her throat, then recited 'Eldorado' by Edgar Allan Poe perfectly. Mieko and I gawped at her like she'd been body-snatched by an alien before our eyes. Who knew there was more to her than enforcing the Seven's rules?

"What?" Vixen snapped after she'd finished. "I like poetry."

"That was beautiful." Mieko sniffed, dabbing her eyes.

Vixen hung her head. "Thanks."

"Now," I said, "let's burn it down."

The three of us stood side-by-side and watched as the flames whooshed along the trail we'd created. The fire swallowed the car in a ball of hungry flames. Even from a distance, the wall of heat made our eyes sting and throats scratch. None of us moved, though. The blaze was mesmerizing. We were all transfixed in equal awe and horror at what we were seeing. I couldn't be sure of what Vixen and Mieko were thinking, but I knew this moment would stay with us for the rest of our lives.

———

None of us spoke on the journey back, but I didn't allow my mind to wander. Our ordeal wasn't over yet. I went through a mental checklist of what we had to do to deep clean the scene, going over each step. Some people recited meditative mantras to keep calm, but not me. Who needs them when you're calculating how many gallons of bleach you'll need?

"Where do we start?" Vixen asked as we arrived back. She nervously inspected the spatters of blood over stools. Some things were beyond saving. We'd have to burn the soft furnishings — no amount of cleaning would erase the DNA traces left behind.

We divided the work between us and worked in silence. When we'd finished, our hands were raw from scrubbing. It'd take weeks to get the smell of products out from under our nails, and we'd have to bathe in cocoa butter to make sure our fingers didn't look like they'd aged fifty years.

I surveyed the scene with satisfaction and wiped the sweat from my brow. "I think we're done for now."

You'd never guess someone had shot themselves dead in the club earlier. My body was exhausted, but my mind wouldn't be able to rest. Not yet.

"You can both crash here," Vixen said.

"I'd rather—" Before I finished speaking, a flicker of fear crossed Vixen's face. She hadn't offered out of the goodness of her heart; with the guys gone, she didn't want to be staying here alone. "I'll stay, but only if I get first dibs on the shower."

"We all have our own showers." Vixen led us up the stairs to the apartment above the club, which she and the guys shared. "Make yourself at home."

Mieko's eyeballs almost popped out of their sockets. "Woah…"

Their pad was more like a freaking penthouse. A huge flat screen, a pool table, and a gigantic corner sofa took up the full length of the room. The three of us could all lie together on it in a starfish pose and still not be touching. It was all open plan with an adjoining state-of-the-art kitchen, which looked like it'd never been used.

"We used to all have our own places, but we ended up staying here most nights." Vixen explained. "Zander figured we may as well renovate."

"No fucking kidding," I murmured under my breath.

"You guys can sleep here." Vixen gestured at the sofa. It looked more welcoming than the bed I had at home. "I'll get blankets. Follow me."

She led us through the living space to continue the tour like we were in an episode of MTV Cribs. Someone with great taste had carefully chosen everything from the carpets to the curtains. It was luxurious, but not in a way that you were too afraid to kick off your sneakers and relax.

"All of our bedrooms are en suite," Vixen continued. "There's a master bathroom at the end for guests."

"You could fit, like, four people in that shower." Mieko peeked around the door like a child eying up a pile of presents on Christmas morning. "I've never even seen one like it before."

"Go ahead, Mieko," I said. She deserved it after tonight. As for me, anything with hot water would be better than the torturous cold hose-down I'd become accustomed to. "Before I change my mind."

"You can use West's bathroom, Candy." Vixen pushed open his bedroom door. "He's a clean freak."

Holy shit. Vixen wasn't exaggerating. West's bedroom and bathroom were absolutely spotless. No photographs or any personal effects were lying around. It looked more like a hotel room than somewhere someone lived permanently. I mean, what kind of psychopath lined up their shampoo bottles in size order?

"What the hell?" I returned to the living area smelling of West's expensive sandalwood shampoo to find Vixen had transformed the room into a blanket fort. How had she put this together so fast? "Who even owns this many comforters?"

"It's like a proper slumber party," Mieko said gleefully, balanced on a mountain of pillows braiding her hair.

"What's next?" I raised an eyebrow. Seeing one of the Razors shoot themselves in the head was one thing, but this totally threw me off balance. "A pillow fight?"

That's what they did at slumber parties, right? When I was a kid, no one ever invited me to stay over at their house. The only invitations I got were from the older guys in Evergreen wanting me to give them blowjobs for a couple of dollars. *Fucking assholes.*

"Ignore her, Vixen," Mieko said. "I think it's great."

Vixen pulled out a bottle of vodka and took a swig. She must have one permanently shoved up her vagina because she seemed able to whip one out at a moment's notice. "Drink?"

"Why the fuck not?" I took it from her. It burned the back of my throat, but I liked the warmth spreading through my body afterward. "It's not like we'll be able to sleep."

Mieko cringed at the strength of the vodka but took a shot. "Doesn't this feel like a dream?"

Vixen collapsed on the sofa. "More like a nightmare…"

"Do you think he had any family?" Mieko asked. We all knew who she was talking about.

"Bryce chose him because no one would miss him." I shook my head and swallowed another mouthful. "The bastard."

"If his family is anything like mine, then he was probably better off not knowing them at all," Vixen pointed out. "Family causes nothing but trouble."

"Let's cheers to that." I held up the bottle. "To family! Who fucking needs them?"

EIGHTEEN

"What's going on?"

The sound of men's voices brought me out of my alcohol-induced slumber. I looked up to find West peering down at me like a specimen in a science experiment. We may have overtaken their man cave for the night, but none of them were more surprised than me to be waking up in the Seven's apartment. It felt like we were in a fucked-up reality TV show — except we had more to worry about than which random guy we'd hooked up with the night before.

"Can you keep it down?" Vixen groaned from a pile of cushions. Beside her, an empty bottle of spirit confirmed my worst suspicions and explained the pounding in my head. "Some of us are trying to sleep here."

"Not anymore," Zander replied, snapping the over-head light on. "Does anyone care to explain to me why my club smells like a morgue?"

"Where's my fucking coffee?" Vixen croaked.

"How did you know we'd be here?" I asked, eyeing

up the breakfast in Rocky's hands.

"Hey!" West objected as Rocky handed me a coffee, which had his name on it.

"Delicious." I took a sip. Perfect, that'd help shift the soul-destroying hangover. Things always seemed to taste better when they were someone else's. "Just how I like it."

"Would you like a coffee, Mieko?" Rocky offered.

She poked her head out of the blanket fortress. "Do you have any juice?"

Who could say no to someone as sweet as Mieko? For once, even Zander was too stunned to make a comeback.

"What would you prefer?" Rocky opened the fridge like a personal butler. "Orange, or mango?"

"Orange," she said, smiling shyly.

"How was your road trip?" I asked. They were all still wearing the same clothes. I did a quick assessment: no blood, no cuts, no bruises, no black eyes, and no missing teeth. It looked like they'd gone for a fucking stroll. When, in the meantime, we had to get rid of a dead body.

"It's none of your business." Zander crossed his arms. "I'm the one that should be asking the questions."

I rose from my mass of covers like a zombie rising from the dead.

"Hang on!" West's mouth fell open. First, I'd taken his coffee. Now, his shirt. The big guy was learning a valuable lesson in sharing today. "Is that my shirt?"

"A fucking shirt should be the least of your worries," I snapped. "What the Sevens do may be none of my business, but it became my business when one of the

Razors broke into the club with a gun last night. Where were all of you then, huh?"

"Do you all have to be so loud?" Vixen brought down a pillow over her face. I'm pretty sure her alcohol level was still way over the legal driving limit judging by the slight slur to her words. "At least wait until I've had a fucking coffee…"

"They did, what?" Rocky gasped. He didn't register the juice he was pouring had spilled over the sides of the glass and onto the countertop. Poor Mieko may not get her juice after all. "You're kidding, right?"

"We'll tell you everything," I said, "after we've eaten breakfast."

No one should head into battle on an empty stomach. Besides, the pancakes smelled fucking divine...

"Tell me again." Zander leaned back in his chair and pinched the bridge of his nose after hearing Vixen's garbled version of events for the third time.

"What more do you need to know?" I asked. We didn't need to relive all the gory details over and over. "The boy showed up, held Vixen hostage, shot himself, and we cleaned up. End of story."

"Why didn't you call?" Zander turned to Vixen in accusation. "We could have dealt with it."

"Because you told me not to disturb you, remember?" she said. Well, that and the fact she was too busy freaking out to think straight. "It doesn't matter, anyway. We sorted it."

"Not all women need a man to come to their rescue, you know," I said. We were up against a ticking clock.

Waiting for the Sevens to swoop in to save the day had been out of the equation. "We can't depend on a knight in shining armor to appear whenever a body needs disposing of."

"There's still one thing I don't understand." West paused. "How did you get out there? To this place in the woods?"

Goddammit. We'd almost gotten away with smoothing over the general details. Mieko looked down at her clasped hands, and I took a keen interest in the sofa stitching. We were keeping our mouths shut. Neither of us wanted to be caught in the middle of a family feud. Vixen would have to own up to it alone. He may forgive her... just.

"We may have borrowed your car," Vixen said. There was more tension in the room than when Vixen had a fucking gun pressed to her head.

West's jaw clenched. "Which one?"

"The Range Rover…" she said, her voice trailing off.

"Where is it now?"

Vixen didn't respond. Where was her usual no-bull-shit attitude when you needed it? Someone needed to put him out of his misery.

"We burnt it," I said matter-of-factly, shoveling a large forkful of pancakes into my mouth before he could ask any more questions.

West's hands balled into fists. I recognized that look. The Hulk wanted to say hello. He jumped to his feet, flipping the table and sending our plates smashing to the floor. Wouldn't throwing a chair have been enough? Those heavenly chocolate chip pancakes didn't deserve to be wasted.

"Come on, West. It had the biggest trunk," Vixen called after him. Somehow, it didn't seem to help the situation. "Wait!"

West was already halfway across the room. He slammed the door behind him with so much force that the entire block will have heard it. Hopefully, he'd cool off before discovering I'd messed up the order of his shampoo collection…

"I suppose you were the mastermind behind all this?" Zander's icy glare landed on me. He could make a compliment sound like the biggest insult. "What about the car plates?"

"Do you think I'm a total moron?" I rolled my eyes. He wasn't the only one with experience in this area. "We removed them."

"I'll get a sanitation team over to clean the club and send someone to remove what's left of the car." Zander's fingers were already flying over the keys on his cell to make the request. "If Mieko has connections to the disposal site, we want nothing coming back to us."

"I haven't been there in years," Mieko mumbled. Her eyes glazed over. Whatever happened to her in the cabin had left lasting damage. The only regret I had about last night was Mieko having to visit that place again. I knew all too well the fear of returning to the places in my nightmares. "My dad used to take me hunting when I was a kid. No one knew we were out there."

"We can't be too careful," Zander said. For once, I agreed with him. We couldn't take any chances with Mieko, regardless of how loose she thought her associations with the location were.

"Were any of you hurt?" Rocky asked. "I can give you a ride to the emergency room?"

For three guys who spent twenty-four hours a day together, their reactions couldn't have been any more different. West couldn't control his anger long enough to stick around, Zander focused on damage control, and all Rocky cared about was whether we needed a bandaid.

"We're fine," Vixen said. "Quit fussing."

"Maybe you should go and check whether West is okay?" I suggested. "He's the one who needs his blood pressure checking."

Zander's brows lowered, letting me know I was treading a very thin line. So fucking what? When you'd spent your whole life walking across a tightrope, you had no fear of falling.

"A car is waiting outside for you both." Zander looked to me and Mieko. Fucking typical. We'd helped save his cousin's life, but were being thrown out without as much as a thank you. Would he have preferred to return to find Vixen's brains splattered all over the walls of his precious club? Gratitude didn't cost a cent. "We have family business to take care of."

"I'll see you out," Rocky said.

"No," Zander ordered, stopping him in his tracks. "They don't need a man to come to their rescue, remember?"

"Touché," I spat.

"We'll see you at work tonight." A snide smile spread over Zander's face. "I would hate for the other dancers to think you were getting special treatment."

I grabbed Mieko's arm and marched out before we had to clean up another crime scene.

"Thanks for breakfast," she called back.

"Don't thank them!" Mieko was too polite for her own good. "Zander Briarly can go fuck himself."

"You don't mind me being here, do you?" Mieko asked nervously. We'd both returned to my apartment after being ousted from the Lapland penthouse like unwanted cockroaches. "I just didn't want to be alone... not yet."

"It's fine." I handed her a spoon. Unsurprisingly, the only thing I had in my freezer was ice cream. There were very few things caramel creaminess didn't make a little more bearable. "Dairy and sugar make everything better, right?"

"We might need more ice cream." She sighed. "I don't know what would have happened if you weren't there. I froze. But you... you knew exactly what to do. If you didn't step in, Vixen could have died."

"But she didn't," I reminded her. When you faced a life or death situation, your natural human instincts came out. Every moment was a battle for survival, and only the fittest made it through. "If you hadn't been there, how would we have known where to take the body? We'd have ended up shoving it in the freezer for the cops to raid."

"That place we drove to—"

"You never have to go there again," I cut her off. "Zander is going to get rid of the car. There'll be no traces left behind."

"My dad was a wicked man." Mieko's eyes misted over. "He used to hurt me. He'd take me out there, and..."

"You don't have to talk about it if you don't want

to." I reached out and took her hand. "You don't need to explain yourself to me."

"Last night wasn't the first time I saw a dead body." Her voice cracked. "My dad. It was an accident. I didn't mean to hurt him. I just wanted him to stop, but I… I… I…"

"You don't have to say it. I know," I said. Physical affection wasn't usually my thing, but I pulled Mieko into a hug. In my arms, she felt so small and fragile. I stroked her hair whilst she wept over my shoulder. "It's okay. It's all going to be okay. He can't hurt you anymore."

Mieko reminded me of how I used to be. When I first started killing, I felt a pang of sadness whenever I took a life. Not for my victims — those fuckers deserved it. But I felt like I'd lost a part of myself I'd never be able to get back. I grieved for a more innocent time, where I knew nothing about how to sever the jugular artery and hoped for a life away from the confines of Evergreen. Now, crying didn't help me release my emotions. I preferred to spill blood over tears. In my twisted way, killing had become a form of therapy.

"How did you know?" Mieko sniffed.

"Because we're the same," I said. "People like us do what we have to do to survive."

"You've done what you had to do to survive too, haven't you?"

"Sometimes there's no other way." After my fifth murder, the numbness set in. Society deems murder unlawful, but wouldn't it be an even bigger sin to allow monsters to walk the streets and ruin even more lives? Mieko did what she had to do to protect herself and, one day, I hoped she'd make peace with her choices.

"After a while, you start to realize that bad people aren't worth your tears. You may not feel it right now, but you're stronger than you think."

"Thanks." Mieko shot me a watery half-smile, then grabbed the tub of dreams. "Do you have any more of this?"

"I'm sure I can find some," I said.

"How do you think Vixen's doing?" Mieko asked. Even after everything that had happened in the last twenty-four hours, she was still worrying about other people. "Zander seemed pretty mad at her, didn't he?"

"Vixen can fight her own battles," I said. It didn't matter what Vixen did, Zander's fierce protectiveness over her would forgive her for anything. "Why do you suddenly care about her so much?"

"I don't!"

"Hold on a second," I said, turning to face her. "Are you blushing?"

"N-n-no!" she lied.

"You can't be serious." I shook my head. "You have a fucking crush on the ice queen, don't you?"

"I don't!" She could deny it all she wanted, but the look on her face told me otherwise. Now, it made sense why she'd defended and felt sorry for Vixen in the past.

I winked. "Sure, you don't."

"Besides, she's not an ice queen." Mieko sulked. Damn, she liked Vixen even more than I'd first thought. "There's more to her than that."

"Just because she recited a verse of poetry doesn't make her any less of a bitch," I pointed out. "But if anyone can make her melt, it's you. Don't say I didn't warn you, though."

Freezer burn hurt like a bitch.

293

As per Zander's orders, Mieko and I arrived for our shift bang on time. There was no way I'd give him the satisfaction of complaining about my hangover, either. No matter how bad my head ached.

"Candy," Scarlett sauntered over on stilt-like heels to greet us. One wrong step and she'd break her legs. "I have a message for you from Zander."

Something felt off… and it wasn't just the lingering sensation from knowing a kid died where we were standing.

"I didn't realize you were his messenger now," I replied. Scarlett must be next in line to straddle the king of Lapland. It wouldn't be long until the crown fucking jewels crushed her like they had her predecessor. "Have you taken up Bella's position as lapdog?"

"He wants to see you in his office." She swished her blonde locks over her shoulder so dramatically that it almost slapped me in the face. "Like, right now."

"What do you think he wants?" Mieko whispered. "Do you think he's still mad?"

"It's Zander," I said as if that was explanation enough. "He's mad all the fucking time. Whatever he wants, it can't be good."

If Zander wanted to fire me, then I'd go out with a bang. Although, hopefully, not in the form of a gun aimed at my labia... again.

"Good luck." Scarlett shot me a fake smile. "You'll need it."

I stormed across the club; my rage growing with each step. I barged into Zander's office without knocking. Why should I play by his fucking rules after his complete lack of gratitude this morning? When he earned my respect, I'd repay it in kind. Until then, he could kiss my ass if he expected me to bow down to his orders.

Zander looked up in disapproval and frowned. "I told you to knock."

"What does it matter?" I challenged. "You were the one who summoned me."

"Take a seat, Candy."

I threw myself down with a huff. "Well?"

"Last night can't go without consequences. You know that, don't you?" Zander drummed his fingers on the desk. "I want you to do something for me."

"If you want me to run another errand, forget it," I snarled. "Why should I do another job to save the Seven's asses and not see a dime for it? If you want my help, you'll need to pay—"

"I want you to leave town," Zander interrupted. He pulled a black briefcase from under the desk and slid it toward me. "This is your cut from the Briarly poker game. You can use it to start over."

"Start over?" My mouth fell open. "You can't just order me to leave."

"I've already made my decision," Zander dismissed, checking his watch in boredom. "There's been a string of disasters since the moment you arrived. We are done cleaning up the mess you leave behind."

"My mess?" I grabbed the suitcase and hurled it against the wall in fury. If he wanted to see a fucking mess, then I'd make his office look like a department store after the Black Friday stampede. "Where were you when I saved Red's life? Where were you last night when a kid held up a gun to Vixen's head?"

"That's exactly my point," Zander said. "All of this started when you came to town."

"Things have been fucked up around here long before I arrived," I sneered. Zander rose to his feet, fists clenched, his stare searing with pure hatred. He didn't realize this was only me warming up. The truth fucking hurt and he'd been used to getting his way for too fucking long. "Don't pretend you're too blind to see it."

"I see everything."

"If you did, you'd be fucking thanking me!" Hell, he should be down on his knees licking my shoes. "If it wasn't for me, Red and Vixen would be dead."

"If it wasn't for you, we wouldn't be in a war with my father," Zander spat in accusation. "His men wouldn't be dead, and last night would never have happened."

"What happened last night was an accident," I said. "You were already in a war. You just didn't want to admit it. If I were you, I'd want me on your side."

"Take the money, Candy."

"I don't want your fucking money!" I kicked the briefcase. "Everyone else may be too afraid of you to say what they really think, but you don't scare me, Zander. You never have."

Suddenly, the office door flew open.

"You can't do this." Vixen fell inside, panting. "You can't fire her."

"This is my club," Zander growled. "I can do what I want."

"Correction!" She raised a finger. "It's *our* club. You told me I can decide which dancers we hire."

"Are you sure about that, Vixen?" Zander asked. "Do you really want Candy to stay?"

"Yes," she confirmed. Who knew burning a body together would win over Vixen's support? "I do."

"Have it your way, Vixen. I'll allow her to stay on one condition…" Zander paused for dramatic effect and his lips curled into a smile, "Candy won't be a dancer. She will become one of us. A Seven."

"What?" I spluttered. "Who says I even want to be a member of your twisted gang?"

"You said that we should want you on our side," Zander replied, using my own words against me. "This is your chance."

"You can't bring someone in without consulting everyone," Vixen intervened. Was she already regretting her choice to vouch for me? "That's not how we do things. It has to be a group decision."

"Let's put it to a vote then," Zander said. As if on cue, West and Rocky filed inside. Both of their expressions were blank. Had this been Zander's plan all along? Did he try offering me money as a final test to prove my loyalty, or was this another one of his mind games? "Are there any objections to Candy joining the Sevens?"

I expected West to speak up. After admitting to torching his car, there was no way he would want me to join his precious gang. If he didn't hate me, then Vixen had spent every waking minute trying to make my life hell. I couldn't imagine she wanted to keep me around. Even Rocky had tried to persuade me to keep my distance… but, a minute later, none of them had spoken.

"It's settled then. We're all in agreement," Zander said, turning to face me again. Had I entered an alternate universe or something? "Joining the Sevens is a lifetime deal. When you're in, there's no getting out."

"This must be your idea of a sick joke," I stammered. "How can you want me to join you? You don't even know me."

Rocky wrung his hands. Well, most of them didn't….

"But we will," Zander said. "Or, you can take the money and leave town. It's your choice."

Could I really trust the Sevens enough to put my life in their hands? I'd always been a lone wolf, but the threat of Hiram loomed over my head like a black cloud. I stood no chance of destroying him on my own, but maybe if I had these guys behind me…

"What's it going to be, Candy?" Zander's eyes burned into mine like hot coals. "Are you in, or are you out?"

I looked at the four people around the room. They were mouthy screwed up violent criminals, but they were also broken... like me. The Sevens had unparalleled loyalty to each other. Even though I would never get my happy ending, maybe it would be possible to find a place for myself somewhere amongst this gang of misfits.

They may have a battle with the Briarlys on their hands, but I was raging a war of my own. I had everything to gain and nothing to lose. What they didn't realize was adding me to their ranks wouldn't help them. It would only rain down a hell of a lot of complications and make them regret ever asking. My decision would change the rest of my life… and theirs.

"I'm in."

DID YOU ENJOY KILLER CANDY?

"Kitten"

A Lapland Underground Prequel Blurb:

My heart is still beating, but does that really make me one of the lucky ones? Nothing in Blackthorne Towers is left to chance. My captor is keeping me alive for a reason…

Obeying his orders will keep me alive, but what is the price I'll have to pay for my life?

When you're surrounded by monsters for long enough, there's only so long you can resist the pull to the darkness… especially if I can get my vengeance.

ABOUT THE AUTHOR

Holly Bloom has a degree in English Literature, but don't let that fool you... she would pick a steamy romance over a Shakespeare play any day!

Holly writes contemporary romance - the dark, gritty and twisty kind. She loves creating badass babe characters, who aren't afraid to speak their minds, and writing about the men who can handle them - often, there is more than one! Why choose, right?

When she isn't working on her next project, Holly spends an unhealthy amount of time watching true crime and roaming around the woods near her home in the UK.

As well as gooey chocolate brownies, Holly's favourite thing in the world is hearing from her readers - her characters may bite, but she doesn't! Promise!

Find out more about Holly Bloom's books at:
www.hollybloomauthor.com

Printed in Great Britain
by Amazon

16479596R00178